HER KILLER CONFESSION

A Carolina McKay Thriller

TONY URBAN
DREW STRICKLAND

D1736351

PACKANACK
publishing

Copyright © 2020 by Packanack Publishing, Tony Urban & Drew Strickland

Visit Tony on the web: http://tonyurbanauthor.com

Visit Drew on the web: http://drewstricklandbooks.com

All rights reserved.

No part of this book may be reproduced in any form or by any electronic or mechanical means, including information storage and retrieval systems, without written permission from the author, except for the use of brief quotations in a book review.

This is a work of fiction. Names, characters, businesses, places, events, locales, and incidents are either the products of the author's imagination or used in a fictitious manner. Any resemblance to actual persons, living or dead, or actual events is purely coincidental.

"In a world where thrushes sing and willow trees are golden in the spring, boredom should have been included among the seven deadly sins."

— ELIZABETH GOUDGE - *THE ROSEMARY TREE*

"Birds born in a cage think flying is an illness."

— ALEJANDRO JODOROWSKY

CHAPTER ONE

THE MAN WHO PRESSED HIS NOSE AGAINST THE REAR WINDOW of her van, painting abstract patterns with his chosen medium of nasal sebum, looked like the specter of death. With the river rushing by outside, for a short moment made more surreal by the three Oxycodone pills she'd popped half an hour earlier, Carolina wondered if she had died and if this man was Charon, come to ferry her soul to the underworld.

Do I even care? She ruminated on it as she watched him peep inside her ride, desperate in his attempts to spy on her. To take her.

Then he spoke, and the illusion was spoiled.

"I'm looking for Carolina McKay," he said, smashing half his face tight against the glass, flattening his features and forcing them out of proportion. He was no longer the painter. Now, he was the subject in one of Picasso's portraits. Not a flattering look.

For Carolina, the previous weeks had been a blur of pain and pills. Pills and pain. She vaguely remembered her mother kicking her off her property, calling her a Judas in her ever-theatrical, over-the-top, kind way, but life consisted mostly of long interludes of delirium and sleep.

Carolina didn't mind being ordered off Beatrice's acreage as life alongside Little Elk Creek brought with it much-needed solitude. With the weather turning colder, even the bugs weren't a bother.

The land was almost heavenly in its serenity. The wind whispered to her through the trees, and the river babbled bedtime stories. The occasional deer or raccoon wandered across the land to remind her the world was still ongoing but didn't try to get her involved. It was far better than she deserved.

She couldn't recall her last foray into town but would need to return soon as her food supplies were dwindling, and hunting animals had never been her bag. She couldn't even recall whether she'd eaten yesterday—not that she cared. Coffee and Oxy kept her functioning.

The man outside her van knocked on the rear panel like the world's most annoying door-to-door salesman.

"Who the fuck is this creep?" she asked aloud, unsure whether she was posing the question to herself or to Yeti.

The super-sized Great Pyrenees had staked his claim to her bed and lounged with his head on her pillow. She would have encouraged him to move, to spare her a night of inhaling dog fur, but the animal was still adjusting to his new home and new master, and she didn't have the heart.

When his calls and knocks went unanswered, the man who looked like death went for the handle; it rattled but was locked. His audacity pissed Carolina off—and she hadn't been in a good mood to start with.

The sound of a would-be intruder made Yeti raise his big head from the pillow and look her way. She didn't have to be a pet psychic to read his mind.

How rude.

How rude indeed.

Carolina reached for the pistol she was used to keeping locked up, then remembered it was holstered at her hip. It still seemed odd to wear it on her person, in the van that served as her home. The world's deadliest fashion accessory. Paranoid even. But it comforted her.

She didn't bother to ensure it was loaded. She knew it was.

"You stay," she told Yeti, who had no qualms with the command and paid her little attention as she moved to the sliding door, curled her slender fingers around the latch, and opened it to the world.

She dropped onto the hard earth, then closed and locked the door. On the chance the man had ill intentions, she did not mind risking her own life—but the dog's was off-limits.

The creep must have heard the clatter and appeared at the back panel, examining her with uncertain eyes.

"Are you Carolina McKay?" he asked.

"No. I'm her stunt double."

His mild confusion shifted, and he tried to smile but failed. "I'm sorry for gawking," he apologized. "I guess it's just... You're not what I expected."

She didn't like the way he was ogling her. "And what was that?"

"I suppose I don't know." His shifted his right hand behind his back, reaching for something.

A gun.

That was her first thought, and her hand went to her own firearm. "Don't do anything stupid," she warned.

The man rose his hand over his head like an outlaw in a bad Western, fingers wagging, overly dramatic.

He's screwing with me.

Now his smile became successful, triumphant. He knew he'd gotten her and liked it. "Don't shoot me, miss; I ain't done nothing wrong." Then he laughed, a coarse sound full of phlegm.

Carolina was no longer scared, but her annoyance grew like weeds in humid weather. "Listen, whoever you are; I came out here for peace and quiet, and you're spoiling both. So, get on with telling me why you're here, or fuck off."

CHAPTER TWO

Dark, leathery skin hung from the man's face and arms in hollow folds, like a balloon that had been stretched to its breaking point before someone let the air out. The way his red-and-white checkered shirt and jeans popped out around his midsection, Carolina suspected there were copious amounts of that same excess skin lurking underneath his clothes.

It was the type of look usually sported by people who'd undergone weight-loss surgery, the kind where they slice you open, hack away at your stomach until it's the size of a ping-pong ball, then send you on your merry way. But this man hadn't needed surgery to lose his weight. He'd done it the hard way.

Cyrus Mankey spat a mouthful of blood into the dirt, and Carolina stared at it, mesmerized. Mixed in with the plasma were coarse bits of tissue—black chunks of impending death. She reminded herself to bury it or toss it into the river before letting Yeti out of the van. The last thing she needed was the dog gobbling up the rotting insides of this strange man.

"My son ain't perfect, but who is?" When Cyrus spoke, his words drew Carolina's attention back to his face. A thin line of red drool snaked its way through the stubble on his chin before disappearing into the folds of his neck and getting lost. His eyes were pale green, the color of foliage at the end of the season when all the chlorophyll was spent.

He stood a little over six feet tall, straight and proud despite his condition. He wore his thick salt-and-pepper hair slicked back—greaser style. Although his health made it impossible to pinpoint his age, she guessed him to be in his late fifties. "And I know, sure as shit he didn't hurt that girl. He don't deserve to spend his life rotting behind bars."

Carolina raised her hand. This was all too much, too fast, and her foggy brain fought to keep up. "Slow your roll there, friend-o. How about you start at the part where you tell me why I should give a shit about you or your supposedly innocent son."

"Not supposedly. He is innocent, goddamn it!" Cyrus's face contorted. He looked like walking death, but a fire burned inside him, and he slammed the side of his fist against her van in frustration. Inside, Yeti gave an annoyed and inquisitive *Woof?*

Carolina aimed her index finger at the man. "Calm yourself. And if you assault my van again, I'll put two in your chest and dump your body in the Little Elk."

Her tone carried enough levity to wet Cyrus Mankey's fuse. "I'm sorry," he said. "It's just, nobody takes this serious. And I thought you'd be different."

"Why?" Carolina asked. "What do you know about me that allowed you to form an opinion?"

"I read about what you did. Finding that serial killer. Not giving up, even though the cops had pinned it on some other asshole. That's exactly what I need here. Someone with tenacity."

Carolina looked away from him, staring at the churning waters of the creek and wishing she were still alone. This was all because of that damned Max Barrasso and his article. No, not an article, an *exposé*. Pretentious dickhead.

The story on his exploitative blog had been picked up by the

AP, and she had been dodging calls from the likes of *Dateline* and 20/20 for interviews ever since. The last thing she wanted after that debacle was celebrity. But even here, in the middle of the damned forest, she couldn't escape her past.

"How'd you find me?"

"I asked about you at the police station. The fat, dopey little deputy, he told me where you were."

Fucking Johnny. Next trip to town, she would tear him a new asshole. "If you read the article, you know I'm not a cop, right?"

Cyrus nodded. "I don't want a cop. Because cops cover for other cops. I want you."

I sure do attract quality men, Carolina thought.

She glanced at a fire ring where she spent the evenings mesmerized by the flames and trying to talk herself out of climbing into them. A folding camp chair stood by it. It was the only chair she had, and the decent part of her knew she should offer it to this man, who looked like he was days away from shuffling off his mortal coil. Instead, she sat in it.

"What was your son convicted of? You mentioned a girl."

"Denton," Cyrus said. "My son's name is Denton."

"Okay, Denton then. He's locked up. This is the part where you tell me why."

"They say he's a murderer."

A quick breeze picked up, blowing Carolina's hair back and exposing her neck. The resulting chill made gooseflesh erupt across her forearms. "Who was he accused of killing? Wife? Girlfriend? Was it a heat of the moment thing, or..."

Cyrus broke eye contact with her. "No, nothing like that. It was a young girl. One he never met and knew nothing about."

Carolina felt a headache coming on, and her hand drifted to her temple, rubbing small, concentric circles. The last thing she needed was to get mixed up with some pedophile's father. "How young?"

"Fourteen."

"Shit," she said.

"Now hold up." Cyrus circled around, returning to her field of vision like an annoying fly that had to keep showing you it was still there. "Denton was only seventeen. He wasn't some pervert. Like I said, he was a good boy."

"That's what every parent thinks, Mr. Mankey. Their son or daughter couldn't do anything wrong. Even when the evidence is as obvious as their own noses."

"You think I don't know that?" Cyrus said. "I'm not fucking dumb. I—" His voice broke into a wheeze that deteriorated into a wet, hacking cough and bent him over at the waist. She half expected the bastard to keel over right there. If he did, she'd add him to the cord wood.

"You all right?" she asked.

He waved away her concern and, after a few moments, the fit passed. He took several shallow breaths before speaking. "Define all right."

"Are you going to die and fall into my fire pit?

"I don't plan to."

"Thank God for small favors," Carolina said.

Mankey straightened up, arching his back and opening his lungs—or what was left of them. "I got diagnosed with mesothelioma last month," he said. "Told me I might hang on until Christmas, but I'm not buying any presents."

Now she felt a little guilty about not offering up her seat. But she figured, at this point, it would only come off as pity. So, she remained in place. "Do you know how you got it?"

"I worked construction. Teardowns mostly. I'm sure I breathed in my share of asbestos and then some."

"They have lawsuits for that kind of thing," she said.

"Fuck do I need with money?" Mankey said.

She considered that. "You could set your family up pretty nice."

"Only kin I got's Denton. And he don't need money, either.

Not unless you can get him sprung from Barbourstown." He stared, his pale eyes boring holes into her. "It's not the dying I mind. I lived my life. Maybe not the way I wanted, but I got to make my own mistakes. Denton didn't get that chance."

So, we're back to this.

"I need to see his name cleared before I'm in the ground." He took a step closer to her, and she got a whiff of sweet smoke. Pipe tobacco. "Please, miss. You've got to help me. I'll pay you whatever you want."

Carolina watched as Cyrus extracted his wallet from his back pocket. It was an ancient piece of leather held together with a rubber band. He dug into it, pulled out a small wad of cash, then thrust the money toward her with a trembling hand and desperate eyes. It was mostly ones with a five mixed in for variety.

"I'm on the draw," he said. "I can give you more when my check comes. Hell, I'll give you the whole check if that's what it takes."

She unfolded the money. A five and twelve singles. Seventeen dollars to spare this man's son a life behind bars. It was pathetic, yet endearing at the same time.

"Just talk to Denton," Cyrus said. "Get his side of the story. If you think he's lying, then I won't push you to go further."

She looked from the man to his money, then back. "All right," she said. "I'll meet with him, but I'm not making any promises beyond that."

Cyrus nodded, relief washing over his haggard face. "That's all I ask."

Carolina took his payment, shoving the cash into her pocket as she wondered what in the hell she'd gotten herself involved in now.

CHAPTER THREE

THE CHOPPED STEAK, DROWNING IN WATERY GRAVY, LOOKED like someone had already chewed, swallowed, and regurgitated it onto the plate, but Carolina didn't care because it tasted damned good. She was growing quite fond of Hank's, the lone diner in Dupray proper, and she dredged a hunk of meat through lumpy mashed potatoes before taking another bite.

After gulping down the food, she chased it with iced tea. It had been a few days since she had an actual meal, and she wasn't wasting any time.

She looked up from her plate and saw Sheriff Elven Hallie staring at her, his jaw shifting side to side as he worked on his tomato and onion sandwich.

"What?" Carolina asked, already loading up her fork for another round.

Elven shook his head, but his eyes remained locked on her. "I've never seen someone eat so... Purposely."

Carolina wiped her face with a napkin and realized she must come across as less civilized than Yeti, who gobbled his kibble from a bowl. Oh well; she was never much of a lady.

Her eyes drifted to the slice of pie that sat to the left of her main course. Just thinking about it made her salivary glands erupt. "You sold me on this place, remember. And that pie." She broke off a chunk of crust and popped it into her mouth, where it melted.

"I didn't realize you'd go full addict," Elven said, chuckling. "I'd suggest trying one of their healthier options. Maybe the grilled chicken salad. But now that you've returned from your Thoreau-esque retreat into the wilderness, I can see you need the calories."

Carolina furrowed her eyebrows. "What the hell is that supposed to mean?" She didn't wait for him to answer. "You know, these days people call that body shaming. Just because I've lost some weight doesn't mean you get to insinuate I have an eating disorder."

She wasn't really mad but wanted to put him on the spot and gain the upper hand. Her clothes had grown a size too big, maybe two, and it wasn't for trying. Sooner or later, she needed to take care of herself, but finding the motivation was a challenge.

Elven's eyes widened in mild shock. "I didn't mean... I just want to make sure you're—"

"Relax, cowboy; I get what you mean. But don't waste your time worrying about me." She looked from her entree to her dessert, trying to decide which to go with next, and found the pie too appealing to delay any longer. It was shocking how fulfilled a piece of this pie could make her feel. She'd had sex that was far less satisfying.

"Changing the subject before I insert my foot into my mouth again," Elven said. "I don't hear from you for weeks, and out of the blue, you ask me here. I suspect it wasn't for small talk."

She twirled her fork between her fingers. "I've been offered a job."

"I wasn't aware you were looking for one."

"Neither was I. It just sort of... found me."

His eyes narrowed suspiciously—and rightfully so. "Tell me more."

"I got a knock at my door this morning from Cyrus Mankey. His son, Denton, was nailed for the murder of a fourteen-year-old girl seven years back. The father believes his son is innocent."

"Of course he does," Elven said.

"He wants me to help him prove it."

"Well, good luck with that," Elven said.

"Do you know anything about the case?"

"The broad strokes. It happened over in Monacan." He set aside his sandwich. "And it wasn't comely."

"What's that mean?"

Elven went into a detached, *just the facts ma'am*, cop mode. "Cecilia Casto was the girl's name. She was young, barely a teenager. Kinda girl you see selling lemonade at the side of the road and buy some even when you're not thirsty because she's so darn sweet."

His eyes narrowed and mouth pinched, as if the memory caused him physical pain. "Any murder is a tragedy, but hers seemed especially so because of the circumstances. She wasn't strangled or shot. Nothing as quick or ordinary as that. It was one of those Satanic jobs."

It was Carolina's turn to lose interest in her food, which annoyed her because there was still a good third of the pie remaining. Mankey hadn't provided her any details of the crime. She should have known it wasn't going to be simple.

"You sure that wasn't just small-town gossip? You know how it goes. A kid listens to heavy metal and draws a pentagram on his Social Studies book, and all of a sudden, he's a devil worshipper."

"It was more than that." Elven checked the restaurant to ensure no one was listening in. They were in the clear, but he dropped his voice anyway. The words came out hushed and halting, like he didn't think they should be said aloud.

"The girl had been decapitated and skinned. They found her body splayed out on a rock, like an altar. Her head propped between her own legs. Several of her internal organs, her heart, her liver, were never found." He folded and unfolded his hands. "Doesn't take a Rhodes scholar to connect the dots."

That wasn't good. That wasn't good at all.

"I promised the old man I'd head up to Barbourstown and talk to the kid. Guess I'll still do that much," she said.

"You have an odd way of passing the time," Elven said.

"A job's a job, right?" Her voice was flat and lacking enthusiasm. Her good mood was gone.

"You do know that a license is required to act as a private investigator in West Virginia, correct?"

Carolina sighed. "Are you going to fine me for operating without a license?"

His smirk was back. "I haven't decided yet."

"You know I didn't hang a shingle out or anything. Stupid fucking Johnny sent him to me. And all I did was tell the man I'd look into it for him."

"Is he paying you?"

"I plead the fifth."

Elven gave a curt nod. "I'll allow it."

She barely held back a laugh. "Thanks, dad."

Elven was ready with a comeback, but she cut him off. "Take off your Sheriff's hat for a minute and answer me honestly. Do you think there's any chance this kid was framed?"

He paused, considering it. "I don't know how they homed in on Mankey the younger, but nothing that happens in Monacan surprises me."

"You mean the police there are corrupt?"

"There are stories," he said. "None I'll share, but Monacan has a reputation, and it's not respectable."

Way to be specific. She wanted to press him further, but she knew the thin blue line would keep him from badmouthing colleagues without proof. "Would you do me a favor and pull up the case file?"

Elven chuckled.

"What's so amusing? Aren't all of the counties linked in a statewide database?"

"No, Carolina. Half the counties in the southern part of our great state are still on dial-up Internet. Heck, you've seen Meredith's filing system. And I'm apt to say hers is better than most."

"Shit," she said.

"Sorry to disappoint. Do you want me to call the sheriff over there? See if I can find anything out?"

The last thing she wanted was anyone associated with Mankey's case to be aware she was poking her nose into their business. "No. I want to keep this under the radar. At least until I know whether it's even worth investigating."

"Understandable." He must have seen the pouting look of disappointment in her face. "I tell you what. I'll have Johnny check the microfiche for articles about the killing. We'll run copies off of whatever he finds. That'll at least give you more to the story than the convict's father tendered."

She smiled. "Thanks, Elven. I'd appreciate it."

"Are you sure you wouldn't rather be my newest deputy than get mixed up in all this?"

There wasn't much she was certain of these days, but this was one of them. "I'm positive."

CHAPTER FOUR

"You're not coming in?" Carolina asked Cyrus.

After parking in the visitor's lot, she climbed out of the van, stretching and unspooling her muscles and ligaments. The four-hour drive to get to the Barbourstown State Correctional Institution had gone by mostly in silence, with only Cyrus's barking coughs and whistling wheezes adding background noise.

She'd considered pressing him about the details he'd conveniently excluded when enlisting her services but didn't see the point. Once she talked to the son, she'd know whether she wanted to waste more time on this goose chase. Nothing the father said would make a difference one way or the other.

Grinding the handkerchief he'd been coughing into between both hands, Cyrus wrung blood from the folds. It dribbled onto the macadam by his feet. "Denton and me don't have what you'd call a traditional relationship. There are some things we disagree on."

"Like what?"

Cyrus adjusted his jeans at the crotch, showing absolutely zero shame while doing so. "Me, for one. He likes to pretend I don't exist."

She wasn't exactly surprised. "Then why did you come? Did you think I was going to lie to you about visiting him and abscond with your seventeen dollars?"

"People have done worse for less." Cyrus grinned, an expression that seemed out of place on his craggy face. "Also, I do enjoy the company of a pretty lady. And I'm running out of time. So, I figured, why not?"

Carolina sighed and turned toward the prison, where featureless gray concrete and barbed wire served as the welcoming committee. She had made it a few yards when Cyrus called to her.

"When you talk to Denton, it might be wise to not mention me," he said.

Even though he could not see her face, Carolina rolled her eyes. She wagged her middle finger in the air, letting Cyrus know he was heard.

"Don't molest my dog while I'm gone," she said and left him in the dust.

A few days earlier, she'd called and received clearance for the visit after agreeing to the rules. No touching, no gifts, and no recording devices. She followed the signs directing visitors, being buzzed through various gates and doorways. Guards, those of the chunky body and crew-cut variety, stared too long as she passed them by. She wasn't sure if it was out of disgust, suspicion, or sad attempts at flirting.

She'd never trusted guards. They were too often men who wanted to be cops but couldn't hack it for a myriad of reasons; so, they settled into being keepers at the zoo. And although she'd sent her share of men to live in places like this, she knew these zookeepers erred toward sadism.

One particularly portly man stopped her at a metal detector. "Put your keys, change, and any metal objects into the bowl." He motioned to a plastic container sitting on a folding table. She obeyed but didn't acknowledge him otherwise. "Now, step through, slowly."

Carolina passed through the metal detector, hoping she hadn't forgotten something that would give the man a reason to pat her down and grope her. If he so much as leaned in for a whiff of her deodorant, she was liable to punch him in the dick.

Fortunately, it didn't come to pass as the detector threw no alerts. She grabbed her keys and coins and continued on.

She'd expected the visitor's center to be the style where the room was divided in half by thick Plexiglas, but instead, she found an open-air room replete with vending machines offering everything from soda, coffee, and juice to chips, candy bars, and pretzels. Some of the machines even peddled personal care items: soap, mouth wash, and shower shoes. Everything cost three times as much as it would in the real world. Legalized price gouging against those who could least afford it.

A dense, musky aroma mixed with raw bleach burned her nostrils as she entered. There were a dozen or so tables and even more plastic chairs. A few were occupied. Men in orange jumpsuits on one side. Families on the other. One woman, openly weeping, held a toddler on each knee while the man across from her watched, stone-faced.

A guard, whose tag identified him as Kaplin, turned to Carolina as she entered. "Name," he said.

"Mine or who I'm here to see."

Kaplin cocked his head and stared open-mouthed. He was one of the larger men she'd seen here, both in height and girth. "Yours," he said, with all the attitude of a teenage girl.

"McKay, Carolina."

He checked his clipboard, then spoke without looking at her. "Table six. The inmate will be brought in soon."

She moved to a table with the number six stenciled on the surface and took a seat, trying to eavesdrop on the other conversations while she waited. None were interesting enough to hold her attention. Most were about families, wives, and girlfriends assuring their men that everyone was holding up well and couldn't wait for them to come home. Mothers telling their sons they were still loved and missed.

She imagined they had these same discussions every weekend and thought it sad, but what else did they have to discuss? No man, at least none worth his testicles, would burden his loved ones with prison gossip.

As the minutes dragged on, she wondered if she'd been foolish to leave Cyrus in her van. Her pistol was locked in the glove box, along with the entirety of her cash and prescription bottle. If he could manage to hot-wire the vehicle, he could disappear with her entire life.

Her foot began to shake, the movement creating ripples that traveled up her leg and made the table tremble as if it sat atop a fault line. One of the nearest wives shot her an annoyed glance, but Carolina was helpless to stop the fidgeting.

After a few more minutes of worrying, a steel door popped, and through it came a man who looked like a younger, healthier version of Cyrus. Maybe Denton Mankey wasn't thrilled with his luck in the paternity lottery, but it was impossible to deny the men were father and son.

The next thing that struck her was how normal he looked. And young. He could have been the guy delivering your extra-cheese pizza or setting up your home network as a member of the Geek Squad. If it wasn't for the pumpkin orange get up he wore.

Denton scanned the room, saw the number six on the table, then spotted Carolina. His mouth turned up in a shy, confused smile as he came to her. Before pulling out the chair and having a seat, he paused.

"Am I at the right place?" he asked.

"You're Denton Mankey, right?"

He nodded and swallowed hard, sending his Adam's apple bobbing in his skinny neck. "Yes, ma'am; I am."

Ugh, she hated this ma'am shit. Whatever happened to miss? "Then sit. And talk to me."

He did both.

CHAPTER FIVE

Cyrus dipped a flaming match into the chamber of his ivory pipe, sucking sweet smoke through the mortise and into his mouth. He felt what was left of his lungs seize in protest as the smoke ebbed over them, but he wouldn't give in and cough. Not just yet. He wanted a few more drags to drown out the taste of blood and rot, which were a constant these days.

He sat on the concrete walkway, back pressed against a prison wall. This was a good day. He liked Carolina. Liked gawking at her. She was the juiciest piece of ass he'd seen in years, and as he smoked, he calculated his chances with her.

She was a cop—maybe not now, but once a cop always a cop; so, that would hurt him. But she seemed desperate and lonely. And he was almost certain she was on something. Pills probably. He was confident, given enough time, he could catch her at a weak moment. He grew hard as he daydreamed about it.

His pleasant thoughts were interrupted by plodding footfalls that came from his left. He swiveled his head toward the sound and saw a familiar face: C.O. Rubanski. The fat bastard with his swaying jowls didn't pay him any attention as he neared. Cyrus planned to remedy that.

He worked the muscles in his throat until a dense ball of phlegm and blood had coagulated in his mouth. Locked and loaded. When Rubanski got himself in the line of fire, Cyrus unleashed it.

The gooey mass collided with Rubanski's khaki uniform pants, the heavy clot oozing down his calf before dropping onto his boot with an audible plop. The guard's body tensed, and he spun toward the old man who had just used his disease as a means of assault.

"I should bust your jaw for that, you son of a bitch!" Rubanski said, his fingers caressing the handle of the club which was holstered on his utility belt.

Until that point, Cyrus had kept his head tilted down, his face hidden in the shadows cast by the midday sun. He looked up a few degrees, still concealing most of his features. "I'm not so sure about that. You boys might have carte blanche when it comes to inmates, but free folks got rights."

Rubanksi pulled the club free, spinning it in his hands. "You're on prison property. That's close enough for me."

"Well, then; let me stand up and save you the trouble of bending over to beat on me." Cyrus rose to his feet, careful not to reveal the amount of pain elicited by that simple movement. Only when he was fully upright did he look the guard in the eyes, revealing his own in the process.

Rubanski's cockiness drained from his pallid face. His eyes, which moments before had been avid and eager, widened in shock. He took a step backward, stumbling as his foot dropped over the curb.

"Watch your step there, boss," Cyrus said.

Rubanski recovered, righting himself and making an attempt at swagger. "Thought they sent you to Paw Paw with the geriatrics and invalids."

"Nah. Not me; I'm a free man."

The guard's eyes darted side to side as he checked the area to see if anyone would come to his aid if shit got real. But they were alone.

Seeing the panic on Rubanski's face was so much fun Cyrus felt his cock grow even stiffer in his jeans. He's always believed violence was the next best thing to fucking. Sometimes even better.

"What's the matter, boss? You need some more C.O.s to back you up? I'll wait if you do. You're half my age and twice my weight, but you know, deep down where it counts, that I'm one hell of a lot meaner than you can ever hope to be."

Cyrus took a quick stutter step toward the guard, who backed away like a rabbit with a rabid wolf on its heels. His feet got tangled up as he retreated, and he went down hard, his shoulder taking the brunt of the fall.

As he stood over the man, Cyrus knew he could kill him. It would have been just deserts for all the times Rubanski had treated him worse than a dog during his years in this hole. Payback for every cruel act these uniformed motherfuckers committed against to the men they were supposed to be babysitting.

He was on the verge of doing it. Of kicking the man's face until it was a pile of flesh and gore. Of stomping his skull until he was ankle-deep in his brains. Mounting anger and the need for vengeance welled up inside of him.

It would be so damned easy. And what did he have to lose?

Instead, he reached out with his right hand and dragged the guard to his feet.

He expected no gratitude and received none. Rubanski jerked his hand away and brushed himself clean of dirt and detritus. "I can't believe they let you out with the civilized people. This state really has gone to shit," he said as he took short, prissy steps toward the entrance.

"You can't keep the devil locked up forever, now, can ya?" Cyrus called after him.

Rubanski shot one more panicked glance his way before disappearing inside.

And Cyrus smiled.

This day just kept getting better and better.

CHAPTER SIX

"Am I supposed to tell you why they say I'm in here? Or do you want to know the truth?"

Carolina examined Denton Mankey. He had the aw shucks face of a farm boy, the kind who'd be happy to help you fix your lawn mower, share his excess end of summer tomatoes, and pull your car out of the snow when you ran off the road. But his pale green eyes belied a harder life. A harder man. He might only be twenty-four, but he'd spent all of his adult years in this prison surrounded by society's worst. That makes a person grow up fast.

"I want to hear the truth."

He stole brief, nervous glances at her, like a man checking out an eclipse even though he knew better. "All right, then. I can tell you that much, but it's apt to be a letdown."

"How so?" she asked.

"Because I don't know shit. I don't know who killed that girl, but it wasn't me."

"Well, then start with the girl. Cecilia Casto." She took an extra-hard look at his face when she said the name, trying to find a tell but seeing nothing. "Did you know her?"

"Monacan's a big county, but there aren't a lot of people in it. I knew of her. Saw her around town sometimes. But if you mean *know her*—like did I party with her—then no. I didn't."

"And you never had any run-ins with her? Maybe asked her on a date and got turned down?"

"She was a kid," he said. But a grin tugged at his lips. "And trust me, when I asked a girl out, the answer was always yes."

Denton had inherited his father's cockiness. She had few doubts that statement was true, though. His golden-brown hair hung in casual curls, and he shared his Cryus' dark complexion.

He could have surfed onto a California beach and fit right in. She imagined, to teenage girls looking for a break from the sad reality of their station, his looks and attitude made him a welcome alternative to the hardscrabble West Virginia boys who were all work and no play.

"Maybe that says more about Monacan than you," Carolina said. "Slim pickings and all."

He took the jibe in stride, breaking into a full smile, and she saw holes where teeth should be. There was some West Virginia in him, after all.

"Either way, I wasn't complaining."

"I bet you weren't," she said. "Did you have a girlfriend at the time of the murder?"

"I did. Regina Gormley."

"She ever visit you here? Send you letters?"

His smile made a slow-motion retreat. "No, ma'am. Everyone turned their backs to me after it happened. Everyone."

She thought of Cyrus. Would it make any difference if he knew his father was her reason for being here? That he believed in his son when no one else did? Maybe, but it wasn't in her place.

"So, tell me about the night Cecilia disappeared." She checked her notes. "June 23."

"I was out with friends. We went to see a movie at the Palisades Drive-In."

"What movie?" she asked.

"The Hungry One or whatever. Something about a girl with a bow and arrow killing other kids or shit. Look, I was seventeen and trying to get laid; I wasn't really paying much attention to the movie."

Carolina remembered what it was like being that age, and while she may have had different priorities, she knew the quality of the film was not what drew teens to the drive-in.

"Were you with Regina that night, or one of your other conquests?"

He nodded. "Regina. And another couple we ran around with. Freddy Cranmer and Odetta Miller."

"Do you any proof you were there? A ticket stub or receipt?"

He shrugged. "Drive-in's cash only. And the only receipt they give you is half of one of those fifty-fifty tickets. Probably got chucked out the window at the end of the show with the stale popcorn. But you ask the others." He tapped his index finger against the table three times. "Ask them. They'll tell you."

"Did they give you an alibi at your trial?"

Denton's eyes narrowed. His face now wary and distrust sprouted. "You seem to know even less about what happened back then than I do. Why are you here asking me all these questions?"

She should have been able to tell him about Cyrus hiring her, but since that was out, it was time to fall back on her best talent. Lying. "Ever hear of the innocence project?"

Some of the suspicion left him. "Yeah. You work for them?"

"I freelance," Carolina said. "But it's the same general principle. And I'm trying to find out whether your case is worth investigating."

"Are you a lawyer?" he asked. "Because you sure don't look like one. Well, maybe a public defender."

Ouch, that hurt. "No. More of a P.I."

"Like Sherlock Holmes?"

"I suppose. Without the pipe, though."

Denton's right nostril curled up in revolt. "My old man smoked a pipe."

Time to change the subject. "Back to your trial…"

He interlaced his fingers, then bent them backwards, popping all his knuckles rapid fire. One of the guards glanced their way, but he was too lazy to investigate further and went back to staring at the wall. "There wasn't no trial," Denton said.

"What?"

His gaze drifted to the table. "I pleaded guilty." The words came out mush-mouthed and shameful.

She stared at him, but he refused to meet her eyes. Carolina couldn't believe how stupid she'd been to waste her time, her energy, on this. She pushed her chair back, raising her butt off the plastic and ready to get the hell out of there when Denton grabbed her wrist. His nails, which hadn't been trimmed in a while, carved crescent moons into her skin.

She checked the guard who'd reacted to the knuckle cracking, but he was oblivious. She pulled, trying to free herself from his grasp, but Mankey wouldn't let go. Now, when she looked at his face, he looked back with wide, pleading eyes. "Wait," he said. "It's not like you're thinking."

She gave her arm another jerk, and that time, it came free. No one else in the room acknowledged the exchange. "You've got two minutes. Make them count."

"How about I show you instead?" he asked. Without waiting for her to reply, he rolled up the sleeve of his jumpsuit. Dozens of small, round scars dotted his arm. Then, he pulled at his collar, revealing a thick, ragged wound that looked like someone had carved away a four-inch-long strip of flesh with a vegetable peeler. Finally, he opened his mouth wide, showing two missing teeth and three others that were jagged and broken.

"Explain," she said.

He tapped the round scars. "Cigarette burns." He dragged his fingers across his neck. "One of those office supply things you use to remove staples, has the long metal teeth?"

Carolina nodded. They had those at her old station in Baltimore and called them Jaws. "And your teeth?"

"Steel-toed boots." Denton sagged back against his chair, as if the memory was too heavy to bear. "Two goddamn days they kept me in a cell, beating the shit out of me. Told me if I'd just sign a confession, they'd stop. I figured if I didn't, I'd be eating hamburgers through a straw the rest of my life; so, they told me to tell them a story. I did, they wrote it down, and I scribbled my name at the bottom."

"Who's they?" Carolina asked. "Who did that to you?"

"Sheriff Reed Bando and his band of jackals."

She didn't disbelieve him, but she wasn't jumping on his bandwagon just yet. Those wounds could have been caused anywhere, maybe even here in the state prison. "Of all the people in Monacan County, why'd they pick you?"

Denton stared at her, unwavering. "Because they needed someone to pin it on. They knew they could do whatever they wanted to me because my family's trash, and that makes me trash, too. Because I'm a Mankey," he said. "And that name's a scarlet letter in Monacan. They knew they could get away with making me take the fall, and they were right."

He sounded truthful, but he'd had seven years to rehearse his sob story.

"Ma'am, I'm not some altar boy who lived a perfect life. But I'm no killer. I don't expect you to believe me straight off, but if you're any good at what you do, all it's gonna take is a little digging, and you'll see. You'll find out I didn't do this."

Every man in prison is innocent, or so the saying goes. But they all deserved a fair chance, and, so far as she could tell, Denton Mankey had been deprived of that.

"Okay," she said. "Then I want you to tell me everything again, starting from the beginning."

CHAPTER SEVEN

"WHAT'S THE STORY BETWEEN YOU AND DENTON?" CAROLINA asked, cruising south at eighty miles per hour on the interstate with no other vehicles in sight. That was a rare advantage of living in one of the most sparsely populated states in the country.

Cyrus pulled the rag away from his mouth. He'd been keeping it there, like a man trying to hold a bad odor at bay, for the duration of the drive. When it came free, she saw blood lingering around his lips and on his teeth. "You've got to be more specific, darling."

"Why are you estranged? And I want details."

"Well, it ain't one of those rambling, Tolstoy kinda tales." He wound down his window, the breeze blowing his hair askew. He grabbed the pipe from his shirt pocket and reached into his pants for matches.

"You read Tolstoy?" she asked, then realized that wasn't the sort of minutia which would aid her investigation and motioned to his pipe. "You can't smoke in my van," she said.

He frowned and shoved the pipe away, petulant. "Some bullshit if you ask me."

"I didn't. Now start talking, or you can walk the rest of the way."

Cyrus folded his arms across his frail chest. "I told you I worked construction. I went where the work was and that was seldom in Monacan. Hard to get close to someone when you only see 'em a couple times a year."

"That's it? Because that seems like all the other vaguely sad father-son story I've heard."

The man slicked back his hair, then used some of the grease to wipe the blood away from his mouth. "You think I beat him or something? Molested him?"

"Maybe," Carolina said. But she didn't think it was that.

"Shit, I wasn't around enough. If I add together all the hours I spent with the boy, I bet it wouldn't total up to a full year. He don't like me because I wasn't a dad to him. I was a stranger who came home a couple times a year. And when I was home, I was more interested in getting his ma in the bedroom than playing catch." He half smirked, half sneered.

"Is his mother around? Because I want to talk to her."

"She's dead," Cyrus said the same flat, unemotional tone he might have used to say, *water is wet.*

"What happened to her?"

Cyrus looked at his lap in the same way that his son averted his eyes before dealing bad news. "Car crash."

"And?" She knew he was keeping something from her.

"And what? People die on the roads every day. 'Specially ones who drive like you."

"Cyrus, if you want me to stay with this, I expect full transparency. If I find out you're keeping anything from me, I'm out, and you'll die with your son behind bars. Is that what you want?"

He huffed and chewed on his lip for a moment before going on. "I'd just got off a six-month gig in Tallahassee. Came home with a wad of cash in my pocket big enough to choke a horse and wanted to celebrate. We hit about every bar in Monacan County. Might've been the best night of my life."

Carolina fought to keep her focus on the road as she stole glances at him.

"We almost made it home. Came around that big corner off route fifteen. Bowie Bend, they call it. Only I didn't make the turn. Ran head-on into a pine tree going about as fast as you are right now."

Instinctively, she eased up on the gas.

"Sandy, she was my wife, she went through the windshield, right into the fat part of the trunk. I was pinned behind the wheel and got to watch her die real slow. Took about half an hour. She couldn't really talk; she just kept mumbling *Wha, wha, wha*—over and over."

That was worse than Carolina had expected. "Damn," was all she could manage.

"I never saw Denton after. They got me for vehicular homicide, DUI, a half-ton of other shit. And that fucking judge didn't take no mercy on me. Twelve years."

"Like father, like son?" she asked. The remark was flippant and callous, and if she'd have taken even a second to think, she wouldn't have said it, but it was too late.

Cyrus spun sideways in his seat, his face flaring red. "Don't you judge my boy for my mistakes!"

In the back, Yeti gave a protective bark, pushing his oversized head between the seats. The dog's arrival diffused the situation before it could get going, and Cyrus slumped against the door panel, breathing hard with pained exertion.

"I'm just saying." He took a big mouthful of air and exhaled a cough. "It's because of who I am that they railroaded him. He deserves better than he got."

Carolina couldn't help but think about her own father. The one that had walked out of her life before she even knew him. And then she thought of Lester. The man who had shown her what a good father was supposed to be like.

"We don't get the fathers we want, do we?" she said.

Cyrus nodded. "That's for damn sure."

Getting involved with these men was foolish. Maybe - probably - dangerous, too. Did she really value her life so little she'd accept such risks? It went against everything she'd been taught, all her instincts. Yet here she was, doing it anyway.

The rest of the drive was in silence. And she didn't mind a bit.

CHAPTER EIGHT

CAROLINA RAISED HER HAND, READY TO KNOCK ON THE DOOR, but froze and stared at the placard—Sheriff. It should be Lester waiting inside the room. She needed his advice, his compassion. But Lester would never be there, inside his office, again. Sooner or later, she had to accept the new reality.

She gave two quick raps that thudded lifelessly against the hollow core door. Then she waited.

After a shuffling of papers came, "Yeah, come on in." She pushed the door open.

Carolina didn't see him at first. No one sat behind the large desk. The swivel chair was also empty.

As she peered around the room, seeing much of the same decor as when Lester was in charge, she wondered why Elven hadn't redecorated yet and made the place his own. If for no other reason than to chase away the ghosts. She knew Elven had loved the man, though, and sometimes, the letting go was the worst part.

"Carolina." Elven's voice floated from the corner of the room, and she found him partially hidden, kneeling beside a filing cabinet with two drawers pulled out. Stacks of files, each two feet high, penned him in.

"Looks like you're in deep over there," Carolina said.

Elven put a hand to his chin and cracked his neck. "You're not kidding." He closed the file he'd been holding, set it atop the others, then climbed to his feet.

"You could use another set of hands around here. Another deputy might lessen your load."

"Did you change your mind since we last spoke?" he asked, his face skeptical, yet hopeful.

"I have not."

He sighed. "Then no; I'm still working through the transition, and that's a nightmare in itself. The last thing I need is to add applications, interviews, and training some greenhorn to everything else I'm trying to get accomplished."

Elven sat in his chair and leaned back into it, stretching out his long frame. "I assume you got my text?" He asked.

Carolina tapped her phone through her pocket. "I did. *Meet me at the office.* Very explanatory. Do you pay per character?"

"I was planning on doing you a favor, but if all you can offer me is sarcasm, I might change my mind."

Intrigued, she sat on the corner of his desk, hovering over him in his chair. If he was anyone else, she would have thought she might be too close, too informal. But Elven didn't seem to mind the proximity. Instead, he only smirked, causing her to wonder even more about the nature of the favor.

"Are you going to tell me what it is, or just gawk at me with that stupid grin?" she asked.

His smirk widened. "Most people don't mind my stupid grin. I can't tell you how many women say the opposite, actually."

Carolina leaned down toward him. "If you think telling me about all the desperate housewives in Dupray who would line up to sleep with you is something to be proud of, then you're either solidifying my low opinion of this place or dragging down what respect I have for you."

"Such ungrateful words from someone who is about to get the file they so desperately want on one Denton Mankey. Perhaps you should strike out on your own. You seem rather self-sufficient, after all."

She looked him up and down, studying him as she tried to determine whether he was being truthful or jerking her chain. "I thought you said you couldn't access it. Something about backwoods Internet problems."

"That is what I said. But the phones still work; so, I made a call."

Carolina jumped to her feet, sending a mug of pens soaring to the floor. This wasn't what she wanted to hear—not after Denton had described how he'd been tortured. "Damn it; I told you not to do that," she said, louder and angrier than she intended. Elven's smile vanished, replaced by confusion and shock. "I didn't want the Sheriff to know I was investigating this. Fuck!"

She spun away, trying to reel in her anger.

"I'm fully aware you have tendencies toward self-aggrandizing," Elven said. The wheels of his chair gave a plaintive screech as he pushed away from the desk and stood. "But that does not mean everyone who surrounds you is a fool."

Carolina forced herself to look at him and found him standing with his arms crossed and a peeved expression on his face. He said nothing else and was clearly waiting on her to make the next move.

"What do you want me to say?"

"*Sorry* would be nice," Elven said. "Because I didn't say anything to Sheriff Bando about you looking into the case."

She felt some of the stress drain from her. "You didn't?"

"Of course not," Elven said.

"Oh." Now she felt like an asshole. It was a familiar feeling, but still an unpleasant one. "What did you tell him then?"

"Well, I called and introduced myself. Puffed him up a bit and told him how I'd heard so many great things about him over the years and I hoped I could be half the sheriff he was."

That drew a derisive laugh from her.

"Yeah, I struggled with that part," Elven said. "Lying isn't my specialty." He stared at her for a little too long before going on. "Then I told him we had some unsolved assaults from a few years back and we considered Mankey a suspect. I said being able to look over his file might help me decide whether or not he was our guy."

"And he agreed to help you?" The news surprised her. Maybe she'd been wrong to assume the worst.

"He did. Said he'd have one of his deputies pull the case file and have it waiting. I told him I'd send my girl over to get it." The smirk was back. She both hated and loved it.

"Your girl?" She asked.

"You know how law enforcement works around here. It's a good ol' boy network. I'm just trying to fit in."

"Don't try too hard. Please." She pulled out her cell phone and searched for the address for the Monacan County Sheriff's Department, then added it to her driving route. It was almost two hours away. "You didn't give him my name, did you?"

Elven shook his head, mocking disappointment. "No names. I just described you."

"Oh God," she said. "I'd hate to hear how that went down."

He took a step closer to her; only the corner of the desk was separating them now. "I told him you were a sight to behold."

From anyone else, she'd have thought the remark sarcasm, but when the words came out of his mouth, she felt her cheeks heat up and turned away before he could notice. "Well, thanks," she said. "I better hit the road if I want to make it there before shift change." She slipped toward the exit.

"I am still waiting for my apology," Elven called as she passed through the doorway.

"You should be used to that by now."

CHAPTER NINE

THE MONACAN COUNTY SHERIFF'S DEPARTMENT WAS A squat, brick building squeezed between a thrift store and a pharmacy like an afterthought. In some place other than West Virginia's deep south, it could have been a library or maybe a doctor's office. But here, its crumbling facade served as home to the county's law enforcement.

A dirt and weed path led the way to the office door, where a pristine Sheriff's badge decal obscured the view through the glass. Carolina didn't waste time trying to peek around it, instead striding inside, where an overhead bell gave a tuneless ding to signify her arrival.

The inside bore the same signs of age as the exterior. Dueling tobacco aromas of smoke and chew served at its air freshener. The vinyl tile floors looked like they hadn't experienced a good scrubbing in years. The mismatched furniture, what there was of it, seemed to have been confiscated from crime scenes.

An overhead fan threw stale air downward, making the dust bunnies, which hid in every available nook, quiver and sway. The overall mood was one of slovenly depression, and it fit the poor excuse of a town she'd driven through to get there. Monacan made Dupray look downright inviting.

No one waited at the desk to greet her, but shuffling footsteps assured her that would be remedied in short order.

A bespectacled man in a blue chambray button-down emerged from a cramped hallway. A glob of Dijon mustard clung to his upper lip like a festering sore. "Sorry," he said. "I was having an early supper."

"I can see," Carolina said. She tapped her lip at the same spot where the excess condiment was residing on his own face.

Rather than wipe it away, he went exploring with his tongue, a dull pink muscle that would have made Gene Simmons jealous. Carolina resisted the urge to shudder as he found it and made it disappear.

"Can I help you?" he asked.

"I expect so. I'm here to pick up a file for Sheriff Hallie in Dupray."

"Oh." His eyes went to the cluttered desk, searching. "Well, I'm not—"

Before he could finish whatever it was he was going to say, a blue spruce of a man in a Deputy's uniform shirt joined them. He rested a hand the size of a catcher's mitt on the secretary's shoulder. "I got this, Lewis. Go ahead and put your bologna on rye outta its misery."

The secretary, Lewis, peered up at the much larger man and nodded. "All right, Donnie."

He left them.

In just those few seconds, Carolina knew this wouldn't be as simple as she'd hoped. But then, what was?

The deputy looked down on her, a professional smile tugging at his lips. He was young, mid-twenties, with shoe-polish black hair and stubble sprouting in random patches like a mysterious fungus across his cheeks and Superman chin. In addition to his hulking frame, he wore the muscles of a gym rat, and she was certain his body-fat percentage was in the single digits.

None of that made up for his ugly mug, though. His broad face was asymmetric, his left eye a good half an inch higher than the right. A deep scar carved its way through that eyebrow and up his forehead before getting lost in his hairline. He had the complexion of a teenage chocoholic, with zits on the verge of bursting and blackheads the size of peppercorns. He was a hard man to look at, but she forced herself.

"Hello there, ma'am. I'm Deputy Donnie Westfall. At your service."

"Is Bando in?" Carolina asked, choosing to drop the sheriff title to insinuate she knew him personally. "Sheriff Hallie sent me to retrieve a file from him."

Donnie looked her up and down. She wasn't sure if he was studying her body language or just studying her body. "Sheriff's not in, but he told me you'd be stopping by. Though, I'm afraid I've been tasked with being the bearer of bad news."

It was par for the course. "And what's that, Deputy?"

"We don't have the file. Sheriff asked me to apologize on his behalf." Donnie's smirk never left his face. "So sorry."

She couldn't believe she'd just wasted two hours driving on these dipshits. She was ready to tell Deputy Donnie what was on her mind when—

"Sheriff also mentioned Hallie was sending a pretty girl on this errand, and I gotta say, that was quite an understatement." He loosed a low whistle between the gap in his front teeth.

Carolina was taken by surprise. Not by the chauvinistic attitude, it went with the territory, but that the man was so blatant about it. Subtlety was a lost art. She caught her own reflection in a convex mirror hanging high above the front desk, providing a view of the office and all its occupants. Her hair was a tangled mess, desperately in need of a hairbrush, if not a blow torch. Her baggy windbreaker was zipped to her neck, concealing her curves. And she was certain the last time she'd bothered to put on makeup was a full season ago.

"Sheriff Hallie spoke with Bando personally. He said the file would be ready when I got here, so I don't understand why I'm getting the run around."

"I'm sorry. I truly am. But a good half our files were destroyed in a flood a few years back. Worst one in these parts in ages. Decades of files, just gone like that." He snapped his fingers. "Sheriff thought maybe the one you were after had survived unscathed and sent me to look for it. But it wasn't meant to be." Still smiling.

"You're sure you looked for the right file?" Her tone bordered on condescending.

He stiffened, unappreciative over being questioned. "Denton Mankey's, right? The guttersnipe who killed poor Cece Casto."

Damn. She'd hoped he was full of shit. And he still might be, but there wasn't much else she could do to prove it. Her only remaining option was trying to pull some information from this hunk of testosterone.

"Yeah, he's the one. It just sucks; I probably wasted twenty bucks in gas, never mind my time." She leaned into the counter, closing the distance between them, and tried to look alluring and desperate, but doing a poor job of both. "I don't suppose you could tell me anything about the case? Something I can take back to Elven? Maybe help him out."

Donnie leaned in, too, close enough she could smell the hot dogs and onions he'd recently consumed. She tried to hide her revulsion. "Not the case specifically—I didn't work it. But I remember Mankey." He paused, and she knew he was going to make her beg for it.

"What was he like?" she asked.

"Real bad apple, that one. Anytime something went wrong, he was one of the first we investigated. Most of the time, he was involved too."

"Like what?"

Donnie shrugged and pulled away. "You ask a lot of questions for the Dupray sheriff's lackey. This is all above your pay grade, don't you think, doll?"

Carolina counted in her head, trying to diffuse her temper before responding. "Just doing my job," she replied through clenched jaws.

"Don't worry your pretty head about police matters now. You go on home and tell your boss you did what he asked. And tell him if he suspects Denton Mankey of doing something wrong, he's probably spot on; the boy never was one to turn down trouble."

Carolina stood, burying her hands in her pockets to resist the temptation to smack the asshole. She was halfway to the door when he called to her.

"You driving back to Dupray tonight?" he asked.

"That was the plan." She saw him standing with his thumbs inside his waistband, his crotch tilted her way.

"Gets dark early this time of year. And the deer'll be jumping. Not real safe to be on the road in those conditions."

"What choice do I have?" Carolina asked, but the dread in her stomach signaled what was coming.

"Well, my shift ends at seven. I got a big place all to myself. And we in Monacan County do pride ourselves on our hospitality."

For a fleeting moment, she wondered if it would be worth it. If she could pry information from him. But despite having almost no concern for her own safety and little respect for herself, even she wasn't ready to stoop so low.

Yet.

"Elven's expecting me back. But thanks for the offer."

Donnie nodded. "Your choice."

She opened the door, the bell chiming above her.

"Be careful out there," Donnie said.

She didn't respond.

CHAPTER TEN

Carolina jerked her phone from the pocket of her windbreaker and dialed Elven's cell. She pinched it between her shoulder and ear as she unlocked her van and climbed into the seat, slamming the door once she was in.

She was not happy, which wasn't unusual. As she threw the van into drive and pulled onto the road, she listened to the speaker ring again and again until finally, it was replaced with an earful of static.

"Elven?"

"Caro—" More static.

She pressed the gas, climbing a small hill where she hoped the reception would improve. "I just left the sheriff's department. They said they don't have the fucking file. The bastard was lying to me, though; I'm sure of it."

"Carol—can't—this is—now?"

Nothing but static between the words. Shit. "Elven, can you hear me?" she asked one more time.

There was more white noise and a few words she failed to

decipher. Then, the phone beeped in her ear. Call Ended. The triangle at the top of the display screen was empty. No signal. Double shit.

She was ready to punch *home* into the GPS but stopped. She'd driven all this way, only to hit a roadblock, but that didn't mean she had to go back to Dupray empty-handed.

ONE OF THE names Denton had assured would provide him with an alibi was Regina Gormley, his on again, off again girlfriend who'd been with him at the drive-in on the night Cecilia Casto went missing. In her research, Carolina had found her address, and now, she cruised down the narrow road for fifteen or so miles until she arrived at Merry Meadows Mobile Home Court. The sign was the only merry thing about the place.

Rows of forty-plus-year-old trailers lined each side of the lane. Many looked abandoned, with broken windows, sagging roofs, and unmowed lawns. Feral cats commandeered deteriorating porches, armies of them ready to keep the rodent population in check. Rust bucket trucks and the occasional car sat at the ready by the few occupied residences.

She checked the house number she'd jotted down. 121. Another twenty yards of dodging potholes and crumbling blacktop, and she was there.

Considering its surroundings, Regina Gormley's trailer wasn't bad. The paint was still white-ish, with maroon trim around the roof and windows. Two pots of fall mums sat on each side of the entryway, and a cardboard jack-o-lantern was taped to the door.

As she exited the van, she caught two children, both under the age of six, watching her from the lawn across the way. She smiled and waved, but they didn't react.

The screen door to their home banged. "Get in here!" bellowed a beanpole of a woman with her hair in curlers. The kids sprinted into the house, and the mother took up the role of gawking at the interloper. Carolina didn't waste time waving or smiling at her.

She climbed the three steps ascending to Regina's trailer and knocked on the door. That action caused World War III to erupt inside.

Dogs barked. Children screamed. A woman retaliated with, "Shut the fuck up!" A slap. Crying. Then stomping footsteps.

"Hold onto Rudy!" The same frustrated voice ordered, and the door opened a solid four inches.

"Yeah?" she asked.

Carolina could only see one eye, a beakish nose, and a mouth with a cigarette dangling from it. "Regina Gormley?" she asked.

"I'm not interested in buying shit, lady," Regina said. "And don't knock on my fucking door again. It makes the dog go crazy." She moved to close the door, but Carolina pressed her hand against it, stopping her before it latched.

"It's about Denton Mankey," Carolina said.

The pressure on the door let up. The woman opened it further, and Carolina could see she was pregnant, seemingly a few short weeks away from popping. Her sweatpants hung below her waist, her thermal shirt above it, allowing her pale, oversized gut to stick out like an albino watermelon.

Behind Regina, one of her kids—its hair was short, and Carolina couldn't tell if it was a boy or a girl—dashed into her legs, causing her knees to buckle. Regina straightened back up and bucked her foot backward, connecting with the androgynous child's arm. It gave a pained scream before taking off running again, full bore, and disappeared out of sight.

Regina glanced inside. "Sissy, watch your brother so he doesn't crawl into the oven again!" Then she was outside, shutting the door behind her, locking in the madness.

"You have any kids?" she asked as she took a long drag on her cigarette.

Thank God no, Carolina thought. "I don't."

"Smart woman." Regina pointed to a red picnic table sitting amongst the weeds that comprised the lawn. Two paint cans, each overflowing with cigarette butts, sat atop it, along with some colored blocks had been built into a lopsided pyramid. They sat across from each other.

"Don't you got to show me a badge or something?" Regina asked.

"A badge?"

"You're a cop, right?"

Sometimes Carolina thought she may as well be painted blue. "No, I'm a private investigator."

"Oh," Regina said. "Well don't they got badges? They do in the movies."

The woman's inquisitiveness surprised Carolina, who realized she'd prejudged her. That was a bad habit she needed to break. "Not in West Virginia. I have a license in my van. I can get it if you want." Please don't call my bluff.

Regina snuffed out her cigarette against the tabletop and added the butt to one of the cans. "Don't bother; I can't leave the kids alone too long or J.R.'s apt to start humping the dog again. So, get on with it, and tell me what you need to know."

"I'm looking into Denton Mankey."

"Yeah, I heard you the first time. That's why I didn't slam the door in your face. I also know his last name; so, you can just save yourself the time and call him Denton. Now, are you gonna ask your questions, or we just gonna sit here and shoot the shit?"

Carolina was more than happy to avoid forced small talk. "Denton told me you were dating at the time the murder happened. Do you remember the night Cecilia Casto disappeared?"

Regina grabbed a pack of generic cigarettes from her pocket. "So, you've seen Denton? How's he doin'?"

Carolina shrugged. "I suppose as good as can be expected, all things considered."

"All things considered. Ain't that the truth?" She flicked a lighter and set the tip of her new smoke ablaze. "Yeah, I remember. We was at the drive-in that night. It was *Guardians of the Galaxy*. And I know it was Wednesday 'cause that's carload night. Nine dollars no matter how many people you squeeze in. That's when we always went."

Carolina jotted down the info. Denton had named a different movie, but she wasn't sure if it was relevant or not yet. "Was it just the two of you?"

"Nope. Went with Odetta and Freddy."

"That would be Odetta Miller and Fred Cranmer?" Carolina asked.

Regina rolled her eyes. "Why the fuck are you asking me questions you already know the answers to?"

"I'm sorry. I'm just trying to verify the information Denton gave me. Will Odetta and Freddy back this up?"

"I doubt Odetta will."

"Why not?" Carolina asked.

"Because she died about three years back. OD'd on Oxy. She'd been on it a good while. Started after she blew a disk in her back. I told her she needed to get help, but she promised me she had it under control. I guess she did, until she didn't."

Carolina felt a little hot at the mention of Oxy, but the sad story only increased her desire to down another pill.

"What about Freddy?" Carolina asked, trying to push aside her craving.

"Yeah, he's still alive."

The trailer door opened and slammed. Both women turned to see a boy of around seven holding a ratty teddy bear in one hand and an orange popsicle in the other. "Momma, I'm hungry, and Sissy won't cut open my popsicle."

"I fuckin' told you to behave. Don't make me get up and teach you some manners in front of this nice lady," Regina yelled. She looked back at Carolina. "Don't worry; I ain't gonna do nothin'. Just need to put a scare into 'em."

The boy disappeared back into the house.

"Do you know where I can find him?" Carolina asked, sticking to the subject.

"I ain't seen Freddy in a while, though I hear you can find him at the bar. Just like old times." She smiled, eyes wistful. "Guess some things never change."

A piercing scream inside the trailer made Carolina jump two inches off her seat, but Regina barely reacted. Still, she knew she was on borrowed time and wanted to ask the most important question.

"Denton confessed to the murder," she said. "He's recanted since then, but let me ask you, do you think he could have done it?"

Regina pulled the cigarette from her lips and tapped a long ash into the yard. "I knew Denton better than most. Spent some of the best times of my life with him. I'm not saying we were some Romeo and Juliet bullshit, but we were close; I knew him here." She tapped her chest with her index finger. Then she went for another hit off the cigarette, her hand trembling. "What was done to that girl were about the most awful things I could ever imagine. There's no way the guy I knew could do something like that. Not to a girl. Not to anyone."

Carolina wanted to press her for more information on the crime, information she still lacked, but she could tell she was losing the woman. Besides, it wasn't fair to get the gory details from this person, who was only involved in the periphery.

"Have the police ever questioned you about any of this?"

The woman rolled her eyes. "Not once. You're the first person to ever ask me about it."

That shouldn't have been a surprise, but it still came as one. It was sounding more and more like Denton's story about being railroaded was true. "Then let me ask you something else. If

Denton didn't murder Cecilia Casto, do you have any idea who could have?"

Regina gaze shifted beyond Carolina, taking in the depressing countryside. "Around here? Could be just about anyone."

CHAPTER ELEVEN

CAROLINA FOLLOWED REGINA GORMLEY'S DIRECTIONS TO Duke's, expecting to discover a run-down, hole-in-the-wall type of place and finding just that. Despite the cool evening air, the front door was propped open with a cinder block, providing a clear view inside.

Just shy of twenty people—most middle-aged or older—were scattered about the interior. A radio blared vintage country music, and some twangy-voiced man droned about losing his home to his bitch of an ex. To the singer, beer seemed to be the solution to all of life's problems, a motto adopted by Duke's patrons.

There was no dancing. No food. No mingling. Just some of the saddest looking men and women Carolina had ever seen leaning against the bar or slouching in booths and drinking away their worries.

She'd thought identifying Freddy Cranmer might be easy—she needed only look for the most obvious drunk. But this place seemed to be an alcoholic's version of an Olympic stadium. Rather than question them one at a time, she did the next best thing and approached the bartender, who looked surprisingly fit for the place and the county.

"Help you?" he asked as he dropped three empties into a metal trash can.

"Maybe," Carolina said. "I'm looking for Freddy Cranmer."

The bartender looked past her, to a corner booth where a drunk slept one off. "What did he do now?"

Carolina thought about blowing him off and moving on to Freddy, but the bartender had been helpful, and she resisted her instinct to be rude. "Nothing, so far as I know. I just want to ask him about an old friend. Thanks for your help."

She crossed half the distance to the drunk before the bartender called to her. "You sure he's not in trouble?"

Carolina glanced back and nodded. "One hundred percent."

"Why don't you come back here and have a seat, and we'll chat," he said. "I'll give you a beer on the house."

This is what she got for being cordial. "Thanks, but I just need to talk to Freddy." That was nicer than what she wanted to say: *Leave me alone, creep.* Her good deed for the day.

"I hate to break it to you, but you have been talking to him."

Carolina turned back at his smiling face. He had a shaved head and dense beard, both of which made him seem older. But, when she took a better look, she could see he was only in his mid-twenties. He was also, contrary to her assumptions, completely sober.

As if he could read the surprise on her face, he laughed. "You look like someone who had low expectations of me. Can't say as I blame you, though."

Carolina hopped onto a barstool and, as promised, Freddy Cranmer handed her a beer. She knew she shouldn't drink, with the pills and the drive home, but when in Rome...

The Coors went down just fine.

"Who sent you here to look for me?" he asked.

"Regina Gormley."

He took a swig from a bottle of water. "Damn. That's a blast from the past."

"I have another one of those," Carolina said. "I'm a P.I. doing some research into Denton Mankey's murder conviction."

If Regina's name brought a fond memory, Denton's did the opposite. "Why would a nice lady like you waste your time over such nastiness?"

"What makes you think I'm nice?" Carolina took another swig of beer.

Freddy examined her for a long moment. "Your eyes," he answered. "There's humanity in your eyes. I don't see that too often, especially in here."

If that was a line, it was one of the more creative ones she'd heard. But she wasn't there to flirt. "Did the police question you about Denton or the homicide?

He dragged a dirty rag across the dirtier bar. "Nope. Why would they?"

"Let's back up a bit," Carolina said. "Do you remember going to the drive-in with him the night Cecilia Casto disappeared?"

He nodded. "Sure do. Double feature. *Hunger Games* and *Guardians of the Galaxy*. I didn't care for either."

That settled up the issue with the differing movies. "Any idea what time the show let out?"

He considered it. "The night comes late that time of year; so, it must've been after midnight. And the drive-in's about forty-five minutes away; I'd guess we got back around one."

"Which is pretty clear evidence against him taking her."

He grabbed a shot glass and filled it with rum, passing it to a patron down the bar. "What's to say he didn't get up to something bad after he dropped us off?"

It was a possibility, but it seemed slim. "It was you, Regina, and Odetta Miller, right?"

"Yeah."

"Which of you were the last to see him?"

"I was," Freddy said. "I lived the furthest outside town; so, he took me home last."

A man down in a booth snapped his fingers to get Freddy's attention. "Give me a sec," he said and went to refill whatever the man was drinking.

When he returned, his friendly demeanor was lacking. "Listen, back then, Denton was my best friend. He stuck by me through a lot of dark days." He pointed to a pin on his shirt. Carolina examined it and saw it was from Alcoholics Anonymous and signaled five years sobriety.

"I wasn't a nice guy, but he never judged me. Not when I got into fights. Not when I puked in his truck. I was closer to Denton than my own brothers. That's why I got so pissed when it came out what he did. And through the grace of God, I've forgiven him, But I'm not getting on board with some bullshit to let him get away with murder, either."

"Did you ever see him act violently? Did he ever join you in those fights you mentioned?"

Freddy finished the last swig of his water, crushed the bottle in his hand, and dropped it into the trash. "Never. He always said he was a lover, not a fighter. That was the truth, too. He saw more pussy than a veterinarian."

She couldn't hold back a smile and thought she'd have to share it with Denton if she saw him again. "You tell me all this, make him sound like a swell guy, yet you still think he killed Cecilia Casto. Why? What makes you so convinced he killed the girl?"

"He confessed. Can you give me a reason why a man would admit to it if he were innocent? Because I've been trying to find one for the last eight years, and I keep coming up blank."

"Denton says the confession was beaten out of him. He has the scars to go along with it."

Freddy huffed. "It would take one hell of a whooping to make me say I butchered a little girl when I didn't. In fact, I'd wager to say you could beat me about to death, and I still wouldn't."

That was the problem with people. They could only view life through their own glasses and thought everyone would behave the same as they would. "You guys were what, seventeen?"

"He was. I was eighteen."

"And there isn't any part of you that thinks a couple of grown men could torture a confession from your teenage best friend?"

"A man who can't control his own mouth ain't got no one to blame but himself."

She wanted to press him further, but a hulking shape stepped into Duke's entrance, blocking all incoming light. She looked and saw deputy Donnie Westfall. "Shit." She said it to herself, but Freddy was close enough to overhear. He followed her gaze, then looked back to her, curious.

"Friend of yours?" he asked.

"Is there a back way out of here?"

Donnie was moving inside, and she didn't have time to explain. Freddy pointed to an unlit hallway at the rear of the bar. "Door back there opens to the alley."

She grabbed her money clip and threw a twenty onto the bar.

"The beer was on me," he said.

"I know. The cash is for pretending like you never met me."

With that, she was on the move, not even casting a glance toward Donnie to see if he'd noticed her. She kept her head down as she hurried down the hallway and pushed against a steel door came open with a scream of protest.

The alley was bereft of people but reeked of vomit and rotting garbage. She crawled over the Andes Mountains of trash bags, one foot sinking into something hot and dense and moist, as she made her way to the street, then checked to make sure Donnie wasn't already out there and waiting for her.

But she'd escaped unnoticed.

Or so she thought.

A yellow slip of paper was pinched between the wiper and windshield of her van. She snatched it away, already knowing what it was. A parking ticket. She looked at the violation line. Scrawled in near illegible handwriting was:

Parked 14 inches from curb.

The fine was $75.

Motherfucker.

Not only did the asshole know what she was driving, now he'd run her plates and find out her name. Find out everything about her. Between that and the mounting costs this job was losing its appeal in a hurry.

She wanted to get the hell out of Monacan but had one more stop to make before calling it a day.

CHAPTER TWELVE

THE SUN SLID LOW IN THE COBALT SKY AS SHE TRAVERSED THE twists and turns of the rural roads. There were no street signs this far out of town; so, she relied on her GPS to lead the way. To take her to the place the newspaper clippings called The Devil's Teeth.

The official name was Loyalhanna Overlook, one of the Appalachia's least-visited hiking paths—probably because it was situated on private property. The body of Cecilia Casto had been found there, in what the aspiring Pulitzer winner who'd penned the first article called *A scene of unimaginable atrocity.*

While the article provided no specific details, as they were deemed too sordid for publication, the wordsmith managed to get across the point. Whatever happened there was unusually bad, going beyond a murder and into something more akin to atrocity.

Although no evidence would remain seven years after the crime, Carolina needed to see the place in person. To put visuals to the name and see if it lived up to the reputation.

She hadn't realized just how far, or difficult, finding it would be. Had she known, she would have come some other time But she'd gone this far already, and turning back would be yet another failure on an unproductive day.

The road dead-ended at an iron gate, beyond which stretched a slim hiking path. A blog, Rogue Hikers, had given her a map to use and warned to "Be alert for copperhead snakes." Through the diminishing light, she wondered, again, how stupid she was to come here. Alone. At sunset. She hadn't even informed Elven about her plans. She could walk up there and break and ankle, or worse, and no one would have a clue to her whereabouts.

She wasn't afraid of dying, but a drawn-out, miserable death alone in the forest held little appeal.

As she checked her phone, she was certain it would still show no signal, and she was right. Oh well; wasn't there some saying about risks and rewards? She skirted the gate and began the ascent, wishing she had a pair of boots and not her low-top Chuck Taylors.

Twenty minutes later and sucking in whooping mouthfuls of air—damn, she was out of shape—she arrived.

At the edge of the clearing, the dirt and weeds transitioned to rock—but not ordinary rocks. These were boulders, more than a dozen of them—each at least ten feet across. She stepped onto one, and its uneven surface, coupled with the drop-off ahead, gave her a brief floating-away feeling.

Between the hunks of stone were crevices over twenty feet deep, the bottoms cluttered with wild foliage and litter. She imagined copperheads were hiding in those depths, too, lounging in the shade and waiting for anyone dumb enough to fall in. Not her. Not today.

It was easy to see why these boulders were called teeth, with their smooth, molar-esque appearance. Beyond them, the land dropped into the valley, which had taken on a fiery glow as the sunlight reflected over the changing leaves. It was beautiful—if you could forget about what happened here.

She couldn't.

Besides, she wasn't there to sightsee—not in the traditional sense. She pulled the newspaper print outs from her pocket and unfolded them. Only one of the articles had photos, and she used them to get her bearings and put herself in the crime scene.

She located the slab of sandstone upon which Cecilia Casto's body had been found and went to it, careful not to misstep and plunge into the chasms between the boulders. Along the way, she saw discarded beer cans and bottles, cigarette butts, drug paraphernalia.

Damned kids. Carolina might have problems, but she didn't litter.

The leaves had already fallen from the maples which called this place home, leaving behind clawing, skeletal branches. On one of them, she saw a carved symbol. An oval with some slashes through the top.

If she allowed her vision to fall out of focus, it almost looked like an animal—maybe a deer. She pulled out her phone and snapped a picture. Something about the raw, primal look of it unnerved her.

Behind the tree, a white pile caught her attention. When she took a better look, she saw it was comprised of animal skulls of varying sizes and shapes, bleached and weathered. While she didn't put much stock in the rumors about this place, the precision used in stacking them seemed too perfect to have been done by drunken teenagers.

There was more. Spray painted pentagrams. Inverted crosses. Random penises. Rather than accentuate the ominous nature of the spot, the graffiti lessened it. Now it did seem like a hangout for kids, a place like thousands of others where rebels came to get drunk and laid and pretend to be bad-asses. Some of the dread she felt being there blew away with the wind.

The slab hadn't been spared from the vandalism. On it, someone had painted a cartoon devil with the biggest dick she'd seen outside of a Hustler cartoon. There was also an eclectic assortment of trinkets. Costume jewelry. Various coins. A weathered Barbie doll. A bouquet of long dead flowers. And someone had written, *Cece Casto gave great head!* Gallows humor at its finest.

Above all of it, etched into the stone, were letters. They seemed random.

e r t o d

The T might have been a plus sign. E.R. plus O.D? All that was missing was *4 forever* and a heart.

There was more, but they were illegible scratches. She dragged her fingers across them, the rough texture pulling at her skin. Even though the rock had been turned a light gray from the sun, the color was deeper in those carvings. It almost looked red down inside the grooves.

It's been seven years, she thought. That couldn't be Cecilia's blood. Not after all this time.

Then there was a sharp pain in her finger. She drew it back and saw real blood.

Her own.

An inch-long slice bisected the pad of her middle finger, and fat droplets leaked out. One of them fell onto the T in the initials, filling it to the brim.

As Carolina stuck her finger in her mouth, sucking the wound clean, she leaned in to inspect what had cut her and found an opaque shard of glass, no larger than a toothpick, embedded in a crack on the rock. In her carelessness, she'd run her finger right across it.

Offering herself up.

That, coupled with the metallic taste of blood in her mouth, made her shiver.

Suddenly she realized the sun had set, leaving behind only the murky remnants of dusk. She could still see the area around her, but in fifteen minutes, it would be pitch black.

And then the unease slammed home.

Not because she thought Cecilia Casto's ghost, or perhaps her killer, would come to steal her life - or her soul - but over more practical purposes. The hike uphill hadn't been fun when she could see where she was going. Making it in the dark would be near impossible, and an impromptu camping trip in an area teeming with copperheads wasn't high on her bucket list.

CHAPTER THIRTEEN

THE DAY HAD BEEN STRESSFUL AND TIRING, LEAVING HER WITH a thudding headache for her efforts. She downed one Oxy as soon as she clambered into the van. It wouldn't do much, but she couldn't drive with her usual dose of three, plus the beer, in her system. Not if she wanted to make it back to Dupray in one piece.

The van's crappy headlights barely brightened the road ahead, forcing her to drive at half her usual speed. At this rate, it would take her until past midnight to get home.

Of course, when you lived in your ride, home was wherever you parked. If she got too tired, she could simply pull off the side of the road, lock the doors, and crash. Figuratively.

Only three miles from the Devil's Teeth, oncoming headlights blinded her. In retaliation, she blinked her high beams, but in this battle of lumens, she was destined to be the loser. She hit them again, for spite, and the oncoming vehicle downgraded to lows.

It was a white pickup, utilitarian and plain. It seemed odd to meet it out here, on this dead-end road, and Carolina slowed, trying to get a look at the driver. She couldn't make out his face before a yellow warning light on his roof came to life, spinning around and around. Then she saw the driver gesturing, his hand pointing to the side of the road. The message was clear enough: *Pull over.*

Carolina flicked off the safety on her pistol, just in case.

The truck pulled alongside her, the driver's side window aligned with her own, and she saw the man was wearing a black cap on which Security was stitched in white letters. His jacket indicated the same. This was better than a Monacan cop, anyway.

"You need some help?" Carolina asked before he could say anything. May as well act as if she was doing nothing wrong, even though she knew the land here was off-limits. Not that the copious signs of vandalism indicated many took such warnings seriously.

The driver was about her age, windburned and possibly Latino, rare in this part of West Virginia. A tattoo on his chest scrabbled at his neck but mostly hid under his collar. His expression was blank and impossible to read. "I was about to ask you the same thing," he said.

"No, I don't think so," she said. "I'm good."

"I'm not so sure about that." He reached toward the passenger seat, and Carolina let her right hand fall to her pistol, just to reassure herself it hadn't run off in the last ten seconds.

The driver drew first.

A flashlight.

She breathed a little easier, even as he blinded her by shining the beam into her eyes. Then he aimed it around her cab, taking a good, long look. Eventually, he settled back into pointing it at her face. Lovely.

"All this land is owned by the Appalachian Coal Company," he said. "You're on private property."

"I am?" She flashed her most apologetic and clueless grin. "Shit. I'm sorry. I didn't see any signs."

He lowered the beam, now aiming it in the general direction of her chest. "Kids might have grabbed 'em," he said. "They'll steal anything that isn't bolted down." Then he smiled too, and Carolina was somewhat convinced her plea of ignorance had been bought.

"I was out birdwatching and got a little lost," she said.

"It happens. Especially at night on these roads."

She could make her exit now, but... "Can I ask what you're guarding? I didn't see anything out here more interesting than a Swainson's Thrush."

"Oh, there's not much. Some old equipment half-buried in the vegetation. It's more about the abandoned mines. Couple a kids came out here last year with their four wheelers and rode them down into the shafts. Two of them didn't make it back out. Dead kids are bad PR."

"Seems to happen a lot out here," she offered, seeing if he'd take the bait. "Kids dying."

"I wouldn't know it. I'm from Arizona. Just moved here in February. Not bad as far as jobs go. Mostly, I just ride around and look at deer. And the occasional lost lady."

"What brought you to a hellhole like this?"

"Online dating," he said, holding up his ring finger to display a narrow, gold band while chuckling, mostly to himself. "Guess there are a few good things around here."

"Sorry; I didn't mean anything by it."

"No offense taken. I guess I should ask you the same. Why are you here?"

For a moment, Carolina considered the truth, but there was no information to be garnered from a man who hadn't even lived in the state when Cecilia Casto was murdered. And the fewer people who knew who she was and why she was here, the better. "Just visiting an old friend."

His smile, which had been quite genuine, faltered. "Not much of a friend to let you out here all by yourself."

"She doesn't know I'm in town yet. Isn't expecting me until tomorrow; so, I thought I'd take in the sights, maybe rough it in my van for the night."

The smile was all the way gone now, replaced with a nervous scowl. "Don't think you wanna be doing that."

"It's okay. I'm a big girl, and it wouldn't be the first time."

"I'm not the superstitious type," he said. "But there's all kinds of rumors about this place. I really wish you'd reconsider."

"What kinds of rumors?"

He looked past her to the black woods. "I don't know. People out here, they got strange ways. My grandmother, she was Paiute, and she told stories about the dread spirits. They watch over places, but if you see them, you die. These woods sort of make me think of that."

"I thought you said you weren't superstitious," Carolina said.

He gave a nervous laugh. "Maybe a little. I'm just saying, though, there's a boarding house on the south side of town. Pretty cheap, too. If you need some money, I'll help you out." He reached behind himself, going for his wallet.

Jesus, he thinks I'm homeless, she realized. Of course, she was, in a way. How bad do I look?

"No, really. I'm good. I'll just head over to my friend's."

"Are you sure?"

She nodded.

"All right then. Drive safe."

"You too. Watch out for the dread spirits."

She meant it as a joke, but he didn't laugh. Didn't even grin. As he flicked off the warning light on the roof, a barred owl unleashed a haunting scream and the man flinched.

"Creepy out here," he said.

It sure was. "Yeah. Maybe your wife should have gone to Arizona rather than you coming to Monacan."

"Don't I know it."

Carolina shifted into gear and continued down the road. The guard lingered behind and, she suspected, would wait there for a while to make sure she wasn't coming back. He needn't waste his time, thought. One trip to the Devil's Teeth was enough.

CHAPTER FOURTEEN

Carolina took the security guard's advice about getting a room rather than crashing in her van. From one outsider to another, it had been a good tip. If Yeti was along for the ride, it might be a different story; but alone, even with her gun, she didn't feel safe pulling off to the side of some dark road in Monacan and sleeping.

She had found the boarding house just at the edge of town. Viola Shafer, who seemed to be both owner and manager, was friendly but cautious when checking her in. Room and board was fifty bucks a night or two hundred a week. She opted for the former and made a mental note to add it to Cryus's growing tab, even though she had little expectations for collecting.

After settling in, she made a quick call to Elven, waking him from a sound sleep, and apologized for putting him on extended dog-sitting duty. He didn't seem to mind, and she filled him in on the day's events, but his voice was groggy, and she didn't keep him, even though he was about the only person she enjoyed talking to these days.

With nothing else to do, she turned on the TV for background noise. Her stomach grumbled, but she hadn't thought ahead and got something to eat. It was fine. A few more pills and twenty minutes later, she was dead to the world.

IT WAS ALMOST eight when she awoke. Downstairs, Viola Shafer had fixed a serving bowl of scrambled eggs and prepared sides of fried potatoes, bacon, and sausage patties. Carolina had planned to skip breakfast and head directly to Cyrus's to update him on what little she'd accomplished thus far, but the smell of the food was far too tempting to resist. After filling her belly, she was on the road again.

The man lived only eight miles outside of town, but the roads were so unkempt and winding it took her half an hour to get there. She'd been expecting a hovel, some run-down trailer or converted camper—Monacan specials—but instead found an actual house.

Crabgrass and random saplings sprouted from the ground around it, giving the property an abandoned look and ensuring it would never end up in Better Homes and Gardens, but the two-story structure was a place she'd have been content to call home. There was no driveway, so she parked on what passed for a lawn and went to the front door.

She knocked, hard and loud, then waited. Harsh coughing echoed from deep in the house. It was a welcome noise. At least Cyrus hadn't died on her since she'd last seen him.

Through the hacking came, "Come in. Door's unlocked."

She twisted the handle and pushed the door inward, noticing the frame was split and had appeared to have once been kicked in and never repaired. Inside, the house bordered on monastic, with only a few pieces of furniture and a couple of end tables and lamps. The kitchen was small but tidy, and she realized, with a twinge of dismay, Cyrus was a better housekeeper than she was.

"Cyrus," she called, still not seeing him.

"Back here," he called out, and she continued on.

The hallway featured a large bookshelf on one side. It was packed with tattered paperback novels, and she glanced at the authors: Melville, Joyce, Dickens, Camus, McCarthy, and Capote. Apparently, he wasn't just pulling names out of his ass the other day when he mentioned Tolstoy. The man was an enigma.

The first room in the hall was the bath. Through a partially open door, she saw the next was a bedroom. As her hand touched the doorknob, she hesitated. Something about walking into a stranger's bedroom was awkward and uncomfortable.

When she widened the door, she was glad she hadn't moved too quickly, as she was looking straight ahead and into the barrel of a shotgun.

She froze and scanned the area with her eyes, heart jumping in her chest. Cyrus was behind the gun, half-sitting in bed, with his back propped against the old headboard. He let out a delighted, raspy laugh that rattled in the back of his throat and set the gun on the bed beside him, where it lay like an uninterested lover.

"Sorry 'bout that," he said. "I've learned the hard way you can't be too careful."

She let out the breath she'd been holding. "I suppose not," she said, stealing furtive glances around the room. It was as tidy and sparse as the rest of the house. All his clothes were put away in the closet and dresser and not lying in a heap on the floor, which was her preferred method of organization.

Maybe she'd have to take some notes from him. Or trade services. He could be her maid to repay his bill.

"You don't gotta stand in the doorway all day. I won't point that shotty at you again." He swiveled in the bed, dropping his feet to the floor. They were a blueish-purple shade, the color of the sunset in the valleys.

He reached to the dresser, where a glass half-full of what looked like tomato juice sat. Then he hocked, his cheeks puffing, and spat into it. Nope, not tomato juice. She felt her breakfast feast do a somersault in her stomach.

After setting the glass aside, his attention went back to her. The sheets had slipped off his body, and he was wearing only baby-blue boxers. The copious amounts of loose skin she'd seen on his arms and face were nothing compared to the spare flesh he wore around his waist. It hung there like he was wrapped in cheap, body-colored fabric. Beyond that unused tissue, bones jutted at a hodgepodge of angles all over his frail torso. He could have been inserted into newsreel footage of prisoners of war and fit right in.

She wondered how he was still alive, then realized it was most likely this case. He was hanging on because he wanted resolution. Maybe redemption, too. Either way, she'd have to work quickly.

There were a few tattoos on his chest and another above on his thigh. All were faded, vaguely green, and indecipherable.

He noticed her looking in the direction of his crotch. "Like what you see?"

Carolina glanced up, startled. A lustful grin stretched across his face.

"Just checking out your body art," she said. "Making sure you don't have any hidden swastikas or eighty-eights."

The remark made him laugh. "There were a bunch of those white-power boys at the prison. Ignoramuses. Besides, I could never join up with them. I like my hair too much." He ran his hand through his locks.

"Your best quality," she said.

Cyrus shifted his hand to his groin, which he gave a good squeeze. "Oh, no. Definitely not."

She wasn't going to bite on that. "Why don't you throw on some clothes, and we'll go for a ride."

"Where?" he asked as he rose from the bed.

"I'll tell you in the van."

CHAPTER FIFTEEN

"I know you're a smart person; so, how the hell can you be so stupid?" Cyrus asked from the passenger seat. He sat with his arms crossed, doing his best impression of a toddler throwing a tantrum.

"What's your problem? I'm investigating the case, like you demanded. And part of being thorough involves interviewing the victim's family."

"Maybe so, but I don't need to be here for this. You think those people want to see the father of the man who's doing time for slaughtering their daughter like the fatted calf?" He reached for his pipe, ignoring her forbidding glare. "They don't give a shit if Denton killed her or not, so long as somebody's paying the price. Guilt don't matter when you got vengeance in your heart."

"Jesus, Cyrus, I'm not a fucking rube. I'm not letting you within a hundred yards of the parents. I just need you to show me the way since their address was unlisted."

His stiff posture softened. "Yeah?"

"Yeah. Now do I make a right or left at the next intersection?"

He led her the rest of the way, eventually telling her to stop beside a long gravel driveway. The mailbox had no name or house number, but he insisted it was the place.

"You wait in the van," she said, pocketing the keys. "Any suggestions on how to break the ice?"

"Why don't you tell them you're a reporter from one of those true-crime shows, and you want them to tell their side. People eat that shit up."

"So, lie?" she asked.

He shrugged. "Pretty much."

"I'm good at that," she said, climbing out of the van and shutting the door, leaving Cyrus alone.

A handwritten sign at the end of the lane read: *Rabbits 4 Sale.* The placard brought with it a stab of sympathy she didn't want to feel. She needed to be focused only on the facts, not walk into their world thinking about everything the family had lost. She tried to shake her sympathy away as she continued up the drive.

The Casto abode was old but well-kept. A fresh coat of white paint had gone over the siding within the last year. The wood porch was freshly sealed. A half-dozen blazing orange pumpkins sat atop the golden wood, accompanied by mums and asters. It was the most welcoming home she'd found thus far in Monacan, and the melancholy feeling came back hard.

Kudos to them for being able to move on with life. Maybe she could take some notes.

Her hand was raised, ready to knock, when she heard a woman's voice from the rear of the house.

"Hold him still now. Don't let him wriggle."

Carolina went to the source and found a woman, a boy, and a pen full of rabbits beyond them. The child, who looked to be ten or less, held one of the animals in his lap. He wore overalls and a white thermal shirt, and his pudgy belly bulged as he held the rabbit tight against it. The woman, who Carolina presumed to be Vanessa Casto, sat beside him. She held a tool in her hand, the glossy metal glinting in the sunlight. She was an old-looking forty-six, her mostly gray hair pulled up in a tight bun. Wrinkles criss-crossed her face like contrails in the sky.

"You got him?" the woman asked the boy.

He nodded. "Yup."

Carolina was close enough to see what Vanessa was holding. Toenail clippers. Only she wasn't cutting the bunny's nails.

She raised the clippers to the rabbit's mouth, using her free hand to open its jaws. The animal's front teeth were yellow and long. Longer than Carolina thought possible. They looked more like tusks than incisors.

Vanessa Casto brought the clippers to those teeth, aligning them perfectly. She'd done this before. The rabbit quivered in the boy's hands but mostly remained frozen. It had done this before too.

Then Vanessa squeezed the clippers with her bony right hand.

Carolina heard the crunch from ten yards away and, for the second time that morning, she was on the verge of losing her breakfast and gasped loud enough the mother and son both observed her sounding the fool.

The boy let the bunny loose, and it hopped to the ground, seemingly unaffected by the recent trauma. Carolina wished she could be so cool.

"Do you have a problem?" Vanessa Casto stood and took a step toward her. The glowering woman looked tough enough to beat the shit out of her.

Still shaken by the sight of the rabbit's teeth being clipped, Carolina lost the story she'd concocted in her head. "I uh, saw the sign out front."

"Yeah?" Vanessa said. "You looking to buy some rabbits?"

Carolina nodded, and Casto tipped her head in the direction of the pen.

"Well, come on and pick out what you want."

Carolina went to her, wondering how in the hell she would transition from bunny buyer to investigator. She passed by the child, whose face was a connect-the-dots puzzle of freckles. He gazed up at her, revealing wide, cornflower-blue eyes that reflected the sunlight like mirrors.

"Morning," she said.

He only watched as she passed by.

"You look a little green around the gills," Vanessa said as she came to a wire cage which sat three feet off the ground. Underneath it was a pile of rabbit poop almost as high as the pen. Inside were dozens of rabbits, crammed into quarters so tight Carolina wondered how they could turn around, let alone thrive. "You all right?"

Carolina nodded again. "I am. The thing with the teeth, it just..." She couldn't stave off a shudder. "I had a bad experience at the dentist when I was younger."

The woman gave a thin smirk. "Their teeth never stop growing. Wild rabbits wear 'em down by chewing and eating hard stuff. But raised rabbits need 'em clipped, or else their mouths grow shut, and they starve."

"Doesn't it hurt? Cutting them like that?"

Vanessa shrugged. "Don't know. I'm not a rabbit." She opened the cage and motioned for Carolina to look inside. "They're five dollars each," Vanessa said. "Or five for twenty."

Deal of the century. Carolina glanced at them, feigning interest, which was a challenge because the cocktail of feces and urine was so pervasive. She pointed to a lop-eared bunny who was entirely white, save for a black spot over its eye. It was adorable, if you were into rabbits. "Is this one a boy or girl?" she asked.

Vanessa's brows knitted together. "Damned if I know. These are meat rabbits. Most folks don't care if they're dining on a buck or a doe. But if you want me to pull it out so you can check for balls, I'll do it."

She was already opening the cage and reaching for the creature when Carolina felt her sad attempt at a ruse had gone on long enough. "I'm not really here for the rabbit," she said.

Vanessa latched the door closed, her expression sour and suspicious.

"I'm an investigative journalist doing some research on the Denton Mankey case. I was hoping I could have a word with you."

Vanessa flinched at the mention of Denton, and Carolina had a feeling this was going to go poorly. "You mean Cece Casto's murder," she said. "Because my girl's the one who matters. It's her name people should remember. Not that piece of walking, talking shit who ended her."

Carolina nodded, regretting mentioning Denton instead of Cecilia. "Yes, of course."

"It's been seven years and three months. What's this for?" Vanessa asked, her skepticism obvious.

"It's for a story on West Virginia crimes. Putting new light on cases people from other parts of the state may have forgotten."

"I never did think my Cece got the attention she deserved," Vanessa said. "If we'd have been a rich family from the suburbs, her face would've been on the national news. But because of where we're from, she barely made the Charleston paper."

The woman had a point. This crime, with its occult undertones, would have been all over the airwaves had it happened in New York or Los Angeles. If the parents had been schoolteachers or stockbrokers, rather than people who sold live rabbits for meat. She couldn't blame Vanessa Casto for feeling as if her daughter had not only been robbed of her life but also her attention.

Vanessa looked past her, and Carolina turned to see the boy staring at them. "Leroy, go inside and get on your math. I'll be in in a bit."

The boy, Leroy, watched a moment longer, then disappeared around the front of the house.

"He's no good at math," Vanessa said. "And I can't hardly follow that common core shit either." She rolled her eyes. "Politicians always fixing shit that ain't broke."

She moved to a small garden area, where two Adirondack chairs flanked a patch of flowers which were leggy and overgrown after a long summer show. Vanessa sat in one chair and, as Carolina moved to join her, she realized this area wasn't just a place to relax; it was also a tiny cemetery with three granite headstones.

One was for Cecilia. Along with her name and the dates of her birth and death were the words "Loving Daughter" and an etched angel looking pensive and skyward. The second was a marker for Ellen Chabol, who died at the age of nineteen, and Suzanna Chabol, who had no dates. The remaining tombstone was for Henry Casto—Beloved Father. His date of death was less than a year after Cece's.

Vanessa noticed her looking. "Henry couldn't handle what happened to Cece. So, one morning he walked out of the house, climbed inside his truck, and swallowed a bullet. Leroy's the one who found him." She stared at the stone, a mixture of regret and anger on her face. Then she looked to the next. "Ellen was my sister. Didn't make it through childbirth. Neither did the baby."

A family so marred by tragedy. How could this woman push on? How could she function and be a capable mother to her son? Carolina admired her fortitude but couldn't comprehend it.

"I'm so sorry," she said, always ready with platitudes.

"So am I." Vanessa kept her attention on the markers for a moment, then forced herself to look away. "What exactly did you want to talk to me about?"

"The case in general. About Cece and what happened to her."

Vanessa Casto slouched back in the chair, weighed down by her grief. "She was the best little girl. I know every parent says that, but she never gave us an ounce of trouble. Liked school. Always got good grades." She huffed out a lone chuckle. "Don't know where she got it from. Me and Henry barely graduated high school."

"Did she have a lot of friends?"

"Not a lot, but enough. She could be on the bashful side, but you put her with kids she got on with, and she could play all day.

That's why I never gave it much thought when she didn't come home that night, not right away. Wasn't anything unusual for her to be out chasing lightning bugs and trying to find the patterns in the stars. We didn't get worried until ten o'clock came around."

"Did you call the police right away?"

"No. We still didn't think it was anything serious; so, we drove around a while, checking out the pond, the grove, the places she usually played. It was only when we got home, and she still wasn't here, when we called Sheriff Bando."

"And how many days was it until Cece was found?"

"It was one eighteen on the afternoon of the third day. I was out here tending to the rabbits when I saw Sheriff Bando coming up the drive. And I swear, every day since, at one eighteen, I just feel like I'm dying inside all over again." A few tears spilled from her eyes, but she hurriedly wiped them away and pulled herself together. She was from tough stock.

"They wouldn't even let us see her. I think that's what did Henry in. The unknowing. He spent every day wondering how bad she was hurt. What she'd been put through. You hear the rumors, it's impossible not to, but what your mind comes up with is a million times worse."

She dragged the toe of her shoe through the mulch, drawing uneven shapes. "I'll never understand why God allows such evil in the world. Why men like Denton Mankey get to take in air when so many good people are underground."

"Did you have any association with the Mankey's? Before, I mean."

Vanessa's head shook back and forth, only a few millimeters each direction. "Knew them by reputation. It was enough to make anyone with sense keep their distance. That and what he did to Virgie Fields."

Fields wasn't a name that had come up in any of her research or the articles that Elven had supplied. "Who's she?" Carolina asked.

"Another innocent soul who had her life ruined by Denton Mankey."

"How so?"

"You go and talk to her. That's her story to tell, not mine."

She wanted to press Vanessa harder but figured she'd take her advice instead. "What about Cece? Did she know Denton? Maybe from school or around town?"

"No. Like I said, we kept our distance."

"Do you know why they suspected Denton? If there was no connection between the two of them?"

Vanessa smiled, but it wasn't a friendly one. It was one filled with spite. Of knowing she had the guy by the balls. "Because of Ottis Moore. He saw that monster trying to talk to my Cece, outside Victor's Gas and Go. Ottis said he was bothering her, offering to buy her a Coke, but she didn't want nothing to do with him. I taught her good."

Another lead. This was more productive than she'd expected. "Did this man, Ottis Moore, see Cece leave the store?"

Vanessa nodded.

"And Denton, did he see him follow her?"

She paused. "Said Denton went the other way. Took off south in his truck, heading toward Dillsburg. But hell, all he had to do was circle back around, and no one would be the wiser. I'm sure that's just what he did."

"Do you know if Ottis Moore was the last person to see her?"

"That's what Sheriff Bando said."

"The sheriff, he really came through for your family, didn't he?"

"I thank God for him every day. He couldn't save my Cece, but he bottled that bastard up where he can't hurt anyone else," Vanessa said.

She closed her eyes for a long while. When they opened again, she was in a different place. "It's getting about time I need to put a casserole in the oven." She rose to her feet, done with the conversation.

"I understand," Carolina said. "Thank you for your time; I do appreciate it."

They moved away from the miniature graveyard, and Carolina was ready to part ways when—

"Are you sure I can't talk you into a rabbit?"

CHAPTER SIXTEEN

CAROLINA DROVE WHILE CYRUS LOUNGED IN THE SEAT NEXT to her, the rabbit with the black spot over its eye on his lap. He lazily stroked the fur on its back, and the rabbit was in Heaven.

"What do bunnies eat, anyway?" Carolina asked.

"My garden every spring." He looked down at the animal nuzzled in his crotch. "You got a name for him?"

Carolina shook her head. "I can't keep him. Yeti would eat the poor thing for lunch."

"Then why'd you buy it?"

"I thought I'd emancipate it. Save it from someone's stew pot. Let him loose to play, procreate. Do whatever rabbits do."

Cyrus shook his head like she was the stupidest person in the history of the world. "You can't turn loose a tame rabbit."

"You can't?" This was news to her. So much for freedom.

"Not unless you want it dead."

Carolina glanced at the creature. "Well, shit."

"Don't worry about it. I'll keep him."

"Are you going to eat him? Wait; don't answer—I don't want to know."

With rabbit-gate settled, she tried to focus on the case and the new avenues she could explore. Ottis Moore and Virgie Fields. Moore might possibly have information in the case, but Vanessa Casto's cryptic comments about the Fields girl had her interest piqued.

"Cece's mother mentioned another family: Fields. Do you know anything about them?"

She caught Cyrus out of the corner of her eye. He shrugged.

"The only Fields I can recall live in Turkey Branch Holler. Don't know 'em personally, though."

"You know how to get there?"

He rolled his eyes. "I know how to get everywhere in this county. Take the third left onto the two lane. It'll lead ya there."

Just after giving her directions, he started coughing. Their drives had been filled with his barking on and off, but this was a whole new level of pain. He shoved the rabbit onto the floor, then bent at the waist, folding onto his knees as the sound exploded from his mouth. His face went red as he struggled to breathe, and his hand fumbled for the door latch. When he found it, he pushed the door open, even though they were doing forty-five. Carolina slowed down in a hurry, lurching the three of them forward and kicking up shale.

It was just in time because Cyrus had his upper body in the open air and retched into the weeds along the side of the road. Carolina couldn't look but heard heavy, wet splatters as whatever he puked up collided with the ground.

After a long minute, he stopped both coughing and gagging and caught some air. He hawked up a thick mouthful and spat to clear his mouth, then leaned back inside the van, panting like Yeti after a marathon of tennis ball fetching.

"I not feelin' too well," he said.

That was the understatement of the decade, she thought. "Let me take you to the hospital."

He turned his head, his bloodshot eyes weak from exertion.

"Why bother? They'll admit me. Poke me. Prod me. Tell me I'm gonna die. Then send Medicaid a bill for twenty grand. I'm finished with hospitals."

The man had a point, and she saw no sense protesting. "Let me drive you home, then."

He waved his hand at her and grabbed the rabbit off the floor. "I ain't payin' you to babysit me. I'll hitch and you can get back to work."

"You think anyone's going to give you a ride?" she asked.

"Who'd turn down a man with a bunny rabbit?" He grinned, revealing blood-stained teeth that did anything but reassure her. Then he stepped out of the van and began walking.

She watched him and thought he was too stubborn for his own good but admired him, too. She drove past Cyrus, leaving him to his own wants.

CAROLINA WAS a third of the way up the rusty and uneven metal ramp before she saw the dog. It was curled in front of the door, enjoying an afternoon snooze in the warm, midday light. The breed was indiscernible, but it was large, with short gray fur that heaved and fell with each breath. She held her own.

She was a dog person, but that didn't mean she wanted to startle one, and she took a step backward. Then another. Then another. Then her foot hit a seam in the ramp, eliciting a twang loud enough to stop her heart. And wake the dog.

It was on its feet in a millisecond, sprinting at her with the speed of a champion thoroughbred. Carolina spun and ran, but her van was parked ten yards away, and she knew her odds were slim. A few more steps, and she was off the ramp and in the dirt, her legs pumping as she ran faster than she could ever remember running before.

Why the fuck am I doing this, she thought. Her van looked to be a million miles away. She could hear the animal's huffing breaths as it closed in on her, its frenzied excitement.

Maybe it's friendly.

She threw a glance over her shoulder. Slobber rained from the open jaws of the dog, which looked like a cross between a mastiff and some sort of hound. My, what big teeth you have.

It was only a few feet from the end of the ramp. Carolina kept running.

Then she heard a surprised—if a dog could sound surprised—yip, and the sound of its nails colliding with the metal, its heavy feet stampeding, stopped.

Another stolen glance revealed the dog on its side. A long, pink cord stretched from its neck to the door of the trailer. She realized it was tethered and had reached the end of its rope.

The dog lumbered to its feet, gave a full-body shake, then plopped its round ass on the end of the ramp and panted.

The door to the home opened, hinges shrieking in protest, and a middle-aged woman stepped into the open. Her blonde hair was permed into tight curls, and she wore a pair of turquoise spandex pants and a tank top; both pieces of clothing were form-fitting, revealing her small, toned body.

"Damn it, Martha; you're gonna break your neck running full-tilt like a moron. You see a squirrel or someth—" The woman's words ceased as she saw Carolina. "Who're you?"

"Hello, ma'am," Carolina said, still catching her breath. If she survived this investigation, she would have to put some of her paycheck toward a gym membership. "My name's Carolina McKay. I'm investigating the murder of Cecilia Casto. Her mother sent me here and told me to talk to Virgie Fields."

The woman pushed up a pair of glasses that had slid to the tip of her nose. "All right. Come on in," she said, motioning for Carolina to follow.

Carolina took a few steps but paused as she neared the dog.

The homeowner looked back and shook her head. "Martha won't hurt you. She just gets excited about new people."

As a rule of thumb, no one thinks their dog will bite, but Carolina hoped the risk was worth the reward. As she reached Martha, the dog's tail whipped gleefully to and fro. "Good girl," Carolina said and extended a hand. Martha lapped at her flesh like it was dipped in chocolate but didn't bite, and she was able to breathe a little easier.

Inside the tight quarters of the trailer, the woman pointed to the kitchenette bench behind the table. Carolina sat in the empty spot. On said table, a calico cat feasted on leftovers which were scattered across two Styrofoam plates.

"Are you Virgie?" Carolina asked.

The woman shook her head. "Nope. I'm her mama, Letty. Get you something to drink?"

Carolina shook her head. "No, thank you."

Letty waved her hand again and opened the fridge. She pulled a small paper cup from a stack on the counter and filled it with tea, then handed the drink to Carolina anyway. "Have a sip. You look parched."

Carolina did as told, even though she wasn't thirsty. The tea was unsweetened and bitter, and she had to fight it down her throat.

"It's good," she lied. "Thank you." She set aside the still nearly-full cup, hoping the cat would knock it to the floor so she wouldn't need to be polite and drink more.

Letty Fields sat on a metal folding chair across from her. "What's this business about Cece? I thought that mess was all settled years ago."

"It was. But we're investigating Denton Mankey, trying to find out if he was involved with other crimes prior to the murder."

Letty sighed. "Well that's bound to be a long list. I don't know where you'd even start."

Carolina didn't like the reply. "Let's start with you. With Virgie. What can you tell me about Denton?"

"I could sit here and give you my opinion, but how about I take you to Virgie instead?"

That worked.

Letty put both her hands on the table and pushed herself to her feet. "Come with me."

Carolina followed her through a living room, then back a narrow hall. The home was larger than her van, yet felt more claustrophobic. And there was a pungent, antiseptic aroma in the air, one that grew stronger as they neared the trailer's two bedrooms.

Letty stopped at the partially closed master bedroom door and motioned for Carolina to enter. "Virgie's in there."

As she reached out, pressing on the flimsy, hollow core door, Carolina knew what waited in the room wouldn't be good. But she hadn't lowered her expectations far enough and managed to be surprised anyway.

Virgie Fields lay in a hospital bed with the head raised to keep her upright, but she slouched to the side like she was toppling over in slow motion and was unable to help herself. She was in her mid-twenties and pretty, but it was evident, looking at her face, the lights were off. She wore an oversized, floral gown. It was loosely tied at the sides, revealing her diaper. She stared vaguely ahead, where a small, flat-screen TV played Looney Tunes cartoons.

Letty pushed past Carolina and went to the bed. She grabbed her daughter's arm and hoisted her up, straightening her. Then she ran her fingers through Virgie's hair, adding some volume to a spot where it had been flattened by her positioning. "There you go, Virgie," she said. "Now you look beautiful."

A small recliner sat beside the bed, and Letty pointed to it. "Go ahead and sit. She likes company. Doesn't get much anymore."

Carolina obeyed. "Hello, Virgie."

She didn't expect to be acknowledged and wasn't. The young

woman's face was a blank canvas, as unseeing and unknowing as a department-store mannequin. It hurt to look at her; so, Carolina turned her attention to Letty, who somehow managed to smile.

"Take her hand," Letty said. "She knows you're here."

This felt wrong. Intrusive. Carolina preferred to remain detached, to pretend as if the victims in the crimes she investigated were nothing more than names. Not people who'd once had lives and dreams. But again, she did as told and reached for the catatonic woman's hand. Her fingers were tight claws, and Carolina had to unfurl them. Virgie Field's skin felt cool, dense, and clammy, like wet playdough. It felt like holding the hand of a dead person.

So, when Virgie squeezed her hand, she had to fight the urge to jump out of the chair and scream.

"I told you she knows you're here," Letty said.

Carolina looked back and forth between mother and daughter like a spectator at a tennis match. "Can she answer my questions?" Carolina asked.

Virgie shook her head. "No, ma'am. She has what the doctors called a catastrophic brain injury."

"Is there any chance she'll recover?" Carolina already knew the answer.

"It's been ten years. This is as good as she's gonna get."

She turned her attention back to Virgie, giving her hand a soft squeeze in return. "You must be a fighter," she said. But she couldn't fathom the reason for existing in a state like this.

"She sure is," Letty said. "You want to know what other horrible things Denton Mankey has done? Take a good look at my Virgie. He did this."

"How?" Carolina asked as possibilities rolled through her head. "Did he attack her?"

"Not physically," Letty said. "When Virgie hit her teenage years, she got rebellious. Drinking, smoking, running with boys. I tried to stop her, told her all the bad things that could happen, but even I didn't think it could get this bad. Her and Denton were friends. Probably more than friends. I know that, I'm not dumb. Anything he said was like the word of God. He'd tell her to run away from home and she did. He'd tell her to help him break into those vacation cabins along the Big Sandy, and she did. He'd tell her to flirt with a guy so he could steal his car, and she did. It's like the word no disappeared from her vocabulary when she was around Denton Mankey."

She pulled a tissue from her pocket and wiped a thin layer of drool from her daughter's mouth. "So, when Denton said they should try huffing bleach, my Virgie was all-too-ready to do it."

"Bleach," Carolina said, mostly to herself. "Shit."

"They bought it at the dollar store, a bottle of bleach and a bucket, and drove to the old wool mill down in Preechner. According to Denton, Virgie went first. She hunched over the bucket, a quarter full, and he put his coat over her head to keep in the fumes. He said he didn't really know how it worked; so, he let her take in some deep breaths. Suck it in real deep. Then, he said, she had some sort of fit."

Letty turned her gaze from her daughter to Carolina, her face hard and emotionless. "He left her there, her head still in that bucket, covered up with his coat. That's how they knew it was him. A mailman found her later that afternoon. No one really knows how long she was there, but she was in a coma for almost a month. When she came out of it... Well, this is my Virgie now.

"The doctors said if she'd have gotten to a hospital right after it happened, she would have been okay. But Denton ran. Left his friend, or his girlfriend, or whatever she was to him, there to suffocate on bleach fumes. That's the kind of man Denton Mankey is."

Carolina had let her grip go limp and felt Virgie Field's hand slip from her own. It dangled at the side of the bed until Carolina picked it up and laid her forearm across her waist, all the while wondering if the man she was trying to exonerate was worth the effort, or if he was right where he belonged.

CHAPTER SEVENTEEN

ONCE CAROLINA WAS OUT OF SIGHT, CYRUS DID A ONE-eighty and headed back to the Casto residence. By the time he reached the top of the long drive, he was dragging ass and felt about a minute away from collapsing and dying in the gravel. It wasn't the dying that bothered him, but he wanted to prove he was right first.

To do that, he needed more than whatever evidence Carolina could uncover. He was short on time, and the legal system moved slower than a slug. If he wanted to clear Denton's name before he was underground, he needed to get Vanessa Casto to understand what she believed was true about Denton was a lie. That Denton was almost as much a victim in this situation as her daughter. Because, if the Castos were on his side, then he could kick this shit into fifth gear.

He made it to the front door, leaning into the frame to steady himself as he knocked, the rabbit still tucked under his arm like a beggar's bundle. He only had to wait a few seconds before he was greeted by the face of a woman who despised him.

Vanessa Casto's eyes turned to saucers when she realized who had darkened her doorstep. "You motherfucker. What right do you have to come on my property?"

"Now Vanessa," he said, holding a hand up, trying to calm her. It had no effect, other than turn her face a deeper shade of red. "I know my presence upsets you, and I don't blame you."

"Upset?" she shouted. "I'm not upset. I'm fucking livid. It's because of your murdering, piece-of-shit son that my little girl is buried in my back yard. And whose fault is it he turned out that way? I reckon its yours!"

"What happened to Cece was terrible," Cyrus said. "But I just need you to put aside your anger and listen to me for a minute. Just a minute, that's all I ask."

She opened her mouth to speak, then stopped. He took it as a sign to continue.

"Denton didn't kill your daughter; Bando set him up."

That was not what she wanted to hear. She muttered one word. "Bullshit."

"It's the truth. There were people with Denton the night your daughter was killed," Cyrus said. "Two people who know he couldn't have done it. And I know there'll be more to come out and prove to you, to everyone, that my boy's innocent."

He studied her, trying to decipher her emotions. "Don't you care about the truth?"

If he thought he was winning her over, he was wrong. Vanessa got in his face, their noses nearly touching. "Your son is trash. You're trash." Now she was pressing against him, shouting, her spittle ricocheting of his face like incoming fire.

"By the look and smell of you, you ain't long for this world. God's punishing for the life you've lived. And the only reason that makes me upset is because you won't live to see your child die."

Cyrus Mankey understood hate. It some ways, it was the hate that kept him alive. But he couldn't tolerate any more of this woman's running mouth.

He grabbed her blouse with his left hand, holding tight as she tried to back away. Then he dropped the rabbit and slipped his right around the back of her neck, his fingers digging into her skin. He felt a pop of hot blood as one of his nails punctured her flesh. No matter how much she struggled, she wasn't getting out of his grasp.

"You listen, and you listen hard. My sins are mine to answer for. Mine, not my son's."

She tried to free herself, but even in the throes of a slow death, he was stronger.

"When my day comes, I'm ready for the devil to drag me down to hell. I'd expect nothing less. But you're gonna find out Denton is innocent. And when that happens, you're going to get on your knees and tell him you're sorry!" He was screaming, and now, it was his spit battering her face. Only his was full of blood. It slithered along the creases in her face, filling them like riverbanks in a storm.

Cyrus's right hand slid around to the front her throat, his thumb pressing into the hollow above her collar bones. She gagged and choked and bawled as she struggled for air.

"Mom?" a child's voice beckoned in the background.

It was enough to snap Cyrus out of his rage. It had been a minute since he'd lost control to that extent, and he felt sick.

He let her go and took a step backward, dropping off the concrete pad and into the crabgrass. Vanessa Casto bent at the waist, coughing. Her son appeared behind him, tugging at her shirt.

"What happened?" he asked. "Who's that man?" He stared at Cyrus with wide, scared eyes.

Cyrus spun around as quick as he could, retreating, and didn't look back as the woman screamed in a hoarse voice.

"I'm siccing Bando on you! You and that lying bitch you sent here. He'll make you sorry!"

As he stumbled down the drive, Cyrus realized he'd just made everything worse. And lost the rabbit. So much for the best-laid plans.

CHAPTER EIGHTEEN

"Need a menu?" the waitress asked. She was a young girl, probably still in high school unless she was a dropout. Her mousy, brown hair hung in ringlets to her shoulders, and she chewed a wad of gum like a cow chews cud.

"Nah," Carolina said. "I'll have a burger and fries."

"You want a coffee, too? Only a buck and endless refills."

Carolina needed coffee to keep everything flowing but couldn't stomach it right now. "Just a Coke."

"Sure thing."

The waitress began to turn away when Carolina stopped her. "Hey," she said. "Do you have a phone book?"

"I think in the back. Give me a sec."

Carolina let her leave. Her phone still had no signal, and she highly doubted Monacan had any internet cafes. If she wanted to find Ottis Moore's address, she had to do let her fingers do the walking.

Ruby's Diner was a converted Airstream camper with no booths, only a counter and eight barstools for seating. It looked like the kind of place where you'd either get food poisoning or consume some of the best, greasy food of your life. Now that Carolina was eating somewhat regularly—for her—her appetite had come back with a vengeance, and she was willing to roll the dice.

After the girl returned with her Coke and the telephone directory, Carolina flipped through the pages before coming to the Ms. She dragged her finger across the page and found it.

Ottis Moore, RR2, Jimtown.

That was all there was. Just a rural route, no street or house number. She jotted down the phone number, then looked to the waitress, who was at the opposite end of the counter waiting on an elderly man in coveralls and a Speedy Mead's Delivery baseball cap. When she finished refilling the man's mug, Carolina signaled for her.

"Can I use your phone? My cell has no bars."

The waitress smirked. "Join the crowd. Don't even know why I pay for mine. Probably only works five percent of the time." She grabbed a cordless phone off a cradle and handed it to her. "It's not out of state, is it?"

Carolina shook her head. "No."

"Okay." The girl left her again.

Carolina punched in the number listed for Ottis Moore. It rang once, then dinged three times. "The number you have reached has been disconnected. If you feel you have received this recording in error, please hang up and try—" Carolina ended the call. So much for that inspiration.

It wasn't the end of the world. She'd hoped to accomplish more, but she could always take an early quit and head back to Dupray. There, she could dig up Moore's address on her own. And if that failed, she could always ask Elven to do it.

It was a short wait before her food was ready, steam still wafting from the burger as the waitress set in before her.

"Anything else I can get you?" the waitress asked.

Carolina shook her head, mumbling a *no thanks* as she was

already one heaping bite into the beef. The waitress smiled and left her alone to feed.

Solitude lasted less than a minute.

The stool beside her groaned under the weight of its new occupant. Carolina tried to be discrete and take him in via her peripheral vision, but he made that moot by speaking to her.

"It's Carolina McKay, right?"

She wiped grease from her mouth as she turned to him. He was average height with a spare tire, bushy-black mustache, and beady, dark eyes that got lost in his plump cheeks as he smiled. The badge clipped to his jacket gave him away, but still, he introduced himself.

"Sheriff Reed Bando," he said, extending a meaty paw. They exchanged a quick, firm, handshake.

"What can I do for you, Sheriff?" she asked, taking a swig of her soda and doing her best to appear unaffected by his arrival.

"I wanted to apologize for not being at the station yesterday when you came by. And to apologize again for the file not being there like I said it would be." He continued to smile, but she knew this was no apology tour and his geniality was as fake as the plastic hamburger mounted outside the diner's entrance.

"Wasn't what I was expecting when I made the drive—but shit happens," she said, deciding it was better to not push any buttons and delay the inevitable.

"Good. Good. I also wanted to clarify some things."

She popped a fry into her mouth, then slid the plate a few inches his way. "Want some?"

Bando waved her off. "Carbs work a number on my diabetes."

"So, what kind of things need clarification?" Carolina asked.

"All things Denton Mankey."

At least it was out in the open now, and he could put the faux friendliness away. His very presence signified he knew she'd been asking questions and he didn't appreciate an interloper in his county.

Carolina's roaring appetite faded, and she wiped her hands on her jeans. "I'm just making sure all the I's were dotted," she said. "I have no agenda, outside of ensuring Denton is as guilty as you say he is."

Bando gave up on the smile. His face looked better without it, less huckster and more lawman. But he was still a sleazy-looking son of a bitch. Beads of sweat sat atop his forehead, some dribbling into his overgrown, black eyebrows where they got lost in the untamed forest. His bottom teeth showed. They were small and rounded off, like he'd had his real choppers replaced with tic tacs.

"Cyrus Mankey may have spun some story and fed you some bullshit, but I can assure you, whatever it was, it ain't true."

Carolina considered asking how he'd paired her up with Cyrus but realized it didn't matter. And she knew in a county like Monacan, little happened without the sheriff's knowledge. He was a glorified guard dog. This was his yard, and he intended to protect it.

"Denton cut off that poor girl's head with a hacksaw. He probably would have cut up the rest of her, too, if those Roush boys hadn't come along when they did." He took a breath and looked out the window, shaking his head before turning back to her.

"It must've been part of his deal with the devil," he said.

A bit of burger fought its way up her throat, and she coughed it back down. "Devil?" she asked, incredulous.

"From what I understand, you've been to the Teeth to see it for yourself. All those symbols. And those trinkets aren't just from kids, you know. They're offerings."

She remembered the pentagrams and other graffiti. How anyone could take it seriously was beyond her. "You actually believe the devil made him do it?"

He flipped from dead serious to his fake smile and even managed a canned laugh. A multi-tasker. "Lord, no. Other folks around here do, though. And what matters is Denton Mankey believed it."

Bando gave into temptation and stole a fry from her plate. He chewed open-mouthed, and she was transfixed by those tiny, candy teeth.

"That boy is crazy *and* mean. A terrible combination."

The two sat for a moment in silence, staring at each other. A standoff.

Carolina knew Bando was waiting for her to acquiesce, but she wasn't prepared to give in. "Thanks for the info," she said.

"It's what I'm here for." He took another fry. "Wish you'd have come to me straight off instead of harassing my constituents, though. Poor form. I'd think a fellow law enforcement official would exercise professional courtesy. But, then again, I'm old-school."

He'd done his homework. For some reason, that surprised her. And the fact that he'd taken time to dig into her past made her more convinced he had something to hide. "I came to your office, remember? But you were nowhere to be found."

Bando leaned in close, still wearing his Cheshire-cat grin that wouldn't fool a blind pig. "Well, now we've met. And I'm telling you this little investigation you're trying to run is over. At least when it comes to anything inside Monacan county borders."

"It's not against the law to ask questions," Carolina said, then took a long drink of the soda, which had already gone flat from melted ice.

"The law is what I say it is." He stood, looming over her, and grabbed his hat from the counter. He reached behind himself, and his hand emerged with his wallet.

Bando withdrew a twenty and dropped it onto the counter, giving a wave to the waitress in the process. "This young lady's lunch is on me, Emma. You keep the change, but I expect it to go in your college fund and not be wasted on make-up. You don't need it, anyway, pretty as you are."

The waitress giggled and waved back. "Thank you, Sheriff."

His switch flipped back, and he was glowering at Carolina. "When you finish your food, I expect you to head back to

Dupray. And stay there. Then we can pretend this never happened."

"And if I don't?" she asked, unable to resist pushing back.

He pulled a set of keys off his belt. "Then I'll bring you up on charges. Investigating without a license. Harassment. And, if I feel like it, I might call the state police and file a complaint against your sheriff buddy for requesting evidence under false pretenses."

Bando took one more fry from her plate, biting it in two and saving the other half for later. "You have yourself a good day now. And drive safe."

He strutted to the door and stepped into the daylight. Carolina saw he'd parked his cruiser beside her van, and he made a point of checking if her inspection sticker was up to date before climbing into his own vehicle.

As he drove off, Carolina grabbed her pills from her jacket, feeling the need rise. She popped two into her mouth and washed them down with the last of the Coke.

As for Reed Bando's advice to get out of Monacan, she would take it. But she didn't plan to stay away long.

CHAPTER NINETEEN

ELVEN HALLIE'S HOME WAS ONE OF THE BEST-KEPT SECRETS IN Dupray. The sprawling, three- story log cabin was tucked a few hundred yards into the forest, invisible from any of the county's roads.

As Carolina traveled up the long, cobblestone driveway, the house took her breath away. The center portion was almost entirely glass, revealing an interior where massive trees had been hand-hewn and turned into support beams. The cedar walls glowed golden, illuminated by a rustic chandelier that must have been fifteen feet from one side to the other. Wood burned in a stone fireplace that stretched from the ground floor to the roof, where wisps of smoke lazily drifted into the evening air.

The home would have fit right in in Vermont or Colorado, and she had to remind herself that, although Elven was now the county sheriff, he came from old money. And lots of it.

She parked beside his Jeep and went to the front door, a slab of oak twelve feet tall. There was no doorbell, only a copper knocker in the shape of a bear. She put it to use.

She'd called Elven on the drive back from Monacan and filled him in. After a gentle scolding for not keeping him informed as to her plans and whereabouts, he relented and told her to come by for dinner. She was still flustered by the encounter with Bando and unsure of Denton's character after seeing the sad remains of Virgie Fields, and a break from it all was welcome.

If she'd have known the mansion she'd be walking into, she might have reconsidered.

It wasn't that she was jealous. She was perfectly content with living in her van. And she'd never had a desire to live like the rich and famous. But somehow, staring at the grandiose abode made her feel lesser. And she didn't like the feeling at all. Now she just wanted to get this over with, and she used the knocker again, three rapid-fire and pounding taps.

"How long are you gonna try knocking until you figure out no one's inside?" he asked.

Carolina spun around, ready with a snarky comeback, but she was startled to see his shirt was off. Sweat glistened against his torso. His physique was remarkable, not quite a six pack - that would have been trying too hard - but the muscles in his chest and arms were those of a man who used them, not built them in a gym. She didn't know why, but she felt embarrassed, as if she'd caught him naked.

"Some scofflaw absconded with your shirt, Sheriff," she said. "Better look for a replacement before you freeze your nipples off." As she spoke, the wind picked up and spread goosebumps across his flesh, confirming her statement.

He shrugged, "I was chopping firewood. Didn't want to get my nice shirt all sweaty." To prove his point, he set aside an ax, which she only then noticed he'd been carrying. So much for her astute powers of observation. "It's unlocked, by the way. You could've just gone in."

Elven pushed past her and opened the door, then held it for her. Despite the chilly weather, she felt the heat coming off him as she passed by.

Inside, it was just as lavish as she pictured from the exterior. Large, open rooms with high end furniture. Vaulted ceilings, lofts. Only the absence of taxidermy animals surprised her—bears, moose, mountain lions; they would have fit right in with stone and wood mansion. But then, she remembered Elven didn't eat meat because he believed animals had souls; he probably wouldn't hunt them, either.

Out of nowhere, Yeti bounded into the room, a stuffed, green cactus filling his mouth. As he chewed on the toy, it emitted muffled squeaks that seemed to work the already-excited dog into a frenzy.

"Hey, handsome," she said as she pulled the toy, saturated and slimy with slobber, from his jaws. "Where'd you get this?"

"I decided to upgrade his toy selection," Elven said. "Hope you don't mind, but the tennis ball you sent him here with looked like it had been around since John McEnroe was relevant."

He moved past her and into a cutting-edge kitchen, where a few pots and pans simmered atop a gas range. Along the way, he grabbed a shirt off the coat rack and slipped it on, buttoning it and tucking it into his jeans before he checked the food.

Whatever he was cooking smelled incredible, but Carolina was still caught up with taking it all in. The biggest TV she'd ever seen in her life was tucked into a corner in the living room. It was flanked by speakers that looked powerful enough to fill an amphitheater.

Artwork, mostly landscapes, decorated the walls. She even spotted an Ansel Adams photograph of Yosemite and, upon closer inspection, discovered it was number fifteen in a run limited to fifty. Yeah, he definitely came from money.

But Elven didn't let his affluence show. At least not now, as an adult. The high school version of Elven was the perfect stereotype of a rich prick. So much for her theory that people never changed.

Yeti trotted to a brand-new, plush dog bed sitting near the fireplace and sprawled in it. The dog was obviously enjoying his new abode, and she couldn't blame him. It was quite an upgrade from her van, with its twenty-eight square feet of living space.

She followed him, noticing a series of framed photos sitting on the mantel. They showed Elven on the high school football team. Elven with his family. Elven's professional portrait in his deputy uniform. And then one that almost made her eyes water.

Elven and Lester. He had his arm around Lester's shoulders, both grinning and holding fly-fishing rods as a river rushed by in the background.

"That was taken at the Bitterroot in Montana," Elven said from behind her.

She flinched with surprise and saw him smirk.

"Sneaky asshole," she said.

"I move like the wind." He picked up the photo, taking it in. "Lester and I went out there two summers ago. I half expected Dupray to burn to the ground with the both of us gone, but somehow, Tank and Johnny kept the ship afloat til we got back."

"Catch anything?"

"A cold. Lester had better luck. Snagged a twenty-eight inch trout." Elven returned the photo to its original spot, then glanced back to the kitchen. "Dinner's ready. Hope you're hungry."

He directed her to a dining-room table large enough to seat twenty, then pulled out her chair. She sat and watched as he went to the kitchen and grabbed two plates. "What's on the menu, chef?"

When he'd made the invite, she was expecting pizza from Hank's, or maybe thawed-out leftovers. Maybe a TV dinner if he was like most of the guys she'd known. But this man had actually cooked a meal. She was impressed.

"Quinoa eggplant rollatini," he said as he set a plate in front of her.

It looked like something from a high-end restaurant, the type of place she never went. She was a diner girl, after all. And now she was wary as she poked at it with her fork like she was afraid it might bite back. "I don't know what that is."

He smiled again, but she could tell that he didn't quite believe her. "Quinoa or rollatini?"

"Both."

Elven picked up his knife and fork. "Just try it. You might be surprised."

That was the kind of thing her mother had said when she was five and had a plateful of uneaten brussel sprouts before her. Such advice hadn't turned out well when she was a toddler, and she didn't expect this to be much different.

She filled her fork a fourth of the way and tentatively brought it to her mouth. The aroma was intoxicating, but still, she hesitated. When she saw Elven staring, she decided it was time to stop being a child and taste it.

Once she did, she no longer cared what it was. It was layered in flavors that made her taste buds erupt. Before she could stop herself, an Mmmm sound slipped from her lips.

"I'll take that as a compliment," Elven said.

"Take it any way you want. I hope you have more."

He laughed, then took a sip of wine. "After you called, I did some digging and found an address for the fellows who found the Casto girl's body."

She was disappointed they were already into the business end as she'd been enjoying a world outside death and misery. But she had no one to blame but herself. "You shouldn't have done that. I don't want you getting into trouble for helping me out."

He waved his fork to dismiss her concerns. "I'm not threatened by Reed Bando. He might be king of the hill in Monacan, but everyone outside county lines knows exactly what he is."

"Still, though, this isn't your responsibility."

"Never said it was. But I like to help my friends."

She was surprised at how much she liked the sound of that word. Friends. In her days at the police academy and on the force in Baltimore, she'd had plenty of acquaintances. Many she'd even have taken a bullet for. But she wouldn't have considered any of them friends.

God, I must be stoned. She took a long swallow of wine, which would do nothing to improve her newfound sentimentality.

"I don't appreciate him telling you to leave town. A little too Hollywood for my taste," Elven said. "And I'm not much for conspiracies, but his actions certainly do raise my hackles."

"Mine, too," Carolina said. "But the more I learn about Denton Mankey's character, the less surprising it seems Bando would have honed in on him. He was no saint."

"I'm sure you'll find the truth, wherever it lies."

Carolina shrugged. She wasn't so certain. "If you say so."

"I do," Elven said. He stared at her, eyes earnest. "You're the best damned cop I've ever worked with. Now I know that's not saying much, but it doesn't change the fact that you're excellent at what you do."

She stared at her plate, which was already half-empty, uncomfortable with this adulation. "I'm not a cop."

"You'll always be a cop, Carolina."

CHAPTER TWENTY

Ottis Moore was the man Carolina wanted to find, but, so far, Elven hadn't been able to obtain a current address, and her internet searches had provided jack and squat. It might be for the best, though, as it would give a few days for things to cool down before she returned to Monacan. The Roush boys, as Reed Bando had referred to them, lived two counties north in Boone, and she decided they would be her mission for the day.

The men were business owners—Beverage D-lite, LLC—and seeing as how it was a weekday, she took a chance and tried their warehouse. A gray, metal-sided pole building filled a vast parking lot. A few box trucks and delivery vans were parked by loading bays, and a tractor trailer was in the midst of a delivery. She followed the sign directing visitors to the office and stepped inside.

A balding, middle-aged man in a button-down shirt sat behind the desk, a telephone pressed to his ear. "So that's three skids a Miller. You want the light or the regular?" He paused, listening, then raised a finger to let Carolina know he'd be with her posthaste.

She took a seat and feigned interest in the magazines sprawled across a low coffee table: *Sports Illustrated. Car & Driver. Men's*

Health. Maxim. She got the feeling they didn't have many females dropping by.

As the secretary wrapped up the order, he shifted his attention to her. "Sorry about that. We're short-staffed, and I'm pulling double-duty. How can I help you?"

"I'm looking for Jeremiah and Daniel Roush. Are either in the office?" Carolina asked, putting on her most winning smile.

Instinctively, the secretary glanced back the hallway; then, he nodded. "It's your lucky day, miss."

Thank God. Finally, someone who didn't call her ma'am.

He grabbed the phone again, punched a single number, then waited. "Jeremiah, there's a beautiful young woman out here for you. Someone must've sent you a strip-o-gram because I know she wouldn't be here voluntarily."

As he laughed to himself over making the most amusing joke in the history of mankind, the secretary grinned so wide Carolina thought the top of his head might fall off. She was less amused but tolerated it. Sometimes, you had to take one for the team. He set the phone on the desk.

"He'll be out shortly."

"Thank you." She wanted to add *asshole* but stopped herself. The day was still young, and there'd be plenty of time to make more people pissed off at her.

A moment later, Jeremiah Roush emerged. He was in his late fifties, with a belly that sagged over his belt and thinning, gray hair brushed forward. He sported wire-rimmed glasses perched askew atop a nose that had been broken at least twice and a cheap, size too big, suit that made him look lazy and unkempt. He stared at her with confused, yet eager, eyes. Maybe he believed the strip-o-gram story and was waiting for her to get on with the show.

"Mr. Roush?" Carolina asked.

He nodded.

"I'm Carolina McKay, and I'm investigating the murder of Cecilia Casto. I'd like to ask you a few questions."

Confusion left his face, replaced with a more dour expression. Dread. He ran short, pudgy fingers through his hair. "That was such a long time ago. I'm not sure I have anything worth telling."

"I understand. But we're at the stage of the investigation where minutia matters, and any details you can provide, even if they seem trivial, will help."

Jeremiah Roush nodded. "Come back to my office, then," he said and turned away from her. She followed. "I assume you want to talk to Daniel, too?"

"Yes, please."

The hall was lined with plaques and certificates, honors bestowed upon the business over the years. It was clear these sons of West Virginia had done well for themselves. Hopefully, they could do well by her, too.

He paused at a closed door, rapped it once with his knuckles, then opened it. Daniel Roush sat inside the room, fingers swiping across his phone's screen. "Daniel," Jeremiah said. "Come back to my office. There's a lady here from the police who's following up on the dead girl we found."

She hadn't told him she was with the police but didn't bother to correct him, either. Daniel Roush almost dropped his phone, then set it aside and jumped up. He was smaller than his father, both in height and weight. His suit fit better, and he might have been able to slide into a business meeting in Philadelphia or New York City without drawing askance glances. Except his bottom lip was puffed out by a pinch of snuff. He brought a White Claw can with him as he joined the parade ending in Jeremiah Roush's office.

The father took a seat behind the desk. There was only one other chair, and Daniel offered it to Carolina. She accepted.

"Thank you," she said. "I wanted to talk to you and your father about the crime scene."

"We told the sheriff everything," Daniel said.

"I know. But the sheriff's office lost all their files in a flood, so we're rebuilding things from scratch." Using Bando's lie against him gave her infinite satisfaction.

Daniel tensed, dismayed by this news. "I try not to think about it. Gave me night terrors for almost two years. I couldn't close my eyes without seeing..." His words trailed off, his face turning ashen.

"Well, let's start about why you were there. You were out riding four-wheelers, correct?"

"Razors," Jeremiah said.

"What are those?" she asked.

"Side by sides. Four wheelers on steroids, I guess. And they have a cage so you don't kill yourself if you roll 'em over," Daniel Roush said.

"All right," Carolina said. "How did you end up there? That land's private property."

"We didn't know," Daniel said, then spit brown juice into his beer can. "They didn't have signs up or anything."

"It's okay. It doesn't matter," Carolina said.

"We were working our way through the Hatfield McCoy trail. Best place to ride in the entire state," Jeremiah said. "We run it a couple times a year. Make a weekend of it. And I'm not going to lie to you—when we're riding, we do our share of day drinking. Ended up going off course—by the time night rolled around, we didn't even know if we were in the state anymore."

Jeremiah stole a glance to his son, who added nothing.

"Okay, then what?"

"We were creeping along through the mountains and saw a light in the distance. It was a fire, flickering tall and bright. So, we rode toward it. Figured there were some campers who could direct us back to civilization. But when we got close, we heard someone shout, and then branches snapping and breaking. Like a herd of whitetail were hauling ass out of there."

"You heard all that over the sound of your ATVs?" She looked back and forth between the two.

"Yeah," Daniel finally joined the conversation. "It was loud. Panicked."

"Did you hear voices?"

"None you could make out," Daniel said. "Just commotion."

"Do you think one person could have made so much noise?" she asked.

They looked at each other, shrugged.

"Okay, so you heard running, then what? What did you see when you got there?"

Daniel looked on the verge of projectile vomiting. He dug the snuff out of his lip with his index finger, wiped it on the top of the can, then set it aside. "I saw a naked girl," he said. "Laid out on a big stone like she was sunbathing at the beach. Except when we got closer, and our eyes adjusted to the light, we realized the body didn't have any skin on it. It was all red and raw. Like a beef fresh outta the slaughterhouse."

"And then I saw her head. It was sitting between her legs, which were spread-eagle." Jeremiah put his elbows on his desk and leaned into his hands. "I didn't think any of it was real, though. I thought someone stole a dummy from one of those Halloween stores because, you know, you just don't believe your eyes. But we went over to it, and," he swallowed hard. "It was real. You could see where the tissue'd been cut, all smooth as if someone took her head off with an ax."

He made a chopping gesture, bringing the side of his hand down on the desk. It rattled a cup filled with hard candy.

Daniel took his turn. "Her head was positioned so she was staring up, like she was looking at the stars. And her jaw was distended, like she was screaming. I was staring at her silent scream, still trying to make sense of it all, when I saw the movement."

Carolina leaned in, curious. "Movement?"

Daniel nodded. "Inside her mouth. I couldn't figure out what it was until I took a close look. Then I saw the worms."

She'd seen her share of decomposing bodies; so, this wasn't a surprise. "You mean maggots."

Daniel Roush stared at her with wide, haunted eyes. "No, ma'am; I do enough fishing to know the difference. These were worms. Earthworms. Her mouth was overflowing with them to the point where some spilled out and writhed along her face. I never saw nothing like it before."

"Hope we never do again," Jeremiah said.

"Aside from her... decapitation, what was the condition of the body? Was it bloated? Gray?"

"Not at all," Jeremiah said. "She didn't even stink."

Three days had passed from Cecilia Casto's disappearance before her body was found. But if what these men said was accurate, she'd been alive most of those days.

"What kind of monster would do something like that?" Jeremiah asked.

Carolina wasn't sure if he was asking it to her directly, or putting it out to the universe, but she intended to find out.

CHAPTER TWENTY-ONE

SHE TOOK BACK ROADS THROUGH MONACAN, AWARE THAT HER panel van, with the solar panels on the roof, was anything but discreet. It had been a few days, but she knew if Bando or any of his lackeys caught sight of her, her visit to the county would be short. Not that she intended to stick around long.

Since interviewing the Roushs, her suspicions about Denton had only grown. The friends who'd accompanied him to the drive-in seemed less important and now didn't come close to clearing him from involvement. That, coupled with him abandoning Virgie Fields with her head in a bucket of bleach, meant she had to see him again, in person. And this time, she wouldn't play nice.

But it wasn't only Denton she needed to speak with. She had to tell Cyrus what she'd found out. And she knew he wasn't going to like it.

It turned out Cyrus was in no state for a serious discussion. She found him sitting beside his vegetable garden, trying to spool wire onto a gas-powered trimmer. It would have been an easy task for most men, but Cyrus struggled. Cording was unraveled all around him, ensnaring his legs and arm. When she saw the bottle of Fireball whiskey lying in the grass, it made more sense.

"On a scale of one to ten, how drunk are you right now?"

He'd been facing away and was oblivious to her arrival. At her voice, he half-turned, revealing a white undershirt stained with blood and puke. The same substances were crusted around his mouth like putrid lipstick. He planted his hands on the ground and tried to push himself into a standing position, only to topple over backwards. "Sumbitch," he muttered.

She took that as a solid nine.

"Is this how you spend your days now? Shitfaced and worthless?" Carolina was fully aware of the irony of judging another for substance abuse, but she preferred to live by the *do as I say, not as I do* mantra.

"Didn' think you were comin back," he slurred. "Figured you fucked me over like all the others." He flailed on the ground like a turtle on its back. She grabbed his shoulders and raised him into a sitting position.

"Can you stand?"

His eyes narrowed as he seemed to consider it. "Doubt it."

"Fantastic." She plopped down on the ground, sitting across from him.

"Why're you here?" Cyrus asked.

"I was going to take you with me to the prison. I need to talk to Denton again about some issues that have come up."

Cyrus rubbed his crotch and leered. "How about you come closer. I'll show you what comes up." He cackled.

Great. It was gonna be one of *those* conversations with a drunk. "I'll pass on that."

"Come on, Car-line," he mumbled. "I'm a dying man. Don't that mean I get a wish or something? One last request. You and me in my bed for a couple hours, I know, then I could die happy."

She supposed she should be flattered, but she wasn't. Up until now, Cyrus had been on his best behavior around her. And while that included outbursts of anger and pointing shotguns at her, it was still better than this. This was pathetic. Then he started to weep and made everything worse.

"I'm sorry," he said. "I just get so lonely. My son hates me. You hate me. I fucked up every decent thing in my life."

His sobbing led to a violent coughing fit, which led to booze and blood spraying from his mouth like water from a fire house. At least he had the courtesy of turning his head. The smell of cinnamon mixed with the barf was almost enough to make her join him in retching.

When he finished, he pulled up and shirt and used it to wipe his mouth. Any delusions she'd harbored about him sobering up and joining her on the trip were gone. The last thing she needed was Cyrus Mankey puking all over her dash. If that happened, she'd have to sell the van. There wasn't enough cleaner in the world to remove the stain from her mind.

"Do you want me to help you into the house before I leave?" she asked.

Even though he was sitting, Cyrus swayed side to side like he was aboard a ship during high seas. "Might be best if I stay right here for a spell."

It was a relief. "Fine. I don't know when I'll be back. I have a lot of shit to sort out, and this isn't looking good."

Despite being drunk, those words got through. "The fuck you mean?"

"I mean the evidence pointing to Denton's innocence was just shot to hell. And if he can't clear this up, I'm out."

The sobbing, apologetic Cyrus flipped off. His version of Mr. Hyde taking over. "Don't you say that, you bitch. You do what I paid you for."

She bit her lip and let the name-calling pass, but she wasn't prepared to leave him off the hook entirely. "Paying me? In case your brain's as rotten as your lungs, I've been paid a grand total of seventeen fucking dollars. I've spent five times as much on gas alone. So, don't think you have the right to boss me, old man."

He blinked, twice, three times. His glassy eyes seemed to clear, marginally. "Told you I'd pay you when I got my check."

"Good thing I'm not holding my breath."

"Third Wednesday of the month," he said. Then he hoisted his right palm skyward. "Swear to God."

She doubted that held much merit, but more arguing would solve nothing. "All right. I'll be back Thursday morning, and I expect you to have cash in hand."

"Yessum."

She returned to the van, slamming the door as she dropped into the driver's seat. In her mirrors, she saw Cyrus watching her. She expected him to be dead before next Thursday, and as she drove, she tried to decide whether she cared.

CHAPTER TWENTY-TWO

"I didn't think I'd ever see you again," Denton said. He sat across from her in the visitor's room and wore his same aw shucks grin.

Today, she wasn't in the mood for it. She was pissed at Cyrus for being a drunk lech. She was pissed with herself for getting neck-deep in a case that looked more likely to be a dead end with each passing day. And she was pissed at Denton for grinning like a fool and not being able to read her body language.

She'd taken two more Oxy before entering the prison and now wished she'd have added a third. "Why would you assume the worst?" she asked.

Denton shrugged, his cheerful demeanor slipping. "Figured you gave up on me by now; I'm kinda used to it."

He walked his fingers along the edge of the table, like a bored kid in church. He looked defeated and hopeless. She could relate.

"For someone who is adamant about being innocent, you don't have much fight in you."

"Ever think I'm tired of getting my hopes up and thinking this time will be different?" He sat back in the chair, crossing his arms.

"I'm sorry if I don't act the way you think I should act or say the things you think I should say, but my whole life has been a series of letdowns. It gets old."

She wasn't in the mood for a *poor me* act. "Hey, if I interrupted your pity party, I'll show myself out."

They stared at each other, waiting for the other person to blink. He did. "You know how many visitors I get in here?" he asked.

She had a fair idea.

"Just you. In seven goddamn years. None of my friends from home. None of the people who wrote me letters and told me they felt sorry for me. Not even my shitass father. Just you."

His story was even worse than she'd suspected. No wonder the guy was jaded, why he expected the worst of people. But this wasn't the time to feel sorry for his situation, not when she had questions and needed answered.

"After what I've learned the last few days, I am close to being done with you," she said.

That snapped him to attention. Denton leaned into the table, his face twisted up in a combination of anger and fear. "What lies did you hear?"

"I've heard some stories," she continued. "And they were pretty convincing."

"Like what? From who?" he demanded.

"First, I want you to tell me about Virgie Fields."

"Oh," he said, the life leaving his eyes. He went back to the walking fingers shtick.

Although nonverbal, it was his answer. What Letty Fields had told her was the truth.

"The first time I was in here, you told me you were a good guy. That the cops railroaded you because of your father's past. Did you really think I wouldn't find out about her?"

He refused to meet her gaze. "We were kids."

"So was Cecilia Casto," she said.

His face twitched as the barb landed hard. "Look, I never said I was an angel. I said I wasn't a killer, and it's the truth."

"Then answer my question about Virgie Fields, and don't sugarcoat. If you lie, I'll know."

Finally, he looked at her. The grin, the confidence, all gone. He looked like student who'd just been called out by the school's toughest teacher. "I try every day to make amends for my past, but it's hard. Especially in a place like this."

Denton fished in his orange jumpsuit pocket and pulled out a wallet-sized photograph. He looked at it for a long moment, then laid it on the table and slid it across to her.

Through the wrinkles and creases, Carolina saw a younger version of Denton Mankey, both arms around a smiling, and alert, version of Virgie Fields. They sat in the grass, she between his legs. His arms were wrapped around her waist. Both wore the giddiness unique to young lovers.

"I was fourteen when it happened. I loved Virgie, I swear it. She stuck by me when my mom got killed. She never judged me for being a Mankey. She was everything good in my life."

Carolina handed the photo back to him and he got lost in it again. "I keep this picture, look at it everyday to remind myself what I did. Or, I suppose, didn't do. I know I shoulda called the cops or an ambulance, but I freaked out and panicked." He took a breath and let the sentence linger while he wiped snot from his nose. "When I saw her start twitching, I got scared shitless. And I ran because I'm a fucking coward."

She didn't think he was lying, and if he was, it was the best performance she'd seen in her life. And she had seen some doozies.

He folded the photo in half and returned it to his pocket.

"If you want to drop me, I understand," he said. "I deserve it."

"Slow your roll," Carolina said. "Before I make up my mind, I want to know what exactly you confessed to."

His misty eyes went confused. "I was on two days with no

sleep. Being beat every other hour. I'm not sure I remember the details. Why?"

"Other than your confession being the main reason you're in here?" She needed to know how the details he'd provided lined up with the facts. But she wouldn't lead him there.

Denton shook his head as he spoke, like he was trying to free his mind of a storm cloud. "I told them I picked up Cece just north of town. I saw her riding her bike, and it was a hot day; so, I offered to buy her a drink and give her a ride home. Then I told them I tried to feel her up, and she got mad and punched me in the balls. I said I lost my temper, took one of those big metal flashlights off the seat, and hit her in the face with it. Said I hit her so hard I killed her."

"Then what?"

"Well, I knew her head had been cut off. Bando told me that when he brought me in. Told me they were questioning me about a girl who'd been beheaded."

Carolina wasn't shocked the police had volunteered that fact, but it still disgusted her. It was a perfect detail to weed out a false confession from a real one, but it only worked when the suspect wasn't spoonfed information.

"I always had my toolbox because I drove an old truck and never knew what was gonna break down," Denton continued. "So, I told 'em I panicked and decided to cut up her body. Said I used my hacksaw."

That was a mistake. On whose part, she wasn't yet certain, but the Roushes were clear the head had been cleanly severed, not sawed off.

"What did you say you did next?"

"I said I took her up to the Devil's Teeth."

"Did they tell you her body had been found there?"

He paused. "They must have"

She wasn't sure if she believed him. "Okay. Did you tell them you did anything else to the body?"

"Like what? Rape it?"

Ugh, why'd he go there? "I don't know. Anything at all."

He considered it. "No. I don't think so. I'm sorry; it's hard to remember lies. The truth's easier."

"What did you say happened after you dumped her body?"

"I said I wanted people to think one of those devil's cults did it. So, I started a fire because I was going to burn her head, like a sacrifice, but I got nervous and took off."

"What about the worms?" she asked.

His brows pushed together. "Beg your pardon?"

"Never mind." She thought he looked genuinely clueless, but she needed one more thing to decide whether he was guilty or not.

"When did you do all of this?"

He paused, thinking. "I don't think I gave an exact time. Said it was around dark, though."

"The same day?"

"Yes."

That was important, and she needed to be certain. "In your confession, you told the sheriff you killed Cecilia Casto the same day you kidnapped her?"

"I told you, yes." Annoyance clouded his voice. "I was homeless. Surfing couches when one was available. Sleeping in my truck when none were. What was I gonna do, put her in Freddy's deep-freeze when his parents were at work? You believe me, right?" he asked, his face painfully earnest.

She wasn't one hundred percent certain of his innocence, but it was damn close. His confession was obviously false as Cece had been alive for days, not left on the ridge to rot in the midsummer sun.

If Bando hadn't been so fired up to close the case, he'd have spotted the gaping hole in the story. Then, she realized, he probably didn't care. He wanted someone in prison, facts be damned, and he got his wish.

But no court was going to overturn a guilty plea based on a recanted confession, even if the confession was obviously bullshit.

To have any chance of freeing Denton Mankey, she had to find out who really killed Cecilia Casto.

"I might," she answered.

That made him smile, one so big and broad it showed his broken and missing teeth. "I don't know if I even care if you can prove I'm innocent. Just knowing you're on my side is the best damned gift I've got in my entire life."

She felt a blush coming on and tried to dismiss his kindness. "That says more about your life than me."

"Maybe so," Denton said. "I never thought of myself as a lucky man. And I don't mean that in a pity-me kind of way; it's just the truth. I never won more on a scratch off than a buck. I always lost on coin tosses. I ended up in here for something I didn't do..." He stared at her, eyes wistful. "But I think, after all these years, my luck's finally changed for the better. And I can't thank you enough."

Never good with the feelings, Carolina waved his way. "I'll send you a bill when this is over."

He nodded, eager. "You better. Because I'll get one of those fat wrongful conviction settlements, and I can pay you as much as you want."

It felt good to see him optimistic. She just hoped she could give him the happy ending he deserved.

CHAPTER TWENTY-THREE

ELVEN WAS CONSIDERATE ENOUGH TO OFFER HER A ROOM IN his house. Even though he had plenty to spare, it felt too much like charity for her liking. She did accept his invitation to park her van in his driveway, though. While she missed the peaceful gurgling of the Little Elk, the cell reception on Elven's property was far superior.

The drive back from the prison, coupled with the stress of the day, had her exhausted by the time she pulled into her parking spot. She needed a few pills and a power nap, but before that could happen, Elven and Yeti emerged from the house. Her reprieve would have to wait.

As she climbed out of the van, Elven chucked a foam football her way. It spiraled perfectly through the air before bouncing off her midsection.

"Good hands," Elven said.

She wasn't in the mood. "The meathead scene was never my bag, remember?" His patented grin faltered, and she felt a little guilty for sticking a pin in his good mood. "Sorry, I'm wiped."

"We won't bother you," Elven said, grabbing the football off the grass. He chucked it toward the house, and Yeti bounded after it. He took a few steps toward the dog, then stopped. "Almost forgot." He dug into his jeans pocket and pulled out a slip of paper.

"What's that?" she asked.

"Three possibilities for Ottis Moore. Two residences and a place of employment. But I'll forewarn you, both properties are up for tax sale; so, he might've moved on."

She glanced at them. All three addresses were in Monacan County. She just couldn't stay out of that place. "Thanks. I guess."

She said the last word through a yawn, not bothering to cover her mouth. If this conversation went on much longer she was liable to fall asleep on her feet. "Anything else?" she asked.

He stared at her a little too hard, like a cop, not a friend. She tried to stand a little straighter, to appear as if she had her shit together, but knew she was doing a poor job.

"Are you sure you want to keep this up?" he asked.

"Keep what up?"

"This quest to exonerate Denton Mankey."

"Why? Did you find something out?"

"No. I'm just wary of you doing this on your own. It's unsafe."

It was her turn to grin. "Aw, Elven... I didn't know you cared."

A low-key blush spread across his cheeks. "I'm serious. You're dealing with some rough characters. The places you're going solo? I wouldn't send my deputies there without backup. Never mind the fact that there are no police in Monacan to have your back if this goes sour."

"I worked in Baltimore, remember? It's one step up from Beirut."

He could only shake his head. "You put your life on the line every time you go out there, and I can't understand why. It certainly can't be the money."

She was fully aware of the risks, but the why part eluded her too. Yes, the thought of an innocent man serving life for a crime he might not have committed horrified her, but he was far from the only person wrongly incarcerated. Was this really about Denton Mankey, or was she after something else? Like redemption?

"It's a job," she said. "Everyone kept saying I needed one, and now, you give me shit over it."

"At least let me give you a gun. For my peace of mind."

She rolled her eyes and pulled her pistol from the holster at her side. "I come prepared."

He nodded, some of his unease fading. "Then let me loan you something else."

"Like what?"

"One of my trucks."

"Why?"

"That van of yours is like driving around with a hit-me sign for everyone to see. I doubt you more than cross the county line before Bando knows you're around. I have an old Ford I use to plow the drive in the winter. It should blend right in."

CHAPTER TWENTY-FOUR

A BACKFIRE EXPLODED FROM THE TRUCK'S TAILPIPE, AND A mushroom cloud of black smoke followed. The Ford was almost forty years old, had serious weight reduction in the form of rust, and chugged like a freight train every time she went over an incline steeper than two degrees.

"I preferred your van to this piece of shit," Cyrus said from the passenger seat.

"I don't recall asking you for your opinion."

"Free country."

"I hope you don't believe that," she said, making a right onto Chickpea Lane.

When she'd arrived at Cyrus's, she saw him beside the garden and thought her premonition had come true and he wasn't just dead, he'd died right where she left him. But as the truck tires crunched, announcing her arrival, he turned her way and gave a genial wave with a hand holding a fistful of weeds. When she told him to hop in, he'd obeyed without protest. Thank you, Doctor Jekyll.

He hadn't bothered with an apology, not that she expected one.

For all she knew, he didn't even remember the incident from a few days prior, and she had no intentions of bringing up the man's failings and addictions. It was all good.

They rolled down Chickpea, reading house numbers on mailboxes as they passed by them.

238

243

249

They were looking for 317, and, soon enough, they arrived.

Only there was no house, just a burned out foundation and the occasional charred beams and joists. A few blackened appliances lingered in the remains, bits of furniture. But no people. And no Ottis Moore.

"Some lead this was," Cyrus said from the shotgun seat.

"Ye of little faith." She punched the next address Elven had provided into her GPS and made a U-turn.

Nearly half an hour later, they came to 19 Waverly Rd. No house there either—only an RV that would have generously been called vintage but more accurately was just old, sagged on flat tires. It had been white, once upon a time, but was now mostly orange with surface rust, although some black mold added dimension. She thought it was abandoned, too—until the door opened.

A man in his sixties popped his head through the opening. He had a wiry mane of dishwater gray hair and a beard that stretched halfway down his chest. He wore pajama pants stained yellow at the crotch and no shirt. In his arms, he held a fat, brown cat.

"This is private property," the man said. "And I do not give you permission to enter."

Carolina hadn't even exited the truck yet and already knew this was going to be fun. She rolled down the window and leaned out. "Sir, we're parked on the berm. That's public property."

The man hopped the ground and took a step toward her. "I know my rights."

"I'm sure you do, and I promise you I have no intention of

violating them. I just need to ask you a couple questions. You can come to me if you prefer."

The man narrowed his eyes but considered it. He closed the door to the RV, then halved the distance between them. "If this is about the taxes, you need to talk—"

"This has nothing to do with your taxes. Like I said, I just need to ask you some questions, and then we'll get out of your way."

He continued to the truck, staying just out of arm's reach, like they might be planning to abduct him. It was then Carolina realized it wasn't a cat in his arms, but a groundhog. It lounged on its back while the old man rubbed its belly in small, even circles.

"Cute pet you got there. What's its name?"

He stared at her like she was the crazy one. "This here is a rodent. It don't have a name. Got hit on the road a few weeks back and has been convalescing in my home ever since."

"That's nice of you," she said, hoping the small talk had broken the ice. "Mr. Moore, I wanted to talk to you about a crime committed some years back. One for which you provided an eyewitness statement to the Sheriff."

"Pardon?" he asked, his expression so clueless she may as well have been speaking Latin.

"About Cecilia Casto," she said.

He didn't reply—only continued his long, confused stare.

"Are you Ottis Moore?" Cyrus asked.

The old man scratched a patch of eczema off his cheek. It left behind a pink welt. "Ottis Moore is an asshole. And I assure you I am not an asshole."

Carolina sagged into her seat. "Sorry for the confusion. Any chance you can tell us where to find Ottis?"

The man had stopped rubbing the groundhog's belly, and the animal gave a whiny squeak of protest, so, he recommenced. "Ottis Moore sold me this residence the summer before last. We finalized the transaction on August the twenty-fourth. I have not seen or spoken to him since—nor do I care to."

Carolina turned the key, and the engine sputtered back to life. "Well, thank you for your help, and I apologize for bothering you."

"No bother," the old man said. "If you find Ottis Moore, will you tell him the air- conditioning unit does not work? He did not disclose that prior to the purchase, and I would like to be compensated."

She gave a quick nod, already pulling away. "I'll be sure to tell him. You and your rodent have a fine day now."

The waste of time, the dead ends, were gnawing at her, and she felt the telltale throb in her shoulder go from a four to an eight. Without thinking, she grabbed her prescription bottle from her jacket pocket and tossed three into her mouth, dry-swallowing them. It was only after they were down the hatch when she remembered she wasn't alone.

But Cyrus, like any good addict, understood the value of discretion and didn't say a word.

THEIR LAST CHANCE for Ottis Moore was the work address. They were two-thirds of the way there when Cyrus, who'd been disinterested thus far, spoke up. "Make a left at the stop sign," he said.

Carolina glanced at the GPS, which was directing her straight ahead for the next twelve miles. "You know a shortcut or something?"

"Or something," he said.

She thought about protesting, but Cyrus had been a decent companion today, and she didn't see any sense in putting an end to that. She turned left at the intersection and continued along the mostly barren street. Ahead, a Gulf gas sign was accompanied by one reading *Jack's Gas and Grub*. On the sign was a hand-painted pig wearing a bib and holding a knife and fork.

"Pull on in," Cyrus said. "I'm hungry."

The squat, cinder-block building was well past its prime. Blue paint peeled from the walls. One window was held together with duct tape. A lone, rust-covered gas pump waited for customers.

"Here?" Carolina asked. "You want to eat here?"

"Yes, I do. And you're joining me. If you don't, I'm firing you."

Carolina's eyes narrowed. "Don't make promises you can't keep, old man." She turned the truck into the empty parking lot, stopping beside the pump. Smoke wafted from a chimney behind the business, and although she thought herself more likely to get trichinosis than a good meal, the sweet smoke was damned alluring.

"What the hell?" she asked, shutting off the engine. "No one lives forever, right?"

She realized it was a crass thing to say to a man with one foot in his grave, but Cyrus only grinned.

"Damn straight," he said.

They left the truck and moved to the entrance, where an *Open* sign hung askew on a screen door. Cyrus, ever the gentleman, held it open for her.

Two walls were lined with varieties of oil and automotive fluids. Another was filled with cigarettes, cigars, snuff, and chewing tobacco. The fourth was behind a glass display case filled with two stainless steel trays loaded with food. Carolina followed Cyrus to it, sidestepping a string of fly tape dangling from the ceiling. You don't get this kind of atmosphere in the cities.

A hulking beast of a man sat behind the case reading the daily news. He didn't look up. "We're all out of brisket," he informed them. "Sold out about an hour ago."

"That's all right," Cyrus said. "We want two pulled pork sandwiches."

"Regular or jumbo?"

"Jumbo."

"Fried jalapenos?"

Cyrus checked with Carolina, who only shrugged. "This was your idea," she said. "What do you recommend?"

"Yeah," Cyrus said to the man. "Jalapenos."

"To drink?"

"Sweet teas," Cyrus said.

"Regular sweet or extra?"

"Extra."

The man finally set aside the newspaper. He worked himself into a standing position, a firecracker of a fart bursting from his wide ass in the process. None of them acknowledged it. "It'll be fourteen ninety-eight."

As he began piling meat into two hoagie buns, Cyrus looked at Carolina with a raised eyebrow.

"What?" she asked.

"Pay the man," he said, shameless.

"This was your idea."

"I gave you all my money. What did you expect?"

"Chivalry," she said as she pulled out a money clip. She grabbed a twenty, a ten, and a five, and laid all three bills on the counter as the man returned, holding their buns in his bare hands. "Give me twenty in gas, too."

They both took their sandwiches, and a moment later, the man passed them plastic cups filled to the brim. "Got seating out back," the man said and pocketed the money. He didn't bother with the two cents Carolina was owed in change.

The seating consisted of hard plastic crates overlooking a mostly-dry creek bed. "You take me to all the best places," Carolina quipped as she plopped onto one.

Cyrus was already one bite into his meal, sauce dribbling down his chin. "You gonna bitch or eat?"

"Why not both?"

He hadn't swallowed the first mouthful but powered into a second. Carolina figured she better get on the ball if she hoped to keep up. She could see the fat man's greasy fingerprints on the bun but didn't let it deter her. She'd undoubtedly consumed worse.

In just one bite, she understood why Cyrus had demanded the

detour. She hadn't even realized she was hungry, but the smoky sweetness tasted like nectar from the gods. She hurriedly chewed and swallowed, then went in for seconds. Soon enough, the hot peppers set her tongue on fire, which she put out with a swig of tea sweet enough to put her into a diabetic coma. It was amazing.

"Told ya," Cyrus said through a mouthful of food.

"That you did."

A cool autumn breeze blew by, knocking crimson leaves off a red maple. Carolina watched them dance back and forth, back and forth, as they drifted to the ground. Despite the shitty seating and the less-than-desirable location, this was a nice moment. One of the few she'd had the last few months. Who would've thought?

They finished their food in silence, too caught up in the eating to bother with small talk. But when the food was gone, the silence became awkward, and Cyrus was the one to break it.

"I've been meaning to tell you something," he said. "I know this job probably ain't what you expected, but I appreciate you taking a flyer on me and my boy. Most people wouldn't do what you're doing."

She was surprised at this rare show of humanity and wasn't quite sure how to respond. "Sure," she said. "I just hope I can find what you want."

"Same."

Since he'd opened the door to a sincere conversation, Carolina decided it was her turn to get something off her chest. "You really should go and see Denton. While you still have time."

He downed the remainder of his tea and stared at the trickle of water below them. She wondered if he was thinking or attempting to ignore her advice. But finally, he countered, "It isn't apt to end well."

"You might be surprised. Especially if he sees your condition."

Cyrus rose to his feet and hawked a ball of phlegm and blood onto the ground. "I was never around to be his daddy when I was well. Doesn't seem fair to burden him with me now that I'm dying."

"It's not just about what you want, Cyrus. If nothing else, getting closure could do him well."

He dropped his empty cup into a dented oil drum serving as a trash bin. "Naw," he said. "Far as he's concerned, I'm already dead. Him seeing a ghost won't do no good. I ruined the boy's life. No going back." He left her there, taking long strides back to the truck.

Carolina started after him. "People change."

He shot her a glance over his shoulder. "Do they?"

In truth, she wasn't sure.

CHAPTER TWENTY-FIVE

"Shit," Cyrus said. "You didn't tell me we were going to a strip club. I'd have put on my fancy silk shirt."

Carolina stared at the brown, metal-sided building that could have passed for a small warehouse if not for the school-bus yellow sign with its blocky black text.

Adult World.

Live Girls Daily.

"That's because I didn't know," she said as she hopped out of the truck and headed to the entrance, Cyrus hot on her heels. The man hadn't moved this quickly in all the time she'd known him.

They stepped into a low-rent pornographic wonderland. Oversized video boxes with titles like *Daddy's Dirty Daughter* and *White Rods in Black Holes*. Magazines making *Playboy* and *Penthouse* look like high art. Then there were the toys. Dildos bigger than her forearm. Rubber vaginas. Feathers and leather and a variety of edible waxes and lotions.

Behind a counter stood the store's lone clerk, a boring man in his forties with boxy glasses and a poor excuse for a beard. He'd been reading a book when they entered but now eyed her suspiciously, and she knew he already suspected her of being a cop.

Carolina turned to Cyrus, hoping the man's presence would put the clerk at ease, only to see him scurrying down a dimly-lit hallway, above which a *Cash Only* sign hung. Bastard.

She didn't want to give the clerk any more time to get spooked and took a direct path to his cash register. He stiffened.

"I'm not a cop." It was as good a lead-in as anything.

"That's what a cop would say," the man said.

"True." She looked for a name tag but found none. "I'm actually a P.I., and I'm looking for Ottis Moore."

The clerk seemed to lose interest. He went back to reading his paperback novel, which she saw was not of the adult variety but was instead a Dean Koontz original. "Won't find him here."

She placed her hand on the counter and tapped her fingers. "That's a shame. It's about a small inheritance he's due."

The clerk's face loosened with curiosity. "Oh, yeah?"

"Yeah."

"Why don't you leave it with me, and I'll see he gets it." He held up two fingers. "Scout's honor."

"Isn't working in a place like this against the scout's code?" she asked.

"Job's a job," he replied, leering. "So how much is old Ottis due?"

"I can't divulge that. When's his next shift? I'll stop back."

The clerk huffed. "Prick stopped showing up for work earlier this year. Never called or nothing."

"Do you have an address on file?"

"Probably, but I really don't feel like digging for it. What do I care if he gets paid after leaving me in the lurch?"

She watched him with steely eyes. "If you're waiting for a bribe, you'll be waiting a long time."

He rolled his eyes. "Okay, okay. I'm a nice guy. You don't gotta be like that." He pulled a binder from below the desk and began flipping through it.

Carolina checked the hall where Cyrus had vanished, but there was still no sign of him. Then she peered down through the glass case and saw an assortment of jewelry, but not the kind you wear in your ears. These were for pierced nipples and dicks. Many were spiked and looked like torture devices.

"All right," the clerk said, bringing her attention back to him. "Ottis Moore. Nineteen Waverly Road. Happy now?"

"Not really," Carolina said. "Seeing as how he doesn't live there any more."

The clerk turned his palms up. "Then I got nothing. Prick's like a fart in a whirlwind. Never know where he'll end up."

CHAPTER TWENTY-SIX

CYRUS WASN'T CONCERNED WITH THE PUMPER OUT FRONT. Let Carolina handle him while he had an afternoon delight. How could she even blame him?

The first two rooms he checked were vacant, but he stuck gold in the third. A woman sat behind a glass window, her back turned. She had long, bleached blonde hair hanging halfway to her ass, and he was already getting hard.

She heard the door open and turned to him. Despite caked-on makeup and a push-up bra, she couldn't pass for eighteen. Still, she was old enough to get him going and not young enough to stop it.

He stared at her expectantly, but she didn't dance. Instead, she pointed to the wall, where there was a slot for money. The sign above it read *five dollars for a show*. He pulled out his wallet and extracted a wrinkled honest Abe, but the machine kicked it back. He was getting frustrated as he stretched it flat and ran it against the edge of the wall and the glass frame, trying to get it in shape. Finally, the machine ate it up without a hitch.

He leaned back as the lights brightened behind the glass, giving him a better look at the girl. Her red lingerie was downright devilish, and although her sashaying was out of time with the music, he didn't mind one bit.

She reached across herself and pulled down one bra strap, then did the same on the other side. A few more spins and twirls, and she moved on to unhooking her bra and letting it fall to the floor but deftly kept her small breasts covered with her hands.

"My name's Diamond," she said with a wink.

"And you shine even prettier than one," Cyrus said. "Now keep up the good work, honey."

Diamond gave him a quick flash of her breasts before covering them again with a forearm while she used her free hand to slowly lower her panties. He caught a glimpse of some hair and wasn't at all concerned the carpet didn't match the drapes.

"You remind me of my grandpappy," she said as she spun around, giving him a good look at her ass crack.

Was that supposed to be sexy? Some sort of fetish role-playing? He was trying to think up a comeback when light spilled into the cramped room. He spun around and saw Carolina.

Diamond hurriedly pulled up her panties. "Hey, it's double the price for two peepers," she snapped. She grabbed her bra off the floor, and he got one good look at her naked chest before she was covered again. Damn it all.

"What the hell do you think you're doing?" Carolina asked.

He dropped his hands to cover his bulging crotch. "Investigating."

Carolina turned to the girl, looking her up and down. "What are you? Sixteen?"

"Carolina," Cyrus said. "This is Diamond. Diamond, Carolina." Neither woman seemed to appreciate the introduction. To save face, he blurted, "Do you know Ottis Moore?"

The stripper looked back and forth between them, wary and maybe a little scared. "What's it to you?"

Cyrus turned back to Carolina, pleased with himself. But she hadn't yet caught on; so, he had to spell it out for her. "She can help us," he said. "But she ain't gonna do it out of the goodness of her heart."

"You pay her," Carolina said.

"I'm broke. You know that."

Carolina glanced at the five dollars a show sign, her nose crinkling in disgust. "Seems like your poverty comes and goes." She grabbed a twenty and held it up for Diamond to see, but the stripper only muttered an annoyed *hmpf*. Then Carolina sighed and took out another twenty.

It must have been the magic number.

"Meet me around back in five minutes," the girl said.

She left the room, which gave Carolina the chance to glare at him without an audience.

She had a fire in her. He liked that in a woman.

CHAPTER TWENTY-SEVEN

CAROLINA IGNORED CYRUS'S PRESENCE AS THEY WAITED FOR the girl, and he was on his best behavior, like a dog that had shit on the rug and was suddenly your best friend.

The rear door creaked open, and Diamond stepped out, her red platform boots crunching in the gravel. The heel was as narrow as a pencil, and not even on her best day could Carolina wear something similar without breaking her neck. Yet here was the girl, sixteen at the oldest, marching along like a majorette in the Rose Bowl parade.

She was in the process of lighting a Newport and sucking a huge drag off it. She held the smoke in for a moment and looked to Carolina as she approached. She let the smoke out, and all of it blew into Carolina's face.

"Sorry," Diamond said, already sucking on her cigarette again.

Carolina shrugged. "Don't mention it."

Diamond extended her free hand expectantly, and Carolina handed her the two twenties, which the girl shoved into her bra. She hadn't bothered changing her outfit, instead only throwing a light jacket over it, and Carolina could see goosebumps muddying her midsection.

"So, what do you wanna know about Ottis?" she asked.

"What can you tell us?" Carolina asked.

Diamond chuckled, smoke blowing out of her nose in a way that reminded Carolina of dragons in cartoons. "He's a weird ass fucker."

"Can you be more specific?" Carolina asked.

"I dunno. He's just weird. Like he never paid no attention to us girls. And, I mean, sometimes we walk around bare-ass naked when there's no customers. Sneaking peeks is half the reason most of these assholes work here. Like Roy in there."

"Maybe he's queer," Cyrus said. Both women glanced at him, then returned their attention to each other.

"He didn't seem like it," Diamond said. "He was a big, fat slob. Those types usually aren't. I dunno. But he didn't seem to care none about sex. Didn't care nothing about anything besides all that hoodoo shit he was always yappin' about."

"Hoodoo?" Carolina asked.

"Mountain magic. Healing spells. Making it rain during dry spells and shit. It's all he ever talked about. That and the toads."

"Toads?" Carolina was beginning to wonder if the girl was stoned.

"Yeah," Diamond said. "The guy who brings toads or something. Maybe he licked 'em. I don't know. Like I said. Weird ass fucker. I didn't pay much attention when he got to ranting about that stuff, honestly."

"Anyone else here into those kind of things?" Carolina asked. "Like a cult?"

Diamond chuckled. "Not hardly." She stopped, remembering something that brought a glimmer of light into her dull eyes. "You know, one time, Sapphire, she only works on the weekends. She had the worst case of clap I ever seen. Ottis, he gave her some green plant to chew on. It smelled nasty as shit, and Sapphire said it tasted like roadkill, but a week later, she was all cleared up. Pussy good as new. About the craziest shit I ever seen." She shrugged. "So, who knows, I guess. Maybe there's a little truth behind his crazy."

"You know where we can find him?" Carolina asked.

"He said he was going to live at some hippy-dippy farm out on Possum Ridge. He said the people there were *enlightened...* Whatever the fuck that means."

She finished off her cigarette in one long drag, then flicked the butt into the gravel and glanced at the store. "Anyway, unless you got another twenty, I gotta scoot. Roy in there clocks my breaks, and he'll rat me to the bossman if I'm out here too long."

"No, we're good. Thank you for your help. But can I offer you a piece of advice?" Carolina asked.

"Depends on the advice."

"Get out of this place. You're so damn young; you could do anything you want with your life. Something better than this."

Diamond laughed again. "I make eight hundred bucks a week, cash money, for doing nothing harder than dancing around in my birthday suit. You tell me what could be better?"

Carolina knew the girl did more than strip to earn that kind of pay. But in a county where the average annual household income was under fifteen grand, her logic was hard to argue against.

CHAPTER TWENTY-EIGHT

As commUNES WENT, THIS ONE WAS UNIMPRESSIVE. THREE large yurts stood side by side, their outer sheaths oversized silver tarps, giving them the look of something out of a low-rent sci-fi film. More than a dozen, but fewer than twenty, men and women toiled in a field, using hand tools to plow the decomposing remnants of the summer crops back into the ground. The sulfurous stench of rotting cabbage filled the air and Carolina's nostrils. It was mixed with stagnant water that laid in shallow pools every five or so yards.

"The fuck is that smell?" Cyrus asked, putting his nose in the crook of his elbow as they walked toward the people.

Carolina was trying not to focus on it, taking deep breaths and holding them until her lungs burned. "Breath through your mouth," Carolina said through an exhale.

He tried and his face turned green. "God damn. I can taste it now, and I've smoked since I was twelve."

Cyrus pulled out his pipe and lit up, and Carolina didn't even consider complaining. She'd take the smell of tobacco smoke over this rancid concoction.

Ahead of them, a scrawny man with gray dreadlocks broke

from the pack of laborers and strode toward one of the puddles. With no modesty, he dropped his linen pants and squatted, directing his bare ass at the water, and began to defecate.

So much for enlightened.

It was impossible to reach the main group without passing by the shitter, and Carolina was unsure whether to acknowledge or ignore him. It turned out she didn't have to make a decision as he spoke.

"Good day, my friends," he said as a heavy log dropped from him, splashing into the water with a plop.

"Good day back at you," Carolina said, looking past him rather than at him.

"Have you come to join our kibbutz?" the shitter asked. "If so, I can assure you, you both would be most welcome."

"I appreciate the invitation, but we're looking for an acquaintance. A man named Ottis Moore."

The shitter nodded and stood, pulling up his pants without taking the time to clean himself in any way. He took a few steps closer and his personal aroma made the fragrance of the fields seem like a floral bouquet. Gnats swarmed around him, some landing in his unkempt mane and squirming inside.

Please don't let him be Ottis, Carolina thought. She didn't know if it would be possible to have a drawn-out conversation with this man without refunding her barbecue.

"You mean Brother Nataraja, as he's now known. Come, I shall take you to him."

They followed the shitter through the field, sidestepping anything resembling puddles, until they came to the group of laborers. There was a three-to-one male to female ratio, and all wore identical, androgynous tan pants and shirts. It was also evident none of them took personal hygiene seriously, and the buzzing insects around them were enough to make Carolina's skin crawl.

"Brother Nataraja," the shitter said. "Your presence is requested."

From Diamond's description, Carolina expected Ottis Moore to be a few cheeseburgers away from professional wrestler size, but the man who separated himself from the group had only a slightly larger-than-average beer gut. He strode toward them, his bare feet sinking deep into the muck with each step. His wiry, blond hair was pulled into a topknot, and he had a good start on a beard, in which small scraps of food were nestled, perhaps being saved for snacks later in the day.

"Can we talk in private?" Carolina asked him, eager to escape from the collective stench.

"Of course," Ottis said, leading the way. "We can sit and talk over here."

They stopped at the edge of the field, beside the yurts. A fallen oak had been sawed into sections that served as seats. Hanging from the trees were a variety of figures and trinkets that looked like mixes between dreamcatchers and something out of *The Blair Witch Project*.

Candles mounted on long poles burned and, thank God, kept away most of the bugs. Two younger women, neither yet in their twenties and both topless, were involved in a heavy-duty make-out session behind one of the dwellings. It was strange ambiance, but far preferable to the field.

While Cyrus couldn't peel his eyes away from the young, partially-nude women, Ottis paid them no attention. It seemed like the asexuality described by Diamond was accurate.

"Tell me how I can help you," Ottis said, his expression relaxed and genial.

"I have some questions about Cecilia Casto's murder."

"Ah," he said, nodding. "Was a shame what happened to her."

"As far as I can tell, you're the last person who saw her alive. Aside from whoever killed her."

"I don't believe that's up for debate, is it? Mankey killed her."

At the mention of his son, Cyrus finally looked away from the show. He aimed his narrowed eyes at Ottis. "That's what you told 'em, huh? That my boy's a murderer?"

Ottis shook his head, unfazed by Cyrus's sudden vehemence. "I never said anything along those lines, sir. I told them the truth. I told them what I saw."

"Which was?" Carolina asked.

He shifted on the log, redistributing his weight. "I saw her riding a bike to the store. She went inside and bought a bottle of pop and some candy. Came back outside, and that's when she and Denton Mankey started talking."

"Talking as in a conversation, or as in he was harassing her?" Carolina asked, ignoring the peeved glare the question drew from Cyrus.

"Chatting. I was beside the store, resting on some old tires and enjoying a marijuana cigarette. I'd say I was ten yards away from them, so I couldn't hear what was being said. But it seemed genial."

"Then what happened?"

"I saw Cece open the passenger door on his truck. Then they kept talking. He said something which made her laugh. And that was the last part I saw."

"Why didn't you see what happened afterward?"

Ottis stole a glance at his dirty, shoeless feet. "Well, I wasn't there by happenstance. I was there because the fellow who did inspections sold meth on the side. And I was one of his better customers." He slapped his belly. "I've kicked the nasty habit. Anyway, he called me in, and we did our deal. Afterward, everyone was gone."

"That's it? You never saw them argue or fight?"

"No. As I said, it seemed cordial enough to me."

"Do you think she went with him?"

"No way of knowing."

"And that's what you told the police?"

He nodded. "Yes, miss. Because it was the truth."

Nearby, a hen gave an angry squawk. Carolina looked toward the sound and found two chicken fighting over an earthworm. That jogged her memory about what the Roushes had seen in Cece's mouth and gave her an idea.

"We were told you're into mountain magic." she said, looking back to the big man. "Something called hoodoo."

"Yes. But it's more than being *into* it. It's a part of everything." He held out his hands and rotated his head. "It's connecting with our world in a deeper level.

"Do you know anything about worms?"

He laughed. "You must be more specific."

"Would there be any reason why they'd be placed in someone's mouth after death?"

There was no laughter from Ottis this time. His face dropped, and he pursed his lips. "Where'd you hear about that?"

Carolina decided to put all her cards on the table. "The men who found Cece Casto told me her mouth was filled with worms. Does that have anything to do with your religion?"

"Hoodoo's not a religion. It's belief. It's about curing people, protecting them. White magic. It's got nothing to do with such perversion."

"Then what does?" Carolina asked.

Ottis shifted his eyes between Cyrus and Carolina, then finally locked them onto Carolina. "That's Der Todesbringer."

She thought he said toads bringer, like Diamond mentioned at Adult World.

"Toads?" She asked.

He stood, wringing his hands together. "Not toads. Todes. Der Todesbringer."

"What's that?"

"Not a what," Ottis said. "A who."

He was on the move, lumbering into the field until Carolina raced after him and caught a handful of his shirt. It felt stiff and unwashed in her grip. "Wait," she said. "I could really use your help here."

Then Ottis looked into her eyes, but it went deeper. Like he was staring into her. Reading her mind. And he took a long look before speaking. "I can see your scourge," he finally said. "It's eating you from the inside out like a cancer. And if you dig deeper into any of this, it'll only accelerate." He pulled himself free of her grasp. "He knows you're after him. And the only way it ends is in brimstone."

The seriousness in his voice unnerved her, and her fear pissed her off. At him for being so cryptic. At herself for letting this dime-store hippie spook her. "Who are you talking about?" she asked.

"Der Todesbringer," he repeated. "The boogeyman."

CHAPTER TWENTY-NINE

Although she had no solid evidence, Carolina felt like she'd accomplished something worthwhile for the first time in the investigation. She didn't want to waste time driving back to Dupray, so she returned to the boarding house to review all the evidence and collect her thoughts. The latter proved easier said than done until she'd taken some pills, swallowing two and chewing the third to speed up the process. As it dissolved against her tongue, she felt the stress of life melt away, replaced with a warm, dull haze that enveloped and caressed her.

How could three little pills make everything so much better?

She spread her growing pile of paperwork on the floor, not even caring that the carpet probably hadn't been deep-cleaned since the first Bush administration. The pile was a hodgepodge of information. The newspaper clippings Elven had given her. Her own notes. Drawings she'd made of the sights at the Devil's Teeth. Summaries of all her interviews so far. Denton's mugshot.

Rather than coming closer to figuring this out, it seemed like she kept finding more questions, more riddles. And now, she had the lone witness against Denton telling her Denton and Cece seemed to get on just fine and that the prime suspect was the boogeyman.

She sat amid the madness, like she was a participant in some fever dream, waiting for her own version of enlightenment.

Then came a knock at the door. And a small, timid voice.

"Miss McKay?"

She went to the door and opened it. Viola Shafer, the owner of the boarding house, stood in the hallway with a plate of steaming-hot food in one hand and a pitcher of drink in the other.

The woman was short and squat, with dull gray hair and a spinster's plain face. She wore a floral-print dress hanging to her ankles—but what fine ankles they were. Carolina thought she probably looked and dressed the same for the last twenty years and would go about life unchanged for twenty more.

"I rang your room but didn't get an answer, so I figured you were busy and brought supper to you. Biscuits and gravy."

Carolina hadn't heard the phone and, in a moment of clarity, wondered if she overdid it on the Oxy. "You didn't have to do that," she said.

"Nonsense," Viola said, passing her by and entering the room. "It's included in your day rate." She set the food on a table for one, then refilled Carolina's Charm City mug with Kool-Aid.

"Will you join me?" Carolina asked. She didn't want the company but thought it only polite to offer.

"Oh, no. I already ate. Thank you."

Carolina sat at the table and dug in while Viola lingered, her prying eyes taking in Carolina's wild jumble of papers. If she hadn't been flying on the pills, she might have told the woman to get out and mind her own business, but she was feeling fine and didn't mind her nosiness in the slightest.

As Carolina cleansed her palate with cherry drink, Viola picked up one of the papers from the floor and showed it to her.

"You have Casto written down here. Is that why you're in Monacan? Because of Cecilia?" she asked.

Carolina nodded, making another forkful of food disappear. "Yeah, I've been looking into it. Can't say I've uncovered much, though," Carolina said, swallowing a belch.

"Our county's dirty secret." Viola rifled through more papers.

"Is it a secret, though?" Carolina asked, interest in her meal waning. "Doesn't everyone here think Denton Mankey was responsible?

"For Cecilia, yes. But she isn't the only one."

Carolina rose from her seat and went to the woman. "What do you mean?"

"Every fourth year, one is taken," Viola said, as if it were common knowledge.

Carolina tried shaking her head, now wanting the opiate fog to dissipate. It didn't work. "One what?"

"One girl," Viola said.

"You're saying a girl is killed every four years in Monacan?"

"They disappear. Most are never seen again. Cecilia was the exception."

Viola's words still weren't sinking in, and Carolina set on the edge of the bed, rubbing her temple. "Who knows about this?"

Viola tittered, nervous. "I'd say anyone who lives in Monacan and has two working ears. Who doesn't know might be a more proper question."

"Who do people think is responsible?"

"Why, Der Todesbringer."

That name again. The boogeyman who sounded as made up as the tooth fairy. "And who is he? Can you tell me anything that might help?"

Rather than answer, Viola pointed to one of Carolina's sketches. The one she'd made of the symbol carved into the tree. "Right there," Viola said.

Carolina picked it up, examined it, then turned it toward her. "I saw this where Cecilia's body was found."

Viola nodded. "Of course, dear. It's his mark."

Carolina stared at the sketch, the figure she'd first taken to be a deer and now realized it wasn't a deer at all.

It was the devil.

CHAPTER THIRTY

Sleep, at least while sober, had been hard to come by for the past several weeks. But after a day on the road with Carolina, Cyrus managed to saw some logs. Until one of the worst coughing and gagging spells he'd experienced in days woke him from a sound sleep.

He lunged forward, hacking blood onto the old quilt that covered his ever-shrinking body. He felt his lungs seizing, his ribcage tearing apart. He couldn't get a breath and half-expected to suffocate with his mouth open. All the while, sweat boiled on is skin.

The coughing wouldn't stop, and he figured this was it. His last hurrah.

At least he got to see some titties on his final day. Life wasn't all bad.

Then he realized he couldn't see his bedroom door. And that his bedroom was filled with dense, black smoke that rolled under the door like the incoming tide.

His quilt and mattress were saturated with perspiration. He peeled the wet blanket off himself and rolled out of bed, head swimming and disoriented. Stumbling through the smoke to his bedroom door, he grabbed the knob, which seared his palm like a steak in a cast-iron pan. Nonetheless, he pushed through the pain and shoved the door open.

His living room and kitchen burned a blinding orange. Fire engulfing the walls, the floors, licked at the ceiling. His bookcase was an inferno, his paperbacks fuel for the hell raging through his modest abode. The one he'd bult all by himself. It has taken him three years and was, without question, his greatest achievement.

But he only had a second to take all of that in before the oxygen in his bedroom collided with the hungry flames, which doubled in fury. A woosh of fire rushed at him, knocking him off his feet and sending him careening into the bed frame.

Something cracked. The bed, a rib, his skull, he wasn't sure. Constellations filled his foggy field of vision.

Still coughing, still in misery, Cyrus scrambled to his feet, grabbed a reading lamp off the end table, used it to smash the glass out of his bedroom window, the one he'd nailed shut years earlier after a break-in. He ran the lamp along with window frame, clearing it of excess glass, popped his head outside, and gulped air like he'd just completed a free dive to the Mariana Trench.

The coarse hacking slowed as oxygen entered what remained of his lungs.

That's when he heard the tires tearing away from his house. Fucking bastards.

But there was no point in trying to chase. Not in his condition. Not wearing only his boxers.

Instead, he turned back to the growing pyre that had been his sleeping quarters, yanked open a dresser drawer, grabbed an armload of clothing. He returned to the window, taking a moment to snatch his pipe and a pouch of tobacco, dove through the cavity, plunging onto the grass outside. He did not stick the landing.

As he crawled away from the burning house, he felt a new fire in his arm. Ready to pound out the flames, he instead saw a gaping, five inch gash on his bicep. Blood gushed.

While he watched his house burn, he used a shirt as a makeshift tourniquet, stopping the bleeding. Then he sat there and watched the last thing in the world that was his disintegrate before his eyes.

CHAPTER THIRTY-ONE

It was nearing 8 a.m. when Carolina rolled up to where Cyrus's house had stood the day before. Things had changed in the last fourteen hours.

The shell of the man's home jutted from the ground like black fingers straight from hell. Even those were few, with most of the structure collapsed inward. Smoke leaked from the ashes, its acrid smell burning her nose as she exited the truck and took in the sight.

Cyrus sat in the grass, enough smoke surrounding him to make it look like he was on fire. But this was pipe smoke. He took a drag of it as he gave her a curt nod. The man was naked, save his underwear, his left arm a scarlet stain, a piece of clothing lashed around it.

"What the hell happened?" she asked as she approached him.

He rolled onto his knees, then got on all fours. Pounds of empty skin sagged from his skeletal body, drooping so low it almost touched the ground. Then he stood, and everything shifted, mostly, into place. If he'd looked awful the first time she'd seen him half-naked, now he was awful times one hundred. She couldn't understand how he was still alive.

"I must've forgot to blow out that candle from the Pottery Barn before I went to bed." His eyes were vacant, maybe in shock.

"Are you serious?" she asked.

"Fuck no, I'm not serious." He shuffled to a lawn chair and plopped into it. "What the hell's it look like? Some asshole burned my goddamn house down."

She wanted to ask the obvious questions: Who? How? Why? But his next remark answered them all.

"People around here want the past to stay in the past." He spat onto the ground, giving his opinion.

"Shit," Carolina said. "I'm sorry, Cyrus."

"Yeah," he said. "Sure."

She was desperate to ask him about the missing girls, to find out if what Viola Shafer had told her had any truth, but the timing wasn't right. Together, they stared at the empty remains of his home and stayed that way until approaching tires drew their attention.

Both looked at the same time and saw Reed Bando's patrol car easing up the drive, eventually coming to a halt beside Elven's pick up. The man pushed the door open with his foot, hitching up his pants as he climbed out. He looked past the two of them, toward the site of the fire, as he strolled into the scene.

A Smith & Wesson .44 magnum dangled from the sheriff's belt, its pearl handle glinting in the morning light. The look on his face dared them to give him a reason to use it.

He homed in on Carolina first, beady eyes squinting down to the size of black beans. "Didn't I politely ask you to leave Monacan?" Bando asked.

"You did. And I did," she said. "For a few days. Now I'm back."

Bando licked his fingers, then straightened his mustache. "I can see. May I ask what's so interesting about Monacan to keep drawing you in?"

She shrugged. "I enjoy the scenery. Besides, it's a free country, right?"

He flashed a humorless smile. "For some folks."

"If you're here about my friend's fire, you're a little late," Carolina said.

"I see that as well," Bando said.

"Don't you have a fire station in this God forsaken county?"

Bando nodded. "Volunteer."

"Why didn't anyone show up?"

Reed Bando looked from her to the house, then back. "Did you call it in?"

Carolina didn't respond, and he turned to Cyrus.

"How about you?"

More silence.

"Well, there's your answer," Bando said. "Next time, try nine-one-one."

"Bullshit," Carolina said. "I bet the smoke was visible fifteen miles away. You expect us to believe this house burned to the ground without anyone reporting it?"

Bando kicked at a piece of charred debris with the toe of his boot. "I'll check with my boys."

"I'm sure you will." Carolina shoved her hands deep into her pockets to prevent herself from slapping the man in the face.

As Bando passed her by, moving toward Cyrus, she could smell whiskey clinging to him like cheap aftershave. She considered commenting on it, asking if it was a little early in the day to start tying one on, but resisted her instinct to cause trouble.

Sheriff Bando gestured toward the destruction, but his eyes were on Cyrus. "Care to tell me what happened here, Mankey?"

Cyrus took a hit on his pipe and didn't answer.

Bando took silence as an invitation to continue his inquiry. "You fall asleep with that thing lit?" Bando asked, reaching out and tapping the pipe with his knuckle.

Cyrus's eyes blazed, and with unexpected speed, he reached out and caught the sheriff's hand in his bony fist. He squeezed it, knuckles going white. "Was it you?" Cyrus asked. "Or one of your lackeys?"

Bando tried to pull himself free, but Cyrus held on tight. "Whatever disease you got inside you must have spread to your brain."

Blood seeped from Cyrus's nostrils as he seethed. "You want me dead, do it now. Draw that piece on your hip, the one you think compensates for your scrawny cock, and put me down like a man."

Reed Bando gave his arm another yank. That time, it worked. Deep indentations, where Cyrus's fingernails had sunk into the sheriff's flesh, turned red and angry. But Bando himself remained cool. "You're upset. It's understandable considering your circumstances."

He extended a handkerchief to Cyrus, who responded by swatting his offering away.

"Listen, there's a reason I drove all the way out here, and I'm afraid it's not a good one," Bando said.

When Cyrus looked at him, Carolina saw apprehension on his face. "Get on with it."

But Bando didn't. He tapped one foot against the ground, nervous. "You might want to sit down for this."

"I already am," Cyrus said.

He had a point.

CHAPTER THIRTY-TWO

The Barbourstown Prison morgue stank of industrial cleaner and pickles. But Carolina knew the latter smell wasn't really pickles. It was formaldehyde.

Mixed in with the aromas was an undercurrent of burned meat, but she thought that might be the lingering effect of standing outside Cyrus's destroyed home. Or so she hoped.

She sat beside Cyrus, each in uncomfortable plastic chairs. They hadn't exchanged a single word during the drive, and neither had become more talkative since arriving. The silence felt natural, though. There wasn't anything to say. Nothing would matter.

Denton was dead and small talk wouldn't bring him back.

The prison mortician had been prattling on for the better part of ten minutes. It had begun with condolences, moved on to paperwork, then shifted to discussions for Denton's final wishes. Not that either of them had a clue.

"Just tell me why the fuck my boy's dead," Cyrus said. They were the first words he'd spoken since Reed Bando broke the news.

Walter Steiner, the mortician, loomed over them. He stood six-

and-a-half feet tall, with broad shoulders, a bowl-cut hairdo, and as much personality as a crash-test dummy. He looked perturbed to have his prepared spiel interrupted.

"Mr. Mankey, if we can just complete these forms, I'll—"

Cyrus kept his gaze on his feet. In the rush to get to the prison, they hadn't even considered that he was shoeless. Despite the circumstances, prison officials wouldn't let him inside barefoot; so, Carolina had to buy a pair of too-large Timberlands for twice the retail price from the prison commissary.

"I'm not signing your goddamn forms until you tell me what happened."

Steiner closed the file he'd been holding, the pages colliding with a hard snap. He grabbed an empty chair and sat across from them. "Inmate Manley was assigned to the lawn care detail."

Cyrus looked at him for the first time, and Carolina could see the hate in him. "Lurch, if you call my son inmate again, I'll kick your teeth in with these ugly-ass boots. His name's Denton."

Steiner shifted in his chair, visibly upset, and Carolina couldn't help feeling a twinge of sympathy for him. Being on the receiving end of Cyrus's wrath was not fun.

"I'm sorry, sir. I'm new and still getting accustomed to the lingo," he apologized before continuing. "According to the guards on duty, Denton was filling up one of the riding mowers when he doused himself in gasoline." He paused and lowered his eyes. "Then he... struck a match and set himself ablaze."

"Bullshit," Cyrus spat out the word, bloody saliva coming with it. The mixture misted Steiner's face, but he resisted the urge to react in any way. "You expect me to believe Denton lit himself on fire?"

Cyrus was red, and it wasn't from the flames that had scorched his own skin hours ago. Carolina saw his body tense and knew he was going to make a move on the man, knew words would do no good, so, she wrapped her arm around his shoulders and drew him into her. To her surprise, he didn't protest or pull away. She felt the fight drain from him as he leaned into her, his body so light he felt like a cardboard version of a man.

The story was indeed bullshit. Denton wasn't suicidal and, even if he were, there were quicker and less painful ways to end your life, even in prison.

"Is there surveillance video?" she asked Steiner.

The man's eyes widened, caught off-guard. "I don't believe so. It happened in the back field, where they plant crops for the food pantry."

"Convenient," Carolina said.

Steiner straightened himself, offended over being on the receiving end of their onslaught. "I don't like to speculate, but I might for a moment here." He gulped a breath. "Most of the men here are anonymous. Just numbers on jumpsuits. But the killers, especially the child killers, have reputations. They have a harder row than the other inmates. Maybe Denton couldn't take it any more. Or," he paused, steeling himself. "Perhaps he was punishing himself for what he did."

His sentiment might have come from good intentions, but it was the wrong thing to say. She expected Cyrus to lose his mind, to maybe kill the man.

Instead, he surprised her by saying, quite calmly, "Show me my son."

Steiner shook his head. "I don't think that's the best idea."

"It's his right," Carolina said.

Choosing his battles wisely, Steiner acquiesced. "Follow me."

There were twelve drawers in the mortuary cabinet. Three rows, each four wide. Steiner grabbed the handle of the last door on the middle row but paused before unlatching it.

"I really don't—"

"Show me," Cyrus said.

Steiner did as told.

Any thoughts Carolina harbored that this might be a sick ruse, that Denton had been locked in solitary, never to again see the light of day, vanished when she saw his body. She'd tried to prepare herself. Failed.

Denton Mankey looked like a chicken placed on a charcoal grill, then forgotten about for hours. His skin was back and hard and cracked. His arms and legs had contracted, drawn into a fetal position. His internal organs had boiled, bursting from his midsection, where they oozed onto the table.

His face had sustained the least amount of damage, which somehow made it worse. Because his kind face was set atop this charred husk nearly unrecognizable as a human being. His mouth was twisted into a grimace, like he was still in pain even after death.

But then she forced herself to look closer, and she realized his expression was that way because his jaw was dislodged and broken. More teeth were shattered. His right eye was sunken, and the skin around the socket was flayed open to the bone.

"Did he beat himself before or after setting himself on fire?" Carolina asked.

Steiner shook his head, not meeting her eyes. He was either in on it, or knew the story was crap. But he was a lackey and wasn't going to speak out either way. "It must've happened when they were putting out the fire. The guards said they panicked."

Carolina glanced at Denton's deep-fried skin. "Yeah, I can tell they were right on it."

"I wasn't there," Steiner said. "But they've got four guards and two inmates who saw the whole thing. I don't think you'll discover anything amiss with their statements."

"Where's the warden?" Carolina asked.

The doctor shrugged. "He doesn't deal with inmate deaths, unless it's..." He looked at Cyrus for a moment, considering his next words. "Unless it's due to foul play, not natural deaths or suicides."

Cyrus didn't look at the doctor; he only kept looking down at his son.

"You tell him we're not going to nod our heads and play along with this," Carolina said. "I want to see the statements from those witnesses, and if they're so much as missing a cross on a t, I'm contacting the attorney general."

The threat was nothing more than hot air. The AG wouldn't get involved in the death of a child killer. No one would care to investigate the brutal death of Denton Mankey.

"Is there anything else?" Cyrus muttered.

The doctor picked up a box, smaller than the one that had held Cyrus's new boots, and pushed it toward him. "These are his personal effects."

Cyrus took it without a word.

With it done, Steiner seemed eager to be away from them. "I'll give you a minute alone with him if you like." He didn't wait for an answer and left the room.

Carolina watched Cyrus as he went through the box. He seemed on the edge of tears, but none came. Instead, he looked miserable. As if he was resigned to a life of disappointment and tragedy. Like he knew nothing would ever break his way.

Carolina felt as if they had a lot in common.

From the box, Cyrus pulled out a stack of envelopes thirty, maybe forty, deep. All were addressed to Denton in the same handwriting. She looked at the upper left corner for the name and address of the sender and discovered the sender to be Cyrus.

That surprised her almost as much as the news that Denton was dead. All this time, she'd been trying to get Cyrus to reach out to his son, and it turned out he already had. Shows how much she knew about their family dynamics.

"Not a single one of them is opened," Cyrus said, his voice flat and matter-of-fact.

Carolina sorted through them and confirmed that. Every one was still sealed. She wanted to shed surrogate tears at the unfairness of it all.

"He saved them, though. That's gotta mean something," Carolina offered in hollow comfort.

Cyrus took the letters back and shoved them into the box, then closed the lid. "If you say so."

CHAPTER THIRTY-THREE

"I'm Sheriff Hallie, and I'm sorry about your son."

Carolina watched Elven and Cyrus size each other up and hoped Cyrus would be cordial. Between the loss of Denton and his home, he was liable to show his wild side, and how could she blame him?

After a moment, Cyrus gripped Elven's extended hand, giving it an extra-hard squeeze. "Thank you." Cyrus tipped his head toward the diner in front of which they all stood. "Carolina told me this place has the best pie."

"Did she now?" Elven smirked and glanced at Carolina with a raised eyebrow. "Well, she's not right all the time, but she pegged that one." He opened the door to Hank's. "You grab yourself a seat and get whatever you want. I already took care of the bill."

Carolina tensed, unsure how Cyrus would react to charity from a stranger.

"You ain't gotta take care of me. I can pay for my own meal," Cyrus said.

"Didn't say you couldn't. I'm just being a good ambassador for Dupray."

"When you put it that way, all right," Cyrus said and shuffled through the doorway. He looked back to Carolina, waiting for her to come.

"Go ahead, Cyrus," she said. "I want to run some things by Elven."

As he strode inside, Carolina and Elven moved down the block, standing in the shade cast by an awning that once served an electronics repair shop.

"That was kind of you," Carolina said.

"What can I say? I'm a giver."

"Thanks for meeting us," she said. "I might have a break, but I need your help."

"You're still working the case? I hate to state the obvious, Carolina, but you can't free a dead man."

She sat on the concrete steps, spent emotionally and physically from a day of drama and traveling, wishing she'd have grabbed a few Oxys before meeting up with Elven. "It's what Cyrus wants. And he's my client, remember."

Elven sat beside her, their legs close enough to touch. She wanted him to hold her and tell her everything would be all right, but that type of comforting didn't fit their friendship.

"Look at what you're putting yourself through. Is it really worth all this?"

She considered the right words, ones which would get him on her side rather than make him think she was crazy. "It's more than proving Denton was innocent. It's about finding the person who decapitated and skinned a fourteen-year-old girl."

That worked.

"What do you need from me?" he asked.

"There are a lot of rumors floating around Monacan."

"Such as?"

"Stories about other victims. I need you to look into the missing person's database and get me a list of anyone who's disappeared from Monacan."

Elven flapped his lips with a long exhale. "That's a bit of a stretch. West Virginia has the sixth-highest per capita missing-person rate in the country. A lot of these people are never found, but it's because they don't want to be. Kids take off. They think they can find a better life, a better job, a better boyfriend, somewhere else." Then he added, "Like you."

She knew much of that was true and understood the desire, especially as a young person, to put this state in the rearview mirror, but there was more to this.

"It's rarely anything sinister," Elven added.

"Tell that to Cece Casto. She's buried in her mother's backyard. I can give you the address."

He gave another exaggerated sigh, as if resigned to losing this battle but not wanting to go down easy.

"I need to see those records. Please, Elven."

He looked toward Hank's. "Your friend gonna be okay by himself?"

She nodded. "He's more capable than he looks."

Elven rose to his feet, heading toward the street. "I really need to learn how to say no to you," he said, opening the door to his Jeep.

"That's fine," she said. "Just don't do it yet."

CHAPTER THIRTY-FOUR

Through the plate-glass window, Cyrus had watched Carolina drive off with her sheriff friend. He ate his meal in silence, aside from the occasional interruption from the waitress to refill his coffee or ask if he needed anything else. She was a cute gal, on the bigger side. Not that he ever minded. It was just more cushion for the pushin'.

On any other day, he'd have charmed her. Said the things that needed to be said. He'd start by telling her her smile tilted up on the right side, and he thought it was adorable. Then, on her next visit to his table, he'd lean in as she was topping off his drink, so her arm would brush across his cheek. She'd apologize, and he'd say it was all right because her skin was about as soft as warm butter, and maybe he'd even reach out and run his fingers across the back of her hand just to show her how sweet she felt.

Then he'd tell her she reminded him of his very first girlfriend, the one who'd moved away when they were young and who he still sorta kinda loved. And he'd tell her just looking at her made his heart beat a little quicker in his chest, and he liked it that way. On any other day, he'd have her in the supply closet by now, her panties around her ankles, screaming his name in his ear.

But this wasn't any other day.

For years, it had seemed like he didn't really have a son. He never saw Denton, never spoke to him. Many days passed where he didn't give him so much as a single thought. But now, it was final. His son was dead. And he didn't know how to react.

The waitress, Rhea, returned, setting an extra large slice of pie in front of him.

"I didn't order dessert," he said.

"I know. But I thought you looked a little blue. And I promise you, there ain't nothing better at putting a smile on your face than a piece of that."

"Oh, I bet I know something else could make me smile, beautiful." His eyes glinted. He couldn't help himself.

She beamed at him, batting his shoulder with her hand. "Try it," she said. "I wanna know what you think."

"Are we still talking about the pie?"

Her face went as red as the bottle of ketchup on the table. "You devil," she said, rubbing his shoulder. "Yes, I'm talking about the pie."

"All right. If you insist."

He sunk his fork into the dessert, loaded it up with a large mound of banana cream filling, and shoved it in his mouth. "It's wonderful," he said, his words muddled as he chewed.

She smiled ear to ear. "I'm glad you like it, hon. Now, you let me know if there's anything else you need. Otherwise, you're all set, courtesy of Sheriff Hallie."

"That's some sheriff you got here," Cyrus said.

"He sure is." She bopped toward the counter, calling over her shoulder, "You know where I'm at if you need anything."

The way she drew out the last word said it all. She was on the menu, but his heart wasn't in it. Piss-poor timing.

The geriatric one booth over slid out of his seat and made a slow-motion shuffle to the exit. As he passed Cyrus by, he threw a smile his way. "Hello," the geriatric said.

"Hello back." Cyrus couldn't comprehend how friendly the people were in Dupray. It was like visiting a foreign country compared to his life in Monacan, where people treated him like something offensive they'd found embedded in the tread of their shoe.

As he worked on the pie, a revelation hit him. No one in Dupray knew him. He had no baggage here. No past. He wasn't the drunk who killed his wife. The asshole who broke their cousin's face in a bar fight. The creep they crossed the street to avoid passing on the sidewalk.

Two more bites, and he finished the dessert, then licked the plate clean. All the while wondering what life would have been like if he had lived somewhere where being a Mankey didn't make people presume he was a bad guy.

He got up from the table, ready to move on. But along the way, he noticed the geriatric had left five one-dollar bills by his plate. Cyrus took a quick glance around to make sure no one was watching before grabbing the cash. He pushed three of the singles into his pocket, then returned to his booth and put the remaining two atop his pie plate.

After all, the waitress was awful friendly.

CHAPTER THIRTY-FIVE

"Meredith is quite perturbed over the excessive use of copy paper and toner," Elven said as he set a thick stack of printouts in front of Carolina.

She'd been busy using his office computer in a completely inappropriate manner, sorting through official reports and records. She hurriedly switched to solitaire, and he pretended to not notice. Immediately, she dug into the paperwork.

"She's liable to bill you," Elven said, as if trying to force her into a conversation. "She lords over office supplies like the Gestapo."

"Uh huh," was all Carolina said. She was sorting the missing-persons reports into two piles. One for men, women over legal drinking age, and children under age ten, and one for girls who fit the profile she'd created in her head.

"That's everything going back to the nineteen-forties," Elven said. When she didn't acknowledge him, he busied himself with straightening a paper clip, using it to clean the underside of his fingernails. "My, it's rewarding to be appreciated."

Carolina glanced up from a report about a 23-year-old woman. "What?" she asked.

"Oh, I'm sorry. I was talking to the wall and must have distracted you."

She narrowed her eyes, confusion dissipating as she caught on. "Thank you, Elven," she said, hoping now he'd let her get back to work.

"Don't mention it," he said.

Ten minutes later, she'd cut the stack down by eighty percent. That left around thirty missing girls. After organizing their reports by year of disappearance, she began to see the bigger picture.

What Viola Shafer had told her was accurate. Every fourth year, a girl had disappeared, dating back to the late 1960s. There were others in-between, but they were easy to eliminate. One girl was being molested by her father. One went missing the same day as her boyfriend. Another vanished after answering a personal ad in a magazine. But the eighteen she found that fit the pattern were one hundred percent matches.

"You've got a hole," Elven said.

He'd been standing over her, looking at the timeline she'd laid out on the floor.

She tilted her head back to see him. Even upside down, he was impressive. "I do?"

He nodded, then used his foot to push apart two papers near the end of the line. "Right there. An eight-year stretch."

Carolina took a closer look. He was right. But so was she. Because a girl had gone missing that fourth year, only she'd been found. "That was the year Cece Casto was killed."

Elven cocked his head like a bird hearing telltale signs of an incoming predator. "Oh."

He crouched down beside her, their shoulders touching, and took a close look at what she'd compiled. "You ever stare at the clouds and see faces, animals?"

She assumed he had a point but could do without the allusions. "Sure."

"You look at anything long enough, and your mind finds a way to make it into something. But they're really just clouds," he said.

He was a smart, logical cop, but he was wrong. That's what she told herself, anyway. Because, in her head, there had to be a bigger picture to this. It wasn't limited to Cece and Denton. It was not just clouds.

"Look at these. All were between twelve and fifteen years old. All vanished without a trace, taking no personal belongings. None were ever seen again." She spun her face toward him, her long hair flying up and brushing across his cheek. "Can you really tell me that's a coincidence?"

He scratched his cheek, where her locks had tickled and birthed an itch. "If you think all these girls were killed by the same person, then you're dealing with a serial killer. But how many serial killers do you know who have a four-year cooling-off period in-between murders? All this, it seems... grandiose."

Carolina knew part was true. Serial killers might start off slow, but they picked up the pace as their cockiness and mania took hold. Then it hit her.

"Maybe it's not a serial killer, not in the traditional sense," she said.

"Then in what sense are you talking about?"

"What if it's a ritual?" Saying it aloud sounded crazy but also made perfect sense. Like she'd just found the impossible piece on the middle of the jigsaw puzzle around which everything else was built.

Elven didn't answer, and she wasn't sure whether that was good or bad.

She stared out the window, remembering the symbols at Devil's Teeth. The name Ottis had mentioned. Viola Shafer recognizing the carving. "You ever hear of something called the Todesbringer?" she asked.

Elven shook his head. "I have not. What is it?"

"I'm not really sure yet, but it keeps coming up. Some legend. Like Monacan's version of the boogeyman."

"You think that's your killer?"

She expected him to laugh in her face, or at the least break into his usual grin, but he looked serious. It was an odd and unwelcome sight on his face. "I'm not sure you should be digging into this on your own anymore," he said.

But she was already gathering together the reports, the ones that hit every fourth year. Elven could be as caring and concerned as he wanted, and it wouldn't change anything. She was in this now.

Until the bitter end.

CHAPTER THIRTY-SIX

CAROLINA FOUND CYRUS TWO DOORS DOWN FROM THE DINER, smoking his pipe under the same awning where she'd begged Elven for a favor. She pulled the truck to the side of the road and cranked the window down on the passenger's side.

"Need a lift, stranger?" she asked.

He hopped in. "Don't a pretty lady like you know better than to give rides to scoundrels like me?"

Carolina threw the truck into gear. It bucked, then lurched down the road. "What makes you think I'm not a scoundrel, too?"

"Quite a pair we make, then." Cyrus seemed in better spirits, or was doing a better job at hiding his feelings. "Saw you slip off with your sheriff buddy. You two a couple?"

"No," Carolina said. "Not that it's any of your business."

She turned on Route 56 west, headed toward Monacan, again. "I need to know more about the Todesbringer. Everyone who mentions it acts like he's the fucking Candyman or something and will appear if they say its name three times. What can you tell me about it?"

"Why do you think I know anything?"

"Cause you flinched when Ottis Moore mentioned it. And you act like you know every nook and cranny in Monacan; so, I suspect you know the legends there, too."

He held his palms up as if he were offering everything he had. "It's just some local mumbo-jumbo. Keeps everyone scared and in their place. There's some horseshit about making sacrifices to him to keep everyone else safe. You know, the greater good."

"Sacrifice what? Children?"

"Girls," Cyrus said.

"That's fucked up." They were out of town, on the open highway, and Carolina floored the gas, but the pickup topped out around sixty. "Viola Shafer told me he takes one every fourth summer."

"Yeah... Sounds about right."

"You think there's any chance some psycho is using this story for a cover? Maybe he knows that no one will look too hard because it'll be written off as the legend?"

Cyrus tilted his head against the door frame, exhausted from his recent ordeals. "Who knows? Sounds like as good a theory as any."

She should let him sleep, to get a break from the nightmare he'd been living the last twelve hours, but there were still a few questions. "I had Elven pull some missing-persons reports. The most recent in Monacan was a girl named Sue Ellen Tanner. Is her name familiar?"

"Yeah; I worked for her daddy some years back. Think I remember hearing about his girl on the news."

"You think he'll talk to us?" Carolina asked.

"We parted in good terms. Don't know why he wouldn't."

Now, she'd let him rest.

CHAPTER THIRTY-SEVEN

A FLEET OF THREE DUMP TRUCKS, TWO BACKHOES, AND several white pickups were scattered around the Tanner Construction warehouse.

"Guess he's moved up in the world since I knew him," Cyrus commented.

They slipped inside the office, a squat ten-by-ten room smelling of coffee and sweat. Dusty Tanner sat behind the desk, a telephone to his ear and a cell phone in his hand, and he was working on both. He barely noticed their entrance, catching it only in his peripheral vision. A slight head nod acknowledged them.

"That's him," Cyrus said of the man Carolina assumed to be an office grunt.

There were no spare chairs in the room; so, they stood and waited until Dusty Tanner finished both of his calls and turned his attention on them. Immediately, his round, red face brightened.

"Holy shit. Cyrus Mankey? Where the hell did they dig you up?" he asked, already on the move. He greeted Cyrus, not with a handshake, but with an embrace tight enough Carolina thought the frail man would shatter like an antique vase. It was also tight enough to start Cyrus coughing, but the man tried to swallow it down and not show weakness.

"Good to see you, Dusty," Cyrus said. "Looks like you've done well since I was on your crew."

"Business has been good to me; that is something I can't deny." He looked to Carolina. "Who's this pretty thing?"

A genuine smile filled his face, revealing a gold tooth. It coordinated with his other accessories. A thick, gold Figaro chair around his neck. A fat, fourteen carat pinkie ring. A gold Rolex gleaming on his wrist.

He was in his late forties, and the middle-age spread had set in, but he still looked fit and full of life. His chestnut-brown hair was styled into a pompadour, and he wore a button-down shirt sagging open at the collar, revealing coarse chest hair. If his last name had ended in a vowel, she could have taken him for a mobster.

"Dusty, this is Carolina McKay, and she might be the only friend I got left."

The statement caught Carolina off-guard, most of all because she knew it to be true.

"Well, then. It's great to meet you," Dusty said. "Cyrus here helped me get this place started. Had some good times together. Real good times."

"That we did," Cyrus said.

Dusty seemed to notice his sorry condition for the first time and lost his smile. "I take it you're not here looking for work," Dusty said.

Cyrus shook his head. "Meso," he said, as if that said it all. "I wouldn't be much help to ya these days."

"I'm sorry to hear about that. Remember Wayne Kelly?"

"Sure do," Cyrus said.

"Meso got him, too. About two years ago now. Damn nasty way to go out."

"I'm finding that out."

They stood there, looking at each other and nodding. Carolina had experienced less awkward silence when getting a pelvic from a male doctor.

"So, what can I do for you?" Dusty finally asked.

"Carolina here wanted to ask a question or two. Figured I'd come along for an introduction."

"Questions?" Dusty asked Carolina. "About what? You have a project?"

She took over from Cyrus, figuring he had done enough already. "I'm investigating Cece Casto's murder, and right now, I'm trying to determine whether there's any connection between what happened to her and your daughter."

His good mood squashed, Dusty turned to a wall of photographs, each held up with thumbtacks. He pointed to a shot of a grinning blonde preteen in a junior cheerleader outfit; she was in mid-air, legs kicked wide apart.

"It's been over three years now," Dusty said. "Hard to believe, but she'd be sixteen and just picking up driving. That was something I was supposed to teach her, being her dad and all. Can't say I looked forward to it. But now, shit, I'd give up everything to watch her grind the gears, stall out at the stop sign." He touched her face in the photo with his index finger, holding it there like wherever the girl was, she'd be able to feel his presence.

"Do you think there's any chance she ran away?" Carolina asked.

He shook his head. "There's no way. Not Sue Ellen. We loved her with our whole hearts. Loved both our kids. I know it's unusual for families these days, but we did everything together, from dinners in the evening to trips to the beach. Called ourselves the four Musketeers."

Carolina nodded. "Did the sheriff's department ever come up with any leads?"

"Reed turned over every rock he could find but had no luck. I know some have low opinions of the man, but what he did for us says a lot about him."

That was not the response she thought she expected.

"One minute, she was fishing with Wayne, the next, she was gone," Dusty said. "It's like she vanished into thin air."

"Wayne's your son?"

Dusty nodded, found a photo of the boy on the wall, pointed. It was a graduation portrait, and in it, he wore a royal-blue cap and gown. "They were thick as thieves, those two. He was even more protective of Sue Ellen than I was."

"Did Wayne see what happened?"

Dusty shrugged. "He stepped away for a few minutes. When he got back, she was gone."

"How old is Wayne now?" Carolina asked.

"Twenty-one."

"Is he still in the area? I might need to ask him a few questions."

Dusty fidgeted on his feet. "He is. But what happened tore him up bad. He feels responsible because they were together. I don't think he'll ever forgive himself."

Carolina could only imagine the guilt. While she and her half-sister, Scarlet, were anything but bosom buddies, watching out for your kid sibling was just something you did if you were a decent human being.

"Understandable," Carolina said.

"Are you thinking the same person who took Sue Ellen killed the Casto girl?" His eyes went to Cyrus. "I never believed it was Denton; I want you to know that."

"Much appreciated," Cyrus said.

"It's one of the avenues we're looking into. I really can't say more just yet."

"Well, if it is, and if you find him, I'd appreciate a crack at the fucker. Whatever it costs." He caressed the gold pinkie ring with the thumb on the same hand, daydreaming about buying revenge.

Carolina ignored that and thanked Dusty for his time, then added, "Any idea where we could find Wayne?"

"Most likely at Micah's Pool Hall," Dusty said. "When you see him, can you tell him it's okay to come home? His mother misses him. And so do I."

CHAPTER THIRTY-EIGHT

A CROWD OF DAY DRINKERS LOITERED IN FRONT OF MICAH'S Pool Hall. None paid much attention to the truck pulling into one of the empty spaces, but Carolina hadn't made it five steps before they broke apart.

"Who ordered bacon?" one of the drinkers said, too loudly, and laughed.

It once again confirmed to Carolina she'd made the right choice when aiming for detective and not undercover work. After having been made, she was uncomfortable leaving the truck unattended and asked Cyrus to wait. He agreed.

The establishment was dimly lit and thick with smoke. The sounds of balls smacking each other loudly, breaking apart, and bouncing off worn felt tables echoed throughout the large room. Aside from a female bartender and an aging barfly, every person in the place was gathered around a pool table in the back right corner. There, a lanky, college-aged man in a Mountaineers hoodie was sinking one ball after another with ease. After each success, someone handed him a shot, and Carolina knew he'd be drunk soon if he weren't already.

She hadn't taken a good enough look at Dusty's photo of his son, but this pool player was the right age, and he seemed to be the center of attention; so, she waited until he finished his latest drink and pushed into the throng.

"Anyone know where I can find Wayne Tanner?" she asked.

The crowd quieted down. Nobody answered her.

She looked at the kid who was on a roll. He chalked his stick while he waited for her intrusion to pass.

"How about you," Carolina asked. "Do you know Wayne Tanner?"

The kid tossed the chalk in the air, catching it with his free hand over and over. "What if I do?"

"If you do, you can tell me where to find him."

He chewed on his lip, then pointed his chin toward a doorway in the back of the hall. "Might be in there," he said.

"Thanks." As Carolina left their table, someone made an oinking sound. She raised her middle finger over her head, and that brought a raucous laugh.

"The five-o flipped you off!" Someone shouted, to more guffaws.

Kids.

The back room was even darker than the main hall, with only a few lightbulbs dangling from cords to illuminate the surroundings. It contained only three booths, all in cracked red vinyl revealing the padding through the gaps. In the furthest booth back, two men leaned over the table and hashed out a drug deal.

Carolina lingered, giving them space. When the transaction was complete, one of them slid out of the booth and stepped toward it. When she saw his aged face, she let him pass by and moved to the dealer.

Wayne Tanner was counting a wad of cash, all small bills, and had little concern over being watched. When he finished, he folded the money in half, deposited it into his pocket, and looked for his next customer.

"What's your bag?" he asked.

He was nothing like his father. Skinny, short, maxed out on tattoos. Not a single piece of gold to be seen. His earlobes were stretched large enough to admit a silver dollar, the holes filled with yellow circles with happy faces. Two rings pierced his left eyebrow, a third, his nose. The third dangled under his nostrils like he was a prize bull. Despite the alternative body art and modifications, he had a tired innocence to him and, she was certain he was 100% sober.

"Kickers or skag?"

In other words, did she want pills or heroin powder? The kid was a mind-reader.

"Kickers." She slid into the booth across from him.

"Forties or eighties?"

Damn, he was a pro. Didn't mess around with rinky-dink five and ten milligram pills. He went straight to the good stuff. She almost said forties to find out the cost—only for educational purposes, of course—but decided she could end the ruse. "Sorry, Wayne; I'm not here to buy. I'm actually here about your sister."

He seemed to wake up, eyes becoming alert, and sat up straight. "Oh shit. Did they find her? Is she alive?" He was half-standing, ready to move.

"It's not like that. I'm just working on the investigation."

He sunk back to a sitting position and managed to look both relieved and disappointed at once. "You one of Bandos?" he asked.

"No. I'm freelance. Not a cop, a P.I."

"Good," he said, but there was doubt in his voice. "What do you want to know?"

"Can we talk about the day she disappeared?"

"Sure," he replied. "We were fishing at Grazier Pond. There's not much in there. Crappies and blue gill, mostly. Nothing with size. But Sue Ellen liked it because the fish there were dumb and easy to hook."

He grabbed a glass of soda and took a drink. "We went a couple times a week during the summer she liked it so much. But after a while, it got boring to me. So, I told Delilah, my girlfriend back then, to come by and keep me company. We were a couple hours into the day, and Delilah pulled out a joint she'd brought. I didn't want Sue Ellen to see, not because she'd tattle, she was cool like that, but because I didn't want to corrupt her. So, I told her to keep fishing, to catch a big one while we were gone, and slipped off into the brush."

Wayne rubbed the bridge of his nose, pinching back tears. "It didn't take us five minutes to disappear that pinner, but it was long enough. When we came back out, she was gone. Like, vanished, gone."

"Did you see any signs of a struggle? Maybe hear footsteps, a car?"

"Neither," he said. "It was like she teleported outta there."

"What did you do? Call your parents? The police?"

"The cops first. Then my dad. He—" His voice broke. "He started screaming. Shit, it was the worst thing I ever heard."

"And no one found anything?"

"No. Nothing. They even brought in some guys with sonar to scan the pond, which was stupid. Wasn't any more than six feet deep, and Sue Ellen, that girl could swim like a dolphin."

"Did the police have any suspects?"

"You mean, other than me?"

Carolina leaned forward. "They thought you did something to her?"

"Bando tried to run me up for it. Said if I smoked the devil's weed, I was capable of anything. Fucking fool kept me in his office the whole next afternoon until my dad came by with Delilah, and she backed me up 'cause I was never out of her sight."

"Do you know if Bando investigated anyone else?"

"Not so far as we were told," Wayne said. He looked past her, to another person lingering at the entryway, and held up his hand. Wait.

"Have you found anything out?" he asked, with too much hope in his voice for her liking.

"Nothing concrete. But I'm trying to see how your sister's disappearance might be connected to the death of Cece Casto and some other missing girls."

Wayne studied her, his blue eyes narrowing. "You're not on that Todesbringer bandwagon, are you?"

"What do you know about it?" she asked.

"We heard all about it after Sue Ellen went gone. That the Todesbringer took her, and we shouldn't waste our time looking or our lives wondering." He reached into a bag beside him and pulled out a gallon baggie of pot, setting it in the table so the man at the doorway could see it and not wander off.

"So, you don't believe it?"

"Believe the boogeyman is lurking on the woods of Monacan, waiting to steal the children? It's a legend, just like the babysitter getting the strange calls that end up coming from inside the house, or the couple on lover's lane who hears a hook scratching at the roof of their car. It's a spooky story people tell their kids to keep them in line. Behave or der Todesbringer will grab you."

Carolina let it hang in the air, then said, "Seems to me, maybe he does."

CHAPTER THIRTY-NINE

WITH NO HOME TO RETURN TO, CAROLINA LET CYRUS SHARE her room in the boardinghouse. She thought he'd offer to sleep on the floor or in the recliner, but as soon as they were in the room, he flopped on the bed and was sawing logs before she could kick off her shoes.

When Viola brought her meal—the night's entree was spaghetti from a can, they couldn't all be winners—Carolina reached out for help. "I don't suppose you have a laptop or a computer I could use?"

Confused eyes answered the question, but Viola spoke up anyway. "What use would I have for one of those?"

I don't know. Joining modern society. "Never mind. Just curious."

With her cell still useless, and at the end of her rope, Carolina used the phone in her room to call the last person she wanted to talk to.

"Who is this, and how did you get this number?" the deep, familiar voice asked curtly.

"Is that any way to talk to the woman who made your career?" she asked.

"Carolina?" Max Barrasso asked. "You get a new phone?"

Despite their rift, the familiarity of his voice was comforting. "No; I'm calling from a boardinghouse."

"Why? Your van shit the bed?"

"Nothing like that. I'm working out of town."

"You're working again?" Bewilderment clouded his voice.

"Yeah. And before you ask, no, you're not getting a scoop this time."

He laughed, smooth and rhythmic. "You still sore? I made you out to be a modern-day Dick Tracey." More laughter.

"What I need is a favor. Can you do that much?" she asked.

"Depends. What's the favor?"

"I need you to use your internet magic to research something call der Todesbringer," she said. "It's some local boogeyman in Monacan County West Virginia. If that helps."

There was only breathing on the other end of the line.

"Max?"

"I'm here. I was waiting for you to say more. Let me verify this. You want me to... Google something for you?"

"Yeah. I need anything you can find out."

"No offense, but this is a little below my pay grade. Why can't you do it yourself?" he asked.

"Because I'm in bumfuck, nowhere, and they still use tin cans and strings to communicate. I have no cell service. There is no internet."

"Damn," he said. "You really need to get out more."

"Tell me about it," she said.

In the background, she heard the clicking of a mechanical keyboard, rapid-fire. She wondered if he was still in his mom's basement or if he'd upgraded since his newfound fame. Maybe he sprung for his own apartment.

"You never told me what you thought," he said.

"About what?" But she knew.

"My **exposé**."

"Oh, that. Didn't get around to it."

"Bullshit. I'm serious. Did you like it?"

Carolina popped the top on her prescription bottle and had a minor panic attack when she realized she was down to fourteen pills. They wouldn't get her through three more days. She had two refills on the script, but she'd need to make getting back to Dupray, and one of her friendly neighborhood pharmacies, a priority. She took three, washing them down with Viola's specialty, cherry Kool-Aid.

"Nothing against your writing, Max, but your article detailed how every decent thing left in my life turned to utter shit. Makes it hard to be objective."

"Oh." He paused, experiencing one of his rare moments of introspection. "All right. I feel you." He sounded like a kid who just found out the brand-new puppy dropped on his doorstep was actually meant for the neighbor.

"But you did a great job," she said. "I mean it."

It was like she could hear him smiling from six hundred miles away. "Cool," he said.

There was more typing then, "Hmm."

"What hmm?" Carolina asked.

"I'm done. But you're not gonna like what I found."

"Why?"

"Because I found squat. A couple websites in German but nothing about West Virginia. Or the US of A, for that matter."

"Are you sure? Maybe you spelled it wrong."

"I'm not an idiot." Max spelled it back for her. He had it correct.

"Makes sense, when you think of it," he said.

"Why?"

"If they don't have Internet, you are, and this is a local legend kind of deal, who's going to put the information online?"

He was right, of course, but it didn't soften the blow. "All right. Thanks, anyway."

"Any time, beautiful. Maybe next time, you can take a case closer to civilization. We got people dying all the time in New York. Come solve a few of them."

"I'll consider it." She hung up the phone before he could try to carry on the conversation. She wasn't in the mood.

"You're not gonna find anything about der Todesbringer on the computer or in books," Cyrus said.

Unaware he was awake and eavesdropping, Carolina jumped at his voice. "Jesus, Cyrus. You about gave me a heart attack." She turned toward him and found him still laying on the bed, staring at the ceiling.

He remained prone and unlooking. "This is Monacan's secret. You want to know about him, you need to go to the source. To Hexebarger."

CHAPTER FORTY

Cyrus waited until they'd been on the road for half an hour before answering her question —who are we going to see? When she got his answer, she understood the delay. If he'd have told her straight off, she would never have agreed to the jaunt.

"We're going to see a witch."

"Are you fucking kidding me? I didn't think you believed any of this." The trip this far had taken them deeper in the mountains than she'd ever been. The road wasn't only unpaved but would have been impassible without the clearance of the truck and four-wheel drive. They stopped passing houses miles ago. She was convinced this wasn't leading anywhere civilized, but the alternative was a night of staring at the same files and asking herself the same unanswered questions.

"Not the fly-on-a-broom kinda witch," Cyrus said.

"Well, thank God for that much." Carolina winced as the truck's front driver's side wheel plunged into a pothole, rocking the vehicle. "Does that make her one of those fancy witches who burns incense and calls herself Rosewater and prays to the Earth goddess?"

"Not exactly. She's... somewhere in between."

His words did nothing to reassure her.

Carolina had been expecting a town, but Hexebarger was nothing more than a deep gash between two hillsides that looked like oil paintings with their sea of orange and yellow autumn leaves.

The truck crept along at five miles an hour until they hit the end of the line. An ancient log cabin mostly concealed underneath a copse of pine trees. A blanket of fallen brown needles several inches thick added an extra layer of insulation to the roof.

Three rust-bucket pickup trucks, all sitting on cinder blocks, were parked to one side. To the other were a half-dozen more campers and RVs, all of which looked like they should have been sent to the salvage yard decades ago. A gas generator chugged away and, in the absence of power lines, Carolina realized it was the only source of electricity on the property.

"How do people live like this?" Carolina asked, mostly to herself.

"More do than you'd think."

The convo was cut short when the door to the cabin opened, and from it emerged a scrawny woman holding a baseball bat. "Who's out there?" she called.

"Wait here until I say otherwise," Cyrus said.

Carolina didn't like the idea one bit. "I'm not going to sit here and watch you get your head bashed in."

"Aw hell, you're too high strung." With that, he was out of the truck.

"Hester Parsons?" he asked.

The old woman tensed. "You manage to miss all the posted signs end of my drive? Get on outta here."

"Ma'am, I'm Cyrus Mankey. Some years back, you gave me a potion, cured my colitis."

The witch narrowed her clouded eyes. "It come back?" she asked.

"Nothing like that. I've brought a friend who needs an education about the ways of the mountains."

Hester Parsons could have been anywhere from seventy to one hundred and ten. She was stooped over to the point where her chest was aligned with her navel. Her ivory hair was almost translucent, revealing a scabby and liver-spotted scalp. If this had been forty years earlier, she might have been wearing a flour-sack dress, but now, her attire was a mismatch of thrift-store finds. She set the baseball bat aside.

"Must be a hell of a friend to bring you all the way down here."

"She's a special one," Cyrus said as he motioned for Carolina to exit the truck and join them.

Once outside of the vehicles, Carolina's nostrils were attacked by the smell of burning hair and charred meat. She scanned the area for the source, taking a good look around. Maybe too good.

She eventually found the reason for the stench. Inside a crude, vaguely circular fire pit, a half-immolated deer smoldered. Its front end lay in the embers, a charbroiled black mass. Its ass rested in the dirt and looked perversely normal.

As Carolina halved the distance between the truck and the cabin, two men emerged from one of the RVs. The taller of the two wore a blaze-orange hunting beanie and nylon chest waders but no shirt. The other was clad head-to-toe in camouflage—but the kind meant for the desert, not the forest. He looked like an Iraq war reject.

Both stared slack-jawed, slobber oozing from their mouths as they watched the goings-on with identical, long faces looking as dim as ten-watt bulbs.

The cap-wearing twin made a noise that sounded like a mutated cross between a pig's squeal and a hyena's laugh.

Eeeeeee-ahahahahahah. Eeeeeee-ahahahahahah.

Caught off-guard by the bizarre call, Carolina jumped sideways, away from him. The other twin bounced up and down, smacking his fat palms against his hefty thighs in a sort of wordless, manic joy.

"Are you on your cycle?" Hester called to her.

Carolina snapped toward her, unable to believe she'd actually said those words. "What the fuck busin—"

"The twins can smell it." Hester motioned them to the hovel passing for her home. "Get in here 'fore they get worked up."

The men's excitement turned more frantic as she passed by them. Squealing. Gesticulating. Hooting. Sniffing. A duet of lunacy.

Carolina thought they were more like things than men and made the hillbillies in *Deliverance* look like Rhodes Scholars. She wanted away from them and ran the last few steps to Hester's cabin. Cyrus held the door for her, and she sneered as she slipped by him.

"You're a terrible fucking tour guide, Cyrus." She thought he might have smirked but didn't respond otherwise.

"I apologize for my boys," Hester said as she ushered Carolina into her home. "They're feral but mean no harm."

Was that supposed to be comforting? "If you say so," Carolina said.

A few lightbulbs hung from exposed wires in the ceiling and did little to illuminate the interior of the cabin. It was probably for the best as, from what Carolina could see, the witch would win no awards for interior design.

Hundreds of jars filled every table, shelf, and much of the floor. They contained everything from liquids, to eggs, to animal parts—to items which were complete mysteries. A variety of furs—rabbit, raccoon, squirrel—were tacked to one wall, drying, as flies crawled over them. A cluster of cats roamed free, but none of them were black. So much for stereotypes.

"What kind of information are you seeking?" Hester asked Carolina, who only then stopped gawking at her surroundings.

She saw no point in dawdling. "I need to know about der Todesbringer."

"Ah. Him," Hester said. She pulled a chair from a table covered in vegetables and dry goods and sat. She motioned for Carolina to do the same, and she did. "What you want to know, girlie?"

"Everything."

"That's a long tale."

"Start with the cliff-notes version," Carolina said, then realized the remark was probably lost on the woman.

But Hester Parsons caught her meaning. "He's older than these hills," she said, raising her arms up at her sides. Arms that were covered in white hairs, so dense they probably kept her warm at night. Her fingernails were thick and deformed, curled and bent in places they shouldn't, ragged at the ends, like rats used them to sharpen their teeth while she slept. "Been here before any of us. Been here longer than time itself."

"Is this thing a spirit or a man or just a legend?"

Hester brought her palms together the way a Christian might do in prayer. "He is everything."

Carolina looked for Cyrus, wanting to cast him a pissed-off glare, but he was distracted by the contents of a cast-iron pot hanging in the fireplace. When she turned back to Hester, the woman was on her feet and beside a cracked window. That seemed impossible, as she hadn't heard her chair scratch against the wood floor, hadn't heard movement of any kind.

Hester motioned toward the darkness outside. "All of this belongs to him. We are but ephemera living on his land, living by his grace." The witch then turned to Carolina, a look of peace and joy on her impossibly wrinkled face. "That's why we give to him our youth. As our thanks."

Now we're getting somewhere. Sort of.

"Is that why girls go missing? One every fourth summer? Is that what happened to Cecilia Casto?"

A jar broke, the explosion making Carolina jump and spin. Cyrus grabbed shards of glass off the floor.

"Let it be, Cyrus Mankey," Hester said, and Cyrus dropped it, the glass disintegrating further. With her eyes, Carolina signaled for him to come over, and he joined them.

"How do we stop him?" Carolina asked. But her gut told her she wouldn't get any answers she liked.

The witch cocked her head, like she was trying to hear a faint sound a mile away. "Stop him?" she repeated. "We don't stop him. He takes what he wants. That's the way it's always been."

Hester reached inside her blouse and pulled out a locket previously concealed by her shriveled prune breasts. She raised it over her head, freeing the necklace, and passed it to Carolina.

When she opened it, she saw a blurry, faded black-and-white photograph of a young girl. A girl around Cece's age. She had hard, dark, sunken eyes and a large forehead. Carolina could see the scant family resemblance between her and the twins and returned the locket and chain to Hester.

"Your daughter?" she asked.

Hester nodded, squeezing it in her tight fist. "He took my Winifred... must be going on half a century now. And I say, thankya." The witch again took her seat.

"Where can we find him?"

"Here," Hester said, knocking her knuckles against the table. "There." She motioned to the world beyond the door. "Everywhere." The last word came out with her head tilted back, her face cast skyward, where moonlight spilled through holes in the roof and gave her bright freckles.

This was all too weird, too insane. Carolina reached over and gave Cyrus a hard slap in the thigh. "In other words, we'll never find him," she said.

Hester lowered her chin, her neck giving three popping snaps. "Maybe not. But I'll tell you one thing, girlie, he knows where to find you." Then she laughed, a hoarse noise, half sigh, half cough. "You stay," she said and climbed to her feet.

She disappeared from the room and Carolina took the opportunity to glare at Cyrus. "I ought to punch you in the dick," she said. "Drag my ass all the way out here for this... madhouse ."

Cyrus twirled his index finger in a circle. "You wanted to know what all this was about. Now you know."

Before she could rip into him again, Hester was back with an armload of goods.

She set two blue jars on the table, unscrewing the lid to one, then handed it to Cyrus. "Drink this," she ordered. "The yarbs in there won't cure your rot, but they'll ease the pain by half."

Cyrus took the jar and gave it a quick sniff. His shoulders twitched, and his nostrils furled, but he drank. Swallow after swallow, tilting both the jar and his head until some of the dense, gray liquid ran from the corners of his mouth and dribbled down his neck. When he finally finished, he set the empty container on the table, beside its mate.

"Take the other," Hester said. "Drink it in the morning, after the sunrise."

Cyrus grabbed it and nodded. "I will."

Then she turned to Carolina and extended her palm. In it was a silver medallion with a crude etching of a bird on one side. Carolina examined it, bemused by the irony of the bird. She made a mental note to ask Cyrus if he'd somehow slipped her middle name – Wren - to the witch.

But she'd heard every word he'd spoken and, as she thought about it, did he even know her middle name? Unless it had been in Max's article, she was certain she'd never told him.

"You keep this on," Hester said. "I cast a spell of protection on it."

The medallion was attached to a string of jute that Hester tied around Carolina's neck. The new piece of jewelry hung to her cleavage, and she noticed Cyrus take a too-long look. She cinched her jacket tighter and stood. It was time for them to disappear.

As they headed back to the truck, the hip-wader-wearing twin emerged from the shadows and skulked toward the fire. He reached down, grabbed the dead deer's hind leg, and lifted it up and down, up and down. Waving it at them.

Cyrus waved back. Carolina jumped into the truck. "Fucking freak show..."

CHAPTER FORTY-ONE

THEY HADN'T MADE IT THREE FEET BEYOND THE ENTRANCE TO the boarding house when Viola Shafer scurried out from her ground-floor room. She was in her nightgown, a head-to-toe number, but still acted embarrassed, as if they'd walked in on her naked.

"A package was delivered," she said, grabbing a cardboard box off the bench sitting beside the guestbook.

"For me?" Carolina asked.

Viola shook her head. "No. For Mr. Mankey." She held the box, wary of getting too close to Cyrus. To keep the peace, Carolina played intermediary and passed it on to him. "Will you be needing anything else this evening?"

"No. Thank you, Viola," Carolina said and watched her hurry, like a scared mouse, back to her room, closing and locking the door behind her.

When she turned back to Cyrus, he was examining the box, which was taped shut.

"What is it?" she asked.

"My luck, a bomb."

"After what you just put me through, you deserve it." She pulled the keys from her pocket and handed them to him; he used the longest one to cut the tape. As she returned the keys to her pocket, he opened the box.

"Hmm," he said, the sound mildly curious.

Moving to his side, she saw the cardboard box contained a metal tin, about ten inches wide by ten high. Cyrus lifted it and gave it a little shake.

"Heavier than I would've thought," he said.

"What?"

"Denton's ashes." There was zero emotion in his voice.

"Already?"

He held it up as if to prove he wasn't lying. "Didn't waste no time," he said. "Almost like they had something to hide."

"Shit, Cyrus. I'm sorry."

He set the metal canister on top of the guestbook. "For what?"

She wasn't sure.

"Do you have a burial plot for him? Or do you need money to buy a headstone?"

Cyrus bit his lips between his teeth. "Never saw much purpose in that." He moved toward the exit, leaving them behind. "I need to get drunk," he said.

"Are you coming back?"

"Haven't decided. Don't wait up."

He was half out the door.

"What should I do with these?" Carolina asked, her hand atop the canister.

Cyrus pointed to the metal trash can next to the door in the lobby.

The thought horrified her. "You can't do that."

"Why not? What good are they going to do me?"

"But, they're... Denton." It sounded as forced as it felt. Those ashes weren't Denton; they weren't his son. They were no more the man than his leftover clothing. Denton was gone.

"Then you keep 'em." Cyrus slipped into the night.

As the door closed behind him, Carolina picked up the tin. It was heavier than she expected, too. She took it to her room and set it on top of the TV, which she tuned in to some old monster movie, then chewed two more Oxycodones and flopped backward on the bed. Her thoughts were racing, but they could do whatever they wanted to.

She'd be asleep soon.

She deserved it.

CHAPTER FORTY-TWO

THE CRUNCH WOKE HER.

Light dribbled into the room, intermixed with the illumination from the TV, and combined, they gave Carolina just enough visibility to see what was happening.

Her door was open. The frame splintered.

Two figures rushed through it.

Coming for her.

She was barely awake, still enveloped in the opioid fog that had carried her to never-never land. It all seemed to be happening too fast and in slow motion at the same time.

She rolled onto her side, feeling as if she weighed a thousand pounds, weighed down by her addiction, her right hand fumbling for the nightstand. For her pistol.

The cold metal kissed her fingers, which closed around the barrel. Salvation.

"Get her gun!" a muffled, male voice shouted.

Then more rushing. Footsteps. Too close.

Carolina tried to spin it in her hand, to take it by the grip so she could aim, shoot—use it as intended. But the drugs had stolen her speed and coordination.

Crushing pain exploded in the side of her head, and she toppled over, the pistol skittering to the floor. Out of her reach. Worthless.

One of the figures moved into her field of vision. It was a thing, not a man.

It was huge, towering over her, almost touching the ceiling. It had no head—only a pointed, shapeless mound atop its torso.

Der Todesbringer.

It was real. And it had come for her.

There was something in its hands. She strained to see it, to make sense of any of this. But how could you make sense out of the impossible?

The thing's chest heaved, its body pulsing and rippling. Its coarse, dense breathing sounded wild and frantic.

It hoisted its right arm. There was a glint of black. Swinging. Arcing toward her.

A tactical flashlight.

The hard metal battered her in the face, breaking some important bone below her eye.

Then everything turned dark.

COLD. Wet. Stinging.

The sensations brought her around, but she was still groggy, still helpless.

She was moving and outdoors.

Icy sleet pricked her skin like needles. Under her, the hardtop slid by too quickly, making her feel sick, like the time she'd rode the Big Bad Wolf at Busch Gardens.

They're carrying me.

Someone, or something had her arms. Someone, or something

her legs. Under the arc-sodium lights, they were still shapes, still blobs, still things.

Her head lolled to the side, and she saw a car approaching. Or, more precisely, herself approaching the car. The trunk was open, and although she was barely there, she knew the score, what would happen.

Carolina squinted, trying to bring her vision into sharper focus, to take in any detail that might be relevant.

The car had no bumper.

It was silver—no—gray. A dingy, stainless steel kind of gray.

There was a logo, one not immediately recognizable like a Ford or Chevy. But what was it?

A cat?

A cougar. A Mercury Cougar. But not the cool muscle car version. This was the boxy 80s model that looked like a two-door version of a granny sedan.

They almost had her to the car. In the car.

She swiveled her head the other way, the movement sending lightning bolts of pain through her body. Further away, someone watched what was happening. A man.

Cyrus?

It was too far to know for certain, the man half-tucked behind a privacy fence covered with ivy.

She tried to scream for him, for anyone, for help.

But no words came. Her mouth was thick, stuffed full with a hand towel, the fibers gagging her.

"Lift her up!"

She was hoisted further, levitating over the trunk. Then she was inside it.

In one fleeting moment, she saw the things abducting her weren't things after all, but men with pillowcases over their heads.

Then, the trunk lid slammed.

CHAPTER FORTY-THREE

SHIT-FACED WAS AN UNDERSTATEMENT.

Cyrus was surprised and impressed he'd managed to stumble from the bar to the boardinghouse without face-planting in the street. By the time he made it, he was so exhausted he had to steady himself against a fence, English ivy tickling his neck as he leaned into it.

He grabbed his pipe and a match. A few puffs would help clear his head. But the first attempt at striking the match was a failure. Round two - the same. On the third, he dropped it but knew if he risked bending down, he was apt to go ass-over-head. If that happened, he'd be stranded until the morning. It was starting to rain, the hard kind of rain that came when the temperatures hovered near freezing. He wouldn't survive a night in the slop.

No big loss.

He reached for a new match but had no chance at trying to light it before he saw two masked men carrying a woman out of the boardinghouse.

Carrying Carolina out of the boardinghouse.

She was too far away, and he was too drunk, to be certain it was her, but no one else in this shithole had hair and a body like hers.

Before he could so much as twitch, she was in the trunk, they were in the car, tires were spinning.

"The fuck..." he muttered.

Forget the smoke. He staggered into the boardinghouse, banging at the silly bell the broad who ran the place kept on the front desk beside a "Ring for service" placard.

You best believe I need service, bitch.

But no one came. Wait until she saw the Yelp review he left her.

He looked for a phone. But who would he call? Sure as hell not 9-1-1. Why hadn't he got Sheriff Hallie's number while he was in Dupray? That was who he needed to contact. That's who could bring some sense to this clusterfuck.

Her phone, he thought. She'd have Hallie's number in her contacts.

Climbing the steps to the second floor took both hands and sheer willpower, but he made it. Then, Cyrus used the wall to guide him down the short hall and to the room.

The door hung ajar and crooked, its top hinge sprung. He hit the light switch and set to hunting.

Not on the tables. Not on the bed.

Not on the TV. Not on the dresser.

He was on his way to the bathroom in case she'd had to pop a squat and left it behind. Because that's what people did these days. Sat on the toilet and stared at their phones because shitting by itself wasn't interesting enough.

But he never made it.

The man who'd been gathering together Carolina's files, her phone, her gun, had heard his drunken stumblebum footsteps and taken refuge in the closet. When Cyrus had his back to it, the man eased open the door, crept carefully across the carpeted floor, and smashed a heavy bust of a grinning Ronald Reagan into the back of Cyrus's skull. Between the booze and the blow, he went down easy.

His face-plant hadn't happened in the street, but in this room. His nose broke his fall and broke itself in the process. He breathed in the rank odor of foot fungus and forty years of accumulated dust in the carpet, the kind buried deep in the padding and there for life. Hot blood gushed from both nostrils, coming out so fast he sucked some of it back in and sputtered, gagged, coughed.

He was still coughing when he was hit again. And again. And again. Then the coughing and choking stopped as his brain went haywire, and it all went black.

CHAPTER FORTY-FOUR

Everything hurt.

Carolina was used to pain. It was like a houseguest who had stopped by for the weekend and never left. But this was different. It wasn't limited to her shoulder or her head. This pain was in her pores, in her cells, in her DNA.

Then nausea hit so fast she had no time to move, not even turn her head, before she retched. Bitter bile and burning stomach acid burst from her mouth, then dove back inside because she was sprawled on her back. Then she gagged and puked again. And again, it drained back into her.

It was like some horrible B-movie: *The Vomit Strikes Back*. If she couldn't stop this revolting cycle, she would choke on her own puke and, despite what little regard she had for living these days, this wasn't how she wanted to go out.

Pushing through the pain, she made it onto her side and, as she barfed again, the fluid spilled beside her, rather than back into her. And she could breathe again. Which also meant she could smell again. The return of her olfactory sense at that particular moment was most unwelcome.

When she opened her eyes, she went blind from the brightness and pinched them closed again. But she needed to know where she was and what was happening; so, she risked raising one lid by a millimeter, then another. And another.

She saw cinder block walls painted a pale green. Puke green, she thought, managing a perverse smile despite the situation. Then she saw a metal toilet with no lid. Then she saw bars.

Just as her tired, confused brain was connecting the dots, the sunlight was blocked as someone stepped between her and the window. She put a hand in front of her face, in case they moved, then risked a good look.

Elven stood in front of her.

But how was that possible?

As he pulled keys from his pocket and unlocked a cell door, the events of the night prior returned in a rush. The men breaking into her room, knocking her out, dumping her in the trunk of the Cougar. Cyrus watching.

She wasn't sure about the last part, but the rest was accurate. Her hand dropped to her side, where she'd grown accustomed to keeping her pistol holstered. No gun. No holster. Just hip. Her fingers dragged through a puddle of vomit on the mattress and came away slimy.

When she looked back to Elven, he was pushing a cup toward her. She took it with the hand that wasn't sticky with puke. The smell of burned coffee roiled her stomach, and she dove for the lidless toilet, the coffee dropping to the floor and battering her like acid rain as she buried her head inside the commode.

"I'll wait until you're finished," Elven said.

It took a while, but when she ran out of things to regurgitate, she rolled away from the stinking toilet, sat on the hard concrete floor of Dupray's drunk tank, and watched Elven shake his head with disappointment.

"I don't think you're up for this," he said, and he took a swig of his own coffee without offering her a swig. It was okay, though; she didn't want to send anything down her throat for a while. Maybe never again.

It was freezing cold, and her clothes stuck fast to her body. They were heavy and wet, and she couldn't stop shaking. She remembered the sleet pummeling her the night prior, but how did she get from the trunk of the Cougar to here?

As if reading her mind, Elven spoke again. "Tank saw my truck in a ditch when he was coming to work this morning. Thought someone stole it and took it for a joyride. Then he found you in the cab. I suppose his initial suspicions weren't too far from the mark."

"What? Why would they—"

He went on as if she hadn't said a word. "The needle was still in your arm," he said, his voice as close to angry as she'd ever heard him.

Carolina checked the crease inside her elbow and saw a small bandage. She peeled it off, found an angry, purple welt, the hole, a speck of dried blood. "I didn't—"

"He thought you were dead. Probably would be if he'd rolled by half an hour later." Elven tilted his head back, softly banging it against the bars of the cell. "He had to Narcan you."

Now the pain, nausea, the vomiting, the tremors all made sense. She had been thrown into the deep end of withdrawal with no warning and no life preserver. "So that's why I feel like shit," she said.

"This isn't a joke." Elven was stern with his words. This felt like a boss chewing her out. Looking down on her, judging her, but never actually yelling. "I never expected this, Carolina. Not of you. I knew you were having problems but I—"

"Elven, it's not—"

He held up his palm, and she took the hint.

Both remained silent for a long moment, Elven composing himself and Carolina trying to find a way to use the shovel she'd been handed to get herself out of the hole rather than dig deeper. She had to wait until Elven was ready for her.

"What do you have to say for yourself?" he finally said.

"I was set up—I think by Reed Bando."

"Did he plant the pill bottles in your van, too?"

"You searched my van?" The question came out louder and more accusatory than wise.

"It was on my property. For all I knew, you were dealing out of it."

"Come on, Elven. Give me a fucking break. You know I was shot. Those pills are for nerve damage."

"That's why you have prescriptions from three different doctors and fill them all at different pharmacies?"

Damn, he'd done his homework. She fell silent.

"If you were in my shoes, you know you would have done the same," he said, his words slow and collected.

Maybe, but she doubted it. "Fine. But I've never done heroin. I've never shot up, Elvin. And if you don't believe me when I tell you that, you aren't half the cop I thought you were."

It was a Hail Mary. And, ever the athlete, he caught it. "I'll give you the benefit of the doubt. I never picked up that vibe from you. With the heroin, at least."

She risked standing. The movement brought the nausea back, but there was nothing left inside her to come up. She grabbed the cell bars to steady herself, her entire body screaming in misery. "There's some real shit going on in Monacan. This is more than just the murder of Cece Casto. And it all revolves around this Todesbringer thing, and it's been going on for ages."

While she rambled, Elven unlocked and opened the cell door. "The boogeyman story you told me about?" Elven asked.

"I know it sounds crazy. But we saw this hoodoo medicine woman—or witch—I'm not sure. She said it's been happening for decades, and the people there are complicit because it somehow watches over them."

Her words picked up speed and, even as she realized she sounded like the paranoid junkie he thought she was, she couldn't stop herself. "The witch said he knew I was getting close, and I think that's why they grabbed me last night. I think they wanted to kill me and make it look like an overdose to keep their batshit craziness covered up."

She took a quick breath. "I feel so close, Elven. I'm so fucking close to unraveling this; I know it."

As chills rushed over her, Carolina wrapped her arms around herself, hands rubbing her skin like she'd just broken the surface of the lake after making the polar bear plunge. Her entire body was experiencing a magnitude four-point-oh.

Elven put his hands on her shoulders as if to keep her from shaking herself to pieces. "You're too deep into this mess to see clearly," he said. "It's time to stop."

"Stop? Now?"

"Yeah," he said. "Look, I was happy to see you passionate about something again, but this is too much. If half of what you think is true actually is, then this is a case for the FBI, not one person without a badge or a license."

This wasn't what she wanted to hear.

"Denton Mankey's already dead," Elven said. "Nothing you dig up is gonna bring him back. If you keep messing around, the people you think tried to kill you might try again, and how many more times do you think you can beat the reaper?"

She put on her best look of sad acceptance and used the pain she was in to manufacture a few fake tears. "I don't like saying it, but you're right."

His permafrost melted, and he began to again look like her friend, not a disappointed parent. Speaking of parents...

"Did you tell Bea about any of this?"

Elven's smirk returned. "Heck, Carolina. Even I'm not that much of a hard case."

"Thank you," she said. "I mean it. And thank Tank for saving me. And tell him I'm sorry."

"Why don't you tell him yourself?" Elven asked.

"I need some sleep. Maybe a few days' worth. Some time to push this shit out of my head."

"Sounds like a good idea."

He led her down the hall, unlocking another door that served as the back entrance to the prison. The discrete exit spared you from the walk of shame.

Even in the sunlight, she was freezing. She needed out of these damp clothes and, as if one of her prayers had been heard, she turned and spotted her van.

"I was sore over finding all those pills and prescriptions," Elven said. "Drove it here and planned to give you the big *You're not welcome on my property speech*, but I think I can skip it. And you are. Welcome, I mean."

His sincerity was like salt in her full-body wound. She wasn't able to get any words out; so, in as much of a surprise to herself as it must have been to Elven, she embraced him. The heat came off him like a woodstove, and she didn't want to let go. Then he wrapped one strong arm around her back and pulled her in even tighter, and she began to think he might be right.

She could drop this and move on with her life, while she still had one. Stay in Dupray and get back on her feet. Maybe even consider the deputy job, if it was still on the table, though she doubted it was now. It wasn't the life she'd ever planned, but maybe it was the one she needed.

With great reluctance, she pulled free of him, then stared into his earnest eyes. "Thank you, Elven."

He squinted, as if this brief exchange of genuine emotion between the two of them had affected him, too. Then he handed over her keys. "Just so it doesn't come as too much of a surprise, you should know I flushed all your pills."

That stung, but she tried not to let it show. "I understand."

"I also called the pharmacies and told them about your doctor shopping and informed them they were not to refill any of your prescriptions."

Motherfucker.

Going with her pills scared her more than anything she'd seen in Monacan, which said more about her state of being than she cared to reflect upon. She put her clammy hand on his chest. "You're a good man, Elven Hallie."

With that said, she was at the van, opening the driver's door, half in the seat when Elven called to her.

"You're not going to do something stupid, are you?"

As she started the engine, even in her wretched condition, she couldn't hold back a grin. "It's like you don't even know me."

He grew smaller and smaller in the rearview mirror as she drove away. Part of her wished she could tell him everything, get him to help, but lives were at stake, and she wasn't going to risk his.

CHAPTER FORTY-FIVE

For the better part of two hours, Cyrus had been struggling to free himself from his restraints with no luck. At least, it seemed like hours. It could have been just one. Maybe only twenty or so minutes. Time passed slow when you were bound and gagged and when your skull felt like a broken bowl held together by its cellophane wrapping.

He was on his stomach, his face pressed into a hard slab of wood that smelled like pine and which had offered him plenty of splinters for his efforts. Rope held his hands behind his back, and that same rope connected his hands to his feet.

Got me trussed up like a Thanksgiving turkey, ready for the oven, he thought while working to loosen the knots.

No matter how much he rocked from side to side, no matter how much he strained, he couldn't free himself. Couldn't even roll over and try to decipher where the hell he was.

Then, for the first time since he regained consciousness, he heard movement. Footsteps, seeping into the room.

He was no longer alone.

Cyrus tried to speak, to hurl some insult - *Untie me, cocksucker,* was what he had planned. But through the gag, it came out jumbled and incoherent. "Uh ti e caw uck er."

That was just embarrassing.

Light, dim and flickering, entered along with the new arrival. Then came a soft thud as a candelabra was set beside him.

His binds tightened as someone grabbed them, pulled on them, and then roughly hoisted Cyrus onto his knees. His joints screamed with pain as his body weight settled onto them, but he refused to make a sound and belie his misery. He might be at this person's mercy, but he wasn't about to show weakness.

The candlelight failed to illuminate the entire room, but it allowed him to take in his immediate surroundings. He saw pewter dinner plates. Wood bowls filled with fruit, much of it rotting and fly-infested. More unlit candles.

Outlines of windows filled the walls, but they were covered in something dense and dark, allowing no light to penetrate. And across from him were two grand doors, the kind that swung open in the middle to admit someone rich or important or both.

Hot breath rustled the hair on his ears. It came in calm, even intervals. Like an obscene caller on the other end of the telephone before he got into the nasty stuff.

Then the voice spoke. "You forgot where you came from. Forgot the rules."

Cyrus tried to snap his head sideways, to ram his noggin into the face of the cryptic motherfucker who was holding him, but that person was just out of reach, and all he did was make himself dizzy.

There came another hard jerk on the ropes, this one forcing him to sit up straight and look dead ahead.

The double doors swung inward and, despite their immense height and size, what passed through their cavity filled the space. It stayed on the fringes of the light, far enough away so all he could see was the outline of its immense frame.

The breath was at his ear again. "You've been looking for Der Todesbringer," it said. "So, we brought you to him."

Cyrus had lived through beatings and tragedies. He'd seen death up close. He'd watched one of the only people he loved die slowly before his eyes, all the while knowing it was his fault. He'd seen his son charred to a crisp and smelled his cooked flesh.

But this was worse. Because what came toward him through those doors was horror on two legs. It was pain and misery and perversion and blasphemy all in one.

It was the boogeyman his mother had warned him about when he was a little boy in his bed. It was the monster he'd seen in his nightmares. It was Der Todesbringer.

The gag did its best, but it couldn't match the ferocity of Cyrus's screams.

CHAPTER FORTY-SIX

"You look terrible."

Beatrice Booth stood in the doorway, arms crossed. Her resting bitch face was out in full force.

"Thanks, Mom," Carolina said. "Can I come in?"

This was the first she'd seen her mother since being kicked out. If she'd had any other option, she would have taken it, but she didn't. So, here she was.

Without a word, Bea turned away from her and moved into the house. As far as welcome mats went, it wasn't much, but Carolina wasn't about to complain.

By the time she made it to the kitchen, Bea was already seated and had a cup of steaming coffee waiting for her. The woman worked fast, despite her age. Carolina wasn't thirsty but grabbed the mug anyway. The liquid was so scalding it made her teeth hurt, but having something in her stomach settled it. Plus, it rinsed the taste of puke from her mouth.

"Are you going to explain what happened this time?" Bea asked, sipping her own brew.

"I can't get into details, but I'm working a case."

"For Elven?" Bea asked, her eyes coming alive.

Carolina knew all her mother wanted from her was to meet a man, settle down, and give her grandchildren like a good, southern daughter. None of those things hit the top twenty on Carolina's bucket list. But right now, she needed her mother's help, and she had to play nice. "We're collaborating," she said.

"Hmm," Bea said, a smirk pulling at her lips. "I'm glad to hear it."

Before her mother could press for more details, Carolina plotted her exit strategy. "Can I use your bathroom to get cleaned up?"

Bea nodded. "Just don't use the hand towels on the rack. They're vintage. I have some from the department store in the linen closet."

In the bathroom, Carolina hit the faucet, turning it on full blast. Her first stop was Bea's medicine cabinet. She jerked it open, pushing aside bottles for elevated cholesterol and high blood pressure. Then she saw something useful: Tylenol-Codeine #3. They were low-dose pills, only fifteen milligrams, and had expired two years earlier, but they were better than nothing. She popped the top, grabbed four, and swallowed them. Then she took four more for the road, dropping them into her pocket.

With that out of the way, she returned to the sink, plunging her hands into the steaming water. She squeezed some antibacterial soap into the mix and used it to wash her face, being extra cautious around her cracked cheekbone. The skin there was swollen and purple and made her look like the loser in a prizefight.

She had two head wounds hidden in her hair and winced as she scrubbed them free of anything that could cause an infection. With the grime cleansed, she caught her reflection and, now bare and exposed, realized how haggard she looked. No wonder Elven was worried about her. She'd picked up long-time hobos who appeared in better health.

But there was no time for vanity. She grabbed one of the cheap towels from the closet and dried herself, then jerked her hair into a ponytail and wrapped a band around it to keep it in place. All that was left was a quick brushing of her teeth, and she was back in the kitchen.

Bea had eggs on the stove. They were still cooking and hadn't made the transition from liquid to solid yet, existing somewhere in the gelatinous middle.

"Sit," she ordered. "Have breakfast with your mother."

There was something in her tone, something very un-Bea. Carolina was used to hearing her sound judgmental, sarcastic, sometimes downright cruel. But those words sounded... lonely.

It was a rare moment of vulnerability from a strong woman who was proud to be a bitch, and Carolina was surprised how much it hurt her to say, "I'm sorry. I can't."

Bea's eye twitched, one quick tell that revealed the pain of the rejection, but she recovered fast. "Neither of my daughters have time for me," she said. "I should be used to it."

Maybe it was the withdrawal, or maybe the subconscious knowledge that she might not come back, but Carolina leaned in and gave Bea a quick peck on the cheek. Then both of them stared, silent and shocked until the moment passed.

"I need to borrow the Volkswagen. Is it still in the garage?" Carolina asked.

"The Passat? It hasn't been driven since your stepfather passed."

Carolina put her hand on her hip. She just couldn't help asking. "Which one?"

Bea scowled. "Vernon."

Carolina thought a moment. Shit, that had to be eight years ago. She wondered what sort of condition it was in. "Keys?"

"They're in the drawer," Bea said, motioning to the one beside the refrigerator.

Carolina fished them out, then took one more look at Bea. "Thanks, Mom. I really appreciate this."

She didn't wait for an answer.

Fortunately, the Passat was backed into the garage; so, Carolina popped the hood and ran jumper cables from it to the van. As she let the battery charge, she plunged into the back of her own ride.

Elven had done a thorough job of searching, but she had a few tricks. When she'd designed her tiny home (hashtag vanlife), she had needed to make every square inch count. Doing so meant creating storage out of thin air. Or under the mattress, in this case. Carolina pulled the Serta to the floor, then lifted away a sheet of plywood. Beneath it was a locked compartment.

She'd stored no pills in there, and damned herself for the oversight now, but it had other items she needed. Her bug out bag. Her *in case shits gets real* bag.

Carolina unzipped the duffel to verify everything was still there. Duct tape. Zip ties. Stun gun. Pepper spray. Burner phone. Revolver. Ammunition. A wad of cash which, last she checked, exceeded eight thousand dollars. She grabbed two hundred-dollar bills and left the rest of the money behind, but took the bag and everything else. A girl could never be too prepared.

After tossing the duffel into the Volkswagen, she returned to the van and grabbed a fresh set of clothes, then added a black, knit ski cap which she pulled low on her forehead. As disguises went, it wasn't much, but it would have to do.

She jumped into the car, crossed her fingers on one hand, and turned the key with the other. The engine roared to life.

"Thank God for German engineering," Carolina said.

CHAPTER FORTY-SEVEN

Bea's expired pain pills were duds. By the time Carolina reached Monacan, the misery and shaking were so bad she could barely keep the car on the road. But she forced herself onward to the one place she might find a reprieve.

"Holy shit. You look like you were in a steel cage match with a black bear and lost," Wayne Tanner said.

She'd found him at his usual hangout, doing deals in the backroom of Micah's Pool Hall. And she didn't intend to waste any time. "How many forties can I get for two hundred?"

Wayne's eyes narrowed, and he examined her more closely, as if suspecting she was part of an undercover sting. "What kind of hinak do you take me for?"

She pressed the two bills against the table. "One who likes cash."

He still studied her, wary. "Why come to me? The way you look, the E.R. would hook you up just fine."

"Takes too long. And they'll want to keep me," she said. "It's for the pain, and I still have a job to do."

She was only half lying. She was in pain, and she did have a job to do. But Wayne understood the situation. "I can toss you seven generics for that." He reached for the cash, but Carolina kept her hand on it.

"Twelve."

He tipped his index finger in her direction. "Lady cop drives a hard bargain."

"I told you before; I'm not a cop."

"So says the cop."

He popped the top on a briefcase beside him, reached inside, and came out with a closed fist, which he held over the table until she released the cash. He took it, then dropped the pills into her waiting palm, one at a time. The moment he'd counted out twelve, Carolina shoved three into her mouth, chewing them like saltwater taffy. The relief was nearly instantaneous, and she slid slumped in the booth as the exquisite fog washed over her.

Wayne cackled. "Another satisfied customer."

Carolina wasn't so stoned as to not realize how pathetic she was. Sitting in this dive, buying drugs from a guy who was barely old enough to drink legally. A guy whose sister was missing and probably dead and part of her investigation. It went against every moral and ethical lesson she'd been taught. But here she was anyway. Just another addict.

"You find anything out about my sister?" Wayne asked, reminding her she still had a case to solve.

"Not yet. I thought I was getting somewhere until…" Her hand went to one of her head wounds.

"Knock on the wrong door?" he asked.

"No. They knocked on mine. Almost killed me."

He leaned into the table with his forearms. "Who?"

"Two guys who looked like KKK rejects. Came into my room, knocked me out, threw me in the trunk of a car, shot me up with H, left me for dead."

"Shit," Wayne said. "Hell of a way to spend a Saturday night."

"I've had better." She was still enjoying the reprieve from her dope sickness, which allowed her brain to focus. "Do you know anyone around here who drives a piece-of-shit Mercury Cougar?"

"What is this? Twenty questions? Thought you came here for a transaction."

She stared him down, not saying a word.

Wayne gave a nervous, high-pitched titter. "Lady cop, even when you are beaten half to shit, you seem kinda scary; I like it."

"That's not an answer."

He glanced around the empty room, double and triple-checking to verify they were, in fact, alone. Then he leaned in close and whispered anyway. "Donnie Westfall drives one."

"The deputy?"

"Mmm-hmm."

"What can you tell me about him?"

"Nothing good," Wayne said. "You know how some people become police so they can catch bad guys, play cops and robbers, and make the world a better place and all that shit, then retire with a government pension?"

She nodded. When she'd been twenty and idealistic, that had pretty much been her reasoning.

"That ain't him. He's the type who becomes police because he can hide behind his badge. It gives him a safety wall. Permits him to treat people like shit." He swallowed hard, then added, "No offense."

"None taken," Carolina said. "Is Reed Bando that type, too? The kind that might be involved with trying to kill me because I poked my nose where he didn't think proper?"

"Nah. Bando ain't too bad. As long as you don't hurt no one or cause him grief, he lets shit slide. Like me, I'm providing a public service here and he knows it, just lets me do my thing. Bando likes to keep everything on an even keel so he can go home every day at five and eat his donuts and watch the evening news."

"Has Donnie Westfall ever given you a hard time?" She needed to know whether this was a personal beef he was trying to get her to settle, or if Westfall was someone worth pursuing.

"Shit, yeah. But I'm not special. He treats everyone like they're his personal cum rags. It's the only reason he's a deputy. It sure ain't because he needs the funds."

"Why? He hit the lottery or something?"

"He's related to those coal barons. The Weiss's. Those fuckers own three-quarters of this county." Wayne spoke like he had a bad taste in his mouth.

She was almost ready to leave when something about what Wayne had just said clicked. Coal barons. And the security guard she'd met after leaving the Devil's Teeth had informed her the land was owned by a coal company. But what was the name? She couldn't recall, and her notes were gone.

"Those people you mentioned, with the mine, what's the name of their business?"

Wayne shrugged. "Beats me. They closed the place down when I was still in diapers."

CHAPTER FORTY-EIGHT

Carolina slouched low in her seat, like West Virginia's lamest gangster, riding dirty in her mother's Volkswagen, as she cruised around the block. The parking lot of the Monacan Sheriff's office contained no Mercury Cougar. Just four pickups - the newest and shiniest had a personalized license plate reading *BANDO1* - and a rust-bucket Jeep Cherokee. This didn't cause her to dismiss Wayne Tanner's information, but she had to put a pin in it, at least for the moment.

It was okay, though, because she had another stop to make: Viola Shafer's boardinghouse.

The aging two-story looked the same as any other day—no police tape roping it off as a crime scene, no deputies mulling about pretending to investigate. She waited outside for a good hour to ensure the latter was true, not wanting to risk walking into another ambush. But during that time, not a single soul came or went.

Carolina pulled the ski cap even lower over her brow, left the safety of the car, and scurried up the walk and inside. On her way in, she grabbed the overhead bell, preventing its cheerful ding, and eased the door shut, whisper quiet. The lobby was empty, so

Carolina rushed through it, ascending the stairs and continuing to what had been her room. Still was, as she was paid up through the next two days.

Anyone taking a quick glance at the entrance to her room might have seen nothing amiss, but Carolina saw the effects of the break-in. The door no longer hung on hinges. Instead, it was perched precariously against what remained of the frame. Near the center was a heel-shaped indentation where it had been kicked in.

She grabbed the knob, lifting the door off the carpet and setting it against the wall, giving her access to the room. Enough daylight spilled through the windows to reveal the place had been ransacked.

The sheets and comforter were off the bed, strewn in a ball on the floor. Every drawer in the room was pulled from its housing, emptied, and tossed aside. All Carolina's personal belongings—her files, her photos, every last note—were gone. Even the two changes of clothes she'd left lay atop the futon had been taken. There was no evidence she'd ever been there.

Except for a wide swath of dust on the shag carpet. It spread from the TV to the dresser. But it wasn't dust. It was ashes.

Denton's ashes.

The bastards had even emptied the poor excuse for an urn, dumping what was left of him onto the floor. Footsteps trampled through them, back and forth, careless, soulless. She considered scooping up what little of it she could salvage, but there was nowhere to put the ashes. No way to save them. The sight of it enraged her.

So, when she heard approaching footsteps, she didn't hesitate to draw her gun as she took cover in the cramped closet and waited. Still in the hallway, the footsteps paused, as if the person they belonged to was examining the now-open door. But it was only a brief interlude, and they resumed again, stepping into the room. Another noise accompanied them: a monotonous squeak. Wheels.

There was a rustling, a cord being unwrapped and plugged in, then a vacuum cleaner roared to life.

With the high decibel distraction, Carolina eased from the closet to take a look at the interloper and saw a back that could only belong to Viola Shafer. She was wearing a heavy sweater, equal parts wool and cat hair, and one of her trademark long skirts that almost touched her orthopedic shoes. Her upper body swayed back and forth, back and forth, in a slow-motion dance as she ran the sweeper across the carpet.

Sucking up Denton.

Without consciously realizing it, Carolina flicked off the safety on the gun as she slipped in behind Viola, then pressed the barrel against the nape of her neck. The woman froze, the vacuum cleaner still roaring but now stationary.

"Turn that fucking thing off," Carolina said through gritted teeth.

Viola hit the power switch with her foot, and the deafening sound subsided, but she didn't move otherwise. Frozen stiff.

"Now, turn around."

Without being told, Viola Shafer raised her hands, like a crime victim who'd just been ordered to *Stick 'em up*. Her entire body quivered as she made the slowest rotation in the history of mankind. When she saw Carolina, her eyes turned to saucers.

"Miss McKay?" It came out like a question, but her face knew the answer.

"How much do you know about what happened here last night?"

Viola's bottom lip quivered. "Someone broke in and robbed your room," she said.

Carolina thought about pistol-whipping her. She'd never done it before, and now seemed like a good time to start. But she held back. "Try again."

"I heard a terrible commotion and, I—" Her voice broke. "I was afraid to come out of my room. I stayed in there until one of the men from the sheriff's department announced himself. He's the one who told me what happened, and I just about went to pieces. Nothing like this has ever happened before."

Carolina thought she was good at spotting a lie and couldn't find one on Viola's face. But she wasn't buying all of what she was selling just yet. "And what did they tell you happened to me?"

"He said you were at the office filing a report."

"You mean he left out the part where I was knocked out, tied up, and thrown in the trunk of a car?"

Viola's wide eyes opened even further. Impossibly far. Carolina wouldn't have been shocked if her eyeballs had fallen clean out of the sockets. She was telling the truth. For the most part, anyway. And Carolina lowered the pistol. She sat on the edge of the bed, regrouping.

"And what cop fed you this pile of horseshit?" Viola flinched at the vulgarity, and that made Carolina feel good for the first time today.

"It was the Palmer boy. Samuel, I think his name is."

The statement surprised Carolina. She'd been expecting her to say Westfall. But this didn't put Donnie in the clear. He might have been the one who taxied her back to Dupray and shot her up with dope.

"What about Bando? Was he here?"

Another no.

"How about the Todesbringer? Maybe he stopped by for tea after shit calmed down."

Viola only stared and trembled.

"Did Cyrus come back here last night?"

"I didn't see him," Viola said. And again, Carolina believed her.

"Fine." She stood, moving toward the door, leaving this pathetic excuse for a woman behind. But then she paused, glanced back, and pointed at the floor with the pistol. "The pile of dirt you're sucking up like it's someone's spilled ashtray. It's a friend of mine. I just thought you should know."

Carolina was almost out of the boardinghouse when she paused at a wall-mounted brochure rack hanging beside the front door. She'd seen it before but paid little attention. The sign above it, in Viola Shafer's perfect printing, read *Local Sights and Activities*.

She scanned the fliers and booklets, which advertised events, such as the Farmer's Jubilee, Mountain Craft Days, and Annual Roadkill Cook-Off. Tucked among them was a thin book: Monacan —A History; it looked to be fifty or more years old, its hardcover stained by decades of grubby fingers. She tucked the book under her arm as she fled.

CHAPTER FORTY-NINE

THERE WAS LITTLE REASON FOR CYRUS TO RETURN TO HIS burned-out shell of a home, but she'd held some crumb of hope maybe he was there, hiding out, waiting for the stink to blow over. But the land was as empty as when she'd taken him from it.

Only what if it wasn't empty? What if the men who'd taken her had taken Cyrus, too? What better way to dispose of his body than to toss it into the remains of his home, where it would be easy to write off his death as having occurred in the fire?

As she approached, wisps of smoke unfurled from the still-smoldering remains, drifting into the afternoon air before getting lost in the sky. She held her breath, having convinced herself she'd find him there. That she'd see her second incinerated Mankey man. That she'd discover that she was truly alone in this mess.

But, when she poked through the detritus with an old spade shovel, she uncovered nothing more than a man's destroyed life story. Chunks of blackened books. Springs from a couch. Dinnerware. Silverware. No dead Mankey. This time.

Carolina breathed a little easier as she retreated to the Passat. Maybe Cyrus did the smart thing and got the hell out of Monacan after he saw what happened to her. Maybe he had the sense to abandon this sinking ship before it went all the way down.

Unlike her.

Why was she still fighting? What did she hope to prove? Denton's innocence held no meaning now. None of the families of the dead and missing girls had asked her to keep digging up old memories. She was sprinting on a hamster wheel of her own design.

What was the point?

A part of her knew this was ego. It was proving she still had the mental acuity and the physical means to do the job she'd been forced out of, the career stolen from her. It was showing the world, yet again, that Carolina Wren McKay could take on the most despicable and unsolvable case and wrap it up in a bow.

But maybe, more than any of those things, this case was the only reason for her to stay alive. Without it, she'd wander off somewhere in her van, lost in her head, until she either got careless and overdosed or she couldn't bear the thought of waking up one more time and put the pistol in her mouth.

Maybe a lonely death was still the future awaiting her, the one playing out like a vignette in some psychic's crystal ball. But for now, at least, she could delay the inevitable.

CHAPTER FIFTY

ANOTHER CRUISE BY THE POLICE PARKING LOT SHOWED ALL vehicles still in their spots; so, Carolina parked across the street, mostly concealed behind a hedge of out-of-control boxwood, and waited. It was nearing 7 p.m., and she knew their shifts would be ending soon, replaced by another round of lackeys.

To help pass the time, she flipped through the book, the history of Monacan. It stunk of cat dander and time, the pages yellowed and foxed. She hadn't expected to find any information on the Todesbringer any more than she expected to find chapters dedicated to Bigfoot or the Mothman. And she found none.

There was nothing about the long history of missing girls or the Devil's Teeth. It was a sanitized, bare-bones version of the county history that showed more interest in foliage and wildlife than the people who lived within its borders.

Mining was also discussed in great detail, which made sense, as it was the area's only real source of income. And the surname getting the most attention was a familiar one: Weiss.

The family was written about in the most glowing terms, hoisted onto pedestals usually reserved for the likes of Andrew

Carnegie or Henry Ford. By reading the book, you'd have thought digging holes into mountains was the industrial equivalent to putting a man on the moon. If the tome was to be believed, the Weiss's were heroes who had put Monacan on the map—until the coal was mined out and Appalachian Mine Company was shut down for good.

If he was indeed a descendant, maybe that was why Donnie Westfall was schlepping shifts on the local police force rather than living the high life. It made sense; even if he was as much of an asshole as Wayne Tanner had painted him out to be, there were far easier ways for a rich man to exert his control over others than with a small-town badge pinned to his chest.

As she pondered Donnie Westfall's psyche, the man himself appeared, stepping from the rear exit of the sheriff's department and striding toward a Ford F-150. It wasn't shiny and chromed-out like Bando's ride, but it was the next-newest vehicle in the lot. Not exactly impossible to buy on a rural county cop's salary, especially one who might have his toe dipped in a plethora of illegal revenue streams and shakedowns. But the vehicle stood out. And she had the impression Westfall liked to stand out.

He exchanged some banter with two other deputies - one finishing his shift, one coming on - words Carolina couldn't overhear. But she wasn't missing any scholarly debates. Then he hopped into the cab of his rig and gunned the engine.

Black smoke roared from the tailpipe as he rolled coal out of the lot, tires giving a loud screech as he took the corner too fast. He'd be easy to tail, and she let several car lengths pass before pulling onto the road.

Westfall lived less than ten miles from the station at 6 Oak Street, in an aging Victorian a decade overdue for a fresh coat of paint. He pulled his pickup into the drive, aligning it with a distinctive, piece-of-crap Mercury Cougar. Even from a block down the street, Carolina could see—or not see—the missing rear bumper, and her suspicions over Deputy Donnie were confirmed.

He was one of the men who grabbed her. Who tried to kill her. And maybe he, not Bando, was the ringleader.

As he loped to his mailbox, snatching a handful of bills and junk, Carolina sunk even lower in her seat, but Westfall was oblivious to her presence. She needed to have a very unfriendly conversation with him, but it could wait for the right moment. Fortunately, she had all the time in the world.

THE SUN HAD SET two hours earlier, but the flickering light of a TV lingered on the ground floor. Carolina felt ready to jump out of her skin, her leg tapping so hard and fast the entire Volkswagen shook. If this car's a-rockin', don't come a-knockin'.

In the battle between her nerves and patience, the former was winning, and it wasn't even close.

She grabbed another Oxy, swallowing it rather than chewing it because she needed to stay sharp for what was close to going down. After what felt like an eternity, the light of the TV flipped off, and Westfall's house went dark.

She waited for another half-hour, in case the man had to drop a large load before turning in for the night. During the downtime, she checked and double-checked her bag, ensuring she had everything she might need. Everything and more. Because she didn't plan on leaving the house without answers.

Carolina hadn't made it two full strides from the Passat when she heard the voice behind her.

"You really suck at being discreet."

She whipped around and drew the gun in one smooth motion. Her index finger curled around the trigger, squeezing, a pound away from firing—when she saw Wayne Tanner.

Immediately, she snapped her finger off the trigger and lowered the pistol. Her heartbeat thudded in her ears, and she took two deep breaths to steady herself. "What the fuck are you doing here?"

"That's what I was going to ask you," Wayne said. He slouched, hands buried in his pocket. "Is this about my sister?"

"I'm not sure yet," she said. "But I intend to find out."

Wayne looked from her to the house, then back. "Sounds like a plan." He moved into the street, gliding toward the Victorian until Carolina grabbed his jacket.

"You aren't going in there."

"The hell I'm not." He shook himself free. "Two's better than one, right?"

"You're from here. You live here. When all is said and done, I get to leave. It's not the same for you." She examined his face and could tell she wasn't getting through. "This could ruin your life. Is that what you want?"

A rueful grin crossed his face. "Ruin my life? That happened when my little sister disappeared while I was getting high, and a hand job, five yards away. My parents blame me for what happened. They say they don't, but they do. And they're right. It was my fault. So, tell me, lady cop, what do I have to lose?"

She tried to think of something, of a convincing reason, but came up empty. It was crazy she was even considering this, bringing him on board as she broke into the house of a sheriff's deputy. Then again, hadn't almost everything she'd done the past few days been crazy?

CHAPTER FIFTY-ONE

They skirted around the house to the rear. A quick try of the knob revealed it was locked; so, Carolina crouched beside her bag, searching for the lock-picking kit she'd used in practice—but never when it counted. As she found it and turned back to the door, she saw Wayne blocking her way.

"What are you doing?" she asked as he ran his hands along the frame. As they drifted across the top, he grabbed something and turned back to her, holding a key.

"Seriously?" she asked.

Wayne shrugged as he slid the key into the lock. "Small-town living."

He opened the door but let Carolina lead the way. Pistol drawn, she took three steps before stepping on something hard resulting in a hollow crack and sent her stumbling forward. Just before she could crash into a pile of unwashed dishes stacked on the kitchen counter, Wayne caught and steadied her. When she looked back, she saw a broken cat-food dish and bits of kibble now scattered in her wake.

She let out a breath and looked at Wayne, who rolled his eyes.

"Jesus," he whispered. "Don't they teach stealth at whatever police academy you went to, lady cop? Because you seem like a total amateur."

"I don't make it a habit of breaking and entering."

"Just put the gun away before you get spooked and shoot the cat. I'm happy to tag along, but I'm not looking to get caught."

She tucked the gun in her jeans as Wayne passed her by. Now, it was her turn to follow. He moved with the skill of a successful burglar, and she assumed dealing hadn't been his first foray into crime.

The ground floor was vacant; so, they moved to the staircase. Looking at such old wood raised Carolina's blood pressure. It was the kind of wood that groaned and cracked and creaked when you walked on it. And they were one misstep away from setting off an alarm in the form of protesting oak, an alarm sure to send Donnie Westfall running and ready to exact some vengeance upon those who dared break into his house.

Halfway through the ascent, they were still in the clear. Then the cat arrived. It was a long-haired version, maybe Persian or a Himalayan. Carolina wasn't sure because she was a dog person. It made the infinity sign around her feet as she stepped, weaving in and out, purring so loudly it sounded like a hundred-pound trolling motor fishing her legs. She tried a gentle shove, but the cat wouldn't be deterred.

Finally, all three of them reached the top landing. No creaks. No alarms. Still in the clear.

Wayne was two yards ahead, and he turned, motioning for her to hurry up. He was perched outside an open door, his eyes darting between the room and Carolina. He opened his mouth, then spoke silent words.

In here.

The cat lost interest in her as she went to the bedroom—a relief. Through the doorway, Carolina saw Donnie Westfall in his bed, naked aside from a shabby pair of tighty-whities. There was a hole in the front through which wiry pubic hair jutted.

She reached into her jacket pocket and extracted the stun gun, ignoring Wayne's questioning look as she crept to Westfall's bedside.

The nightstand was littered with his wallet, keys, spare change, and revolver. No sense leaving the latter there, within reach, should things take a fast detour south; so, she added it to her waistband, feeling a bit like a wild-west lawman with a gun on each hip.

As Westfall's chest rose and fell, soft whistles escaped his lips. They seemed effeminate coming from his bulky frame, not the coarse snores she would have suspected.

It seemed too easy. So easy she began to wonder if this was a setup. What if Wayne Tanner had led her there because it wasn't Bando who let his business as a drug dealer go by unpunished, but Westfall?

She spun back to Wayne, eyes wild and panicked. He stood in the same place, hands still in pockets. He raised his brows in the universal sign for *What?*

Then, "The fuck?"

It was Westfall. Bedsprings squeaked as he moved, and by the time she turned to him, the big man was propped on his elbow and half-way to a sitting position. His hand jutted toward the stand, to where his revolver had been, and came up empty. Then he was on the move, coming at Carolina, who raised the taser, jabbing the prongs into his bare chest.

They locked eyes an instant before she squeezed the trigger.

Westfall's entire body went rigid. His head snapped back, ligaments straining in his neck as saliva foamed from his mouth. He collapsed sideways like a falling tree, bouncing off the bed, head colliding with the nightstand on the way to the floor.

He landed face down, and Carolina zapped him again.

For spite.

CHAPTER FIFTY-TWO

WESTFALL WAS SO HEAVY THE TWO OF THEM WERE HELPLESS to carry him out of the bedroom; so, Carolina settled on zip-tying his feet together and duct-taping him to a wooden chair that had been tucked in the corner. She imagined him sitting on it each morning and evening while he put on and removed his boots. For good measure, she ran several loops of tape around his torso and hips. He wasn't going anywhere.

When he was immobilized, she'd added a strip of tape across his mouth. Not because she took him for the screaming type, but for the satisfaction of peeling it off and ripping free a cluster of facial hair in the process. She was halfway through that part now.

"Almost there," she said, giving the tape another small tug. Then another. And another. His skin was red and raw and smooth underneath. Finally, she ripped it clean off, leaving behind a two-inch, hairless strip of flesh surrounded by stubble.

Donnie Westfall shook his face, then sneered as he looked at her. "I don't know what the fuck you think you're up to, but you're good as dead now, bitch."

"You tried that once," Carolina said. "Didn't take."

"As soon as I get out of here, you're done."

"What makes you think you're getting out of here?" she asked.

She noticed him working at his restraints, not making a show of it, trying to be discreet. She wondered if he might be strong enough to snap the zip ties. Even if he was, she had the guns. The real guns and the stun gun. They were all laid out on his dresser and within reach.

"Tell me where Cyrus is," she ordered

"Who?" He half-smiled.

She didn't like that at all and backhanded him across the mouth, splitting his lower lip. A rivulet of blood trickled down his chin, dripping onto his chest. "I'm not here for the games. I know what you did to me. I saw your piece-of-shit Cougar before you locked me in the trunk. So, get to talking, or I can promise you one miserable fucking night."

Westfall full-on grinned now. Blood smeared across his teeth, giving him the look of a wild animal enjoying a fresh kill. "You're mistaken, doll. I'm just a public servant."

Carolina grabbed the taser, brought it toward his crotch. "I heard if you get shocked in the sack with one of these, you'll be impotent. How about we try it out. See if it's true."

She pressed it into his underwear, waiting for him to back down, but before he could--

"Carolina," Wayne called out from a nearby room. "You need to see this."

"Sounds like your boyfriend needs you," Donnie said. "Is Wayne Tanner your dealer now? Sounds about right to me. Trash associates with trash. Tell me, what kinda arrangement do you two got worked out? Blowjob for heroin? Bareback for pills? I'm sure you both fill each other's needs just fine."

"Carolina?" Wayne repeated, his voice wavering, scared.

She jammed the stun gun into Westfall's crotch and fired one million volts into his scrotum. As his body spasmed, she spoke into his ear. "I can do this all night, doll."

The sound of his piss raining onto the hardwood floor filled the room as she left him.

CHAPTER FIFTY-THREE

"WHAT IS IT?" CAROLINA HISSED, ANGRY AT BEING PULLED away from the smug asshole. At Westfall being able to leverage Wayne's involvement and use it against her. How dare the prick think he had the upper hand?

Wayne didn't seem to notice or care about her tone. Instead, he knelt, motionless, in front of a fireproof lockbox.

"Wayne?" Carolina put her hand on his shoulder and only then noticed he was crying.

The spare bedroom was full of old furniture and an eclectic assortment of junk, but Wayne had done a thorough job of tossing it. It looked as if he'd pulled the box from under a jumble of tools and chunks of drywall.

When Wayne turned to Carolina, his face was ashen. "The dumb motherfucker left the key in the lock after all that effort to hide it. Kinda defeats the purpose."

He held up the box. The lid was open, and inside was a stack of Polaroid photos. They were upside down, and Carolina could see names scrawled in sloppy printing on the backs.

"What are those?" she asked, already reaching for them.

Wayne pulled the box away. "I don't think you should."

She didn't take his advice.

When she flipped the photos over, image side up, she understood the haunted look on his face, his insistence she not look. Because these were photos of the missing girls. Dozens of them, some so old the paper had turned ecru and brittle, the colors in the images faded by half.

But the content was the same, regardless of the condition. The photos showed the girls alive and tied up. Being tortured. Assaulted. Skin being sliced from their bodies. And worse.

She leaned into the wall to steady herself as she went through them; the cumulative effect of seeing murder after murder after murder made each one hit harder. Carolina turned to Wayne, who was still crying, and saw a photo in his grip. It was folded in half, and he clutched it so tight and hard his skin had gone ghost white.

"Your sister?" she asked, already knowing the answer.

He nodded.

"It's okay. Let me see," she said.

"No. Nobody needs to see her this way." He shook his head. "It's so much worse than I ever thought."

He tried tearing it apart, but couldn't manage. Instead, he crumpled it into a ball, then looked up at her. "What are we gonna do now?" he asked.

Carolina snatched a hammer from the assortment of tools. "Will you do whatever I tell you to do? Because if you're not up for this and want to leave right now, I won't judge you."

Wayne wiped his eyes, trying to harden himself but doing a poor job. "I'm not going anywhere."

CHAPTER FIFTY-FOUR

Donnie Westfall wore a grin that could only be described as shit-eating when Carolina and Wayne reentered his bedroom.

"Thought you forgot about me. Figured maybe you came to your senses and ran while you still had two working legs." He began to chuckle, but something, maybe the look on their faces, or maybe the way Carolina gripped the hammer, clued him in, and he went serious.

Carolina grabbed a fistful of his greasy hair and dug the claw end of the hammer into his acne-riddled cheek, popping one of the sores and spilling putrid pus.

"Hey, now. Why don't you just let me go? You can still get out of here, no harm, no foul," he said.

"It's too late for that." She lined up the hammer with the top of his hand, drew back.

"Come on," Westfall said. "Ask me your fucking questions. I'll answer 'em."

She wanted screams, not answers, and swung the hammer into Westfall's left hand. A loud crunching sound filled her ears, but Donnie didn't scream. So she swung again. And again. And again.

Somewhere along the line, the man did scream, but Carolina was so lost in rage she couldn't hear him. By the time she was finished, his hand looked like ground chuck. It barely resembled an appendage, nothing more than a quivering mass of bone, shredded flesh, and exposed fat and tissue. One of his fingers was so destroyed it hung by a loose flap of skin, dangling like a clock pendulum. Carolina grabbed it with her blood-slicked grip and ripped it off.

"What the fuck, you fucking crazy bitch!" Donnie yelled. "I'm gonna kill you both; you hear me?"

"You mad, Donnie? Was that your jerking off hand? Or do you use the other one?"

She eyed up his right and went to work.

"Please, please, please," Donnie said between tears. Snot ran from both nostrils, seeping between his lips as he tried to speak.

"Please? I bet those girls said please, didn't they? I bet they begged you to stop. You and your fucked-up psycho friends." She used the hammer to tilt his held back so she could look him in the eyes. "Did you show any of them mercy? The girls in the photos? Cece Casto? Sue Ellen Tanner?"

Westfall sucked in deep, hitching breaths. "Stop," he begged. "Just stop."

With both hands destroyed, she wondered what to attack next. His balls seemed tempting but too obvious. Instead, her eyes went to his teeth. Those slightly bigger-than-average incisors with the gap in between. She knew what needed to happen.

"If you want to hurt him, go ahead," she said to Wayne. "But don't kill him."

Wayne stared at her, wide-eyed and traumatized, as she left the room.

Thirty seconds later, she was back. Her fist closed over what she'd gone after. What she couldn't wait to put to use.

She flipped around the lever of the toenail clippers and brought the blades to Donnie's mouth. "This is for the girls in the Polaroids."

"Wait!" Donnie screamed. "Wait, wait, wait!"

"Hold his head still," Carolina ordered Wayne. The young man did as told, but his hands shook.

She pushed the clippers around Westfall's left front tooth, the blades scraping across the enamel, digging into it. The sound made her arms break out in goosebumps. Then she gritted her own teeth and squeezed.

The noises Donnie made when she was smashing his hands were an angelic symphony compared to the hellish misery that erupted from his mouth as his incisor cracked in half. A drop of blood seeped from the visible, pink pulp.

The deputy before her was a sobbing, blubbering, bleeding mess. And he deserved all of it and more. But, finally, Carolina felt this had gone far enough.

She took a staggering stack backward, only then realizing her face and clothing were splattered with his blood. She wiped it away from her eyes and mouth, smearing it like warpaint.

"Where is Cyrus?" Carolina asked.

Westfall tried to raise his head, which was sloppy on his neck, like a gear with loose ball bearings. "Took him to der Todesbringer," he said.

"Then what?"

"Don't know. Didn't stick around."

"Who is he? Who is the Todesbringer?"

Westfall stayed silent, bloody drool draining from his mouth, wincing with every inhale and exhale as the air hit the exposed nerve of his tooth.

Carolina grabbed his hair again, brought the clippers to his other tooth. It didn't have the effect she wanted.

"Kill me if you want, but I can't tell you." He met her gaze, his eyes wide in fear. "If I do, I'm damned."

She reached into her pocket and pulled out the photos, shuffling through them until she found the one she wanted. It showed Donnie Westfall holding a naked girl, one no more than twelve or thirteen. Her body was drenched in blood. Her face a mask of abject horror. And, in the photo, he smiled as he clutched her barely-there breasts.

"You're already damned." She let the clippers fall to the floor, grabbed Donnie's undershirt from a nearby dresser, and shoved it into his mouth. Then she ran a loop of duct tape around his head to hold it in place. Next, she pressed the photo against his forehead and ran a strip of tape across it to hold it fast.

She leaned in close, her lips almost touching his ears. "Have fun wiping your ass with hooks for the rest of your miserable life."

Finished, she regathered her supplies and picked up the duffel. "Let's go," she said to Wayne.

"What about him?" Wayne asked.

"Someone'll find him soon enough. If not, they'll come poking around when he starts to stink."

CHAPTER FIFTY-FIVE

CAROLINA SLUMPED IN THE PASSAT, HEAD SPINNING. SHE didn't have time to consider what she'd done, not when she needed to get to the bottom of this rabbit hole.

"There are other men in those pictures. Their faces aren't visible, but they're there, holding the girls, hurting them. There has to be a connection with the Weiss's," she said. "Westfall's related to them. The Devil's Teeth is on the property they own. Girls have been vanishing for decades, most never found. And nobody did a thing to stop it. That only happens if the people responsible are powerful."

"What are you talking about?" Wayne asked, reminding her he was in the passenger seat. She glanced over at him and saw his hands twisting in his lap. She put her own over them to settle him.

"Listen to me. What happened in there, Westfall earned what I did."

"Okay." He was unconvinced.

"I mean it," she said. "Don't let that piece of shit take up space in your head. Not now, anyway."

He gave a weak nod, and she knew she was losing him. She had to act fast.

"Do you know where they live? The Weiss's?"

Giving him something to focus on besides the torturing of Donnie Westfall seemed to snap him out of his shock. "They have some big estate out on Sheep Ridge."

"Can you take me there?"

He nodded. "I can, but it's not close."

THE SUN PEEKED over the mountains, turning the sky a brilliant mix of blues, purples, and oranges. If she weren't coming from such a scene of horror at Westfall's house, Carolina might have thought it a beautiful sight.

Wayne had been right. The drive to the Weiss's was long and painfully quiet. The visions of the girls, stripped naked, tortured, raped, and worse, kept cycling through her head. Their fragile, broken bodies. The terror on their faces. No matter how hard she tried to focus on the curves and crests in the road, she couldn't stop seeing them.

Finally, after miles trapped with her own thoughts, Wayne lifted a hand and pointed to the left. A decrepit iron gate hung askew on broken hinges. Atop it was a single letter: W.

She pulled off the road beside a mailbox with the address 6 Sheep Ridge. There was no space to drive through the gate; so, she shut off the engine.

"Now what?" Wayne asked.

"We walk."

She was out of the car first, squeezing through the gap and stepping onto a crumbling brick driveway, now mostly overtaken by weeds. Wayne came through behind her, and she could feel him close on her heels.

Ahead of them lay the Weiss Estate. It looked more like a

southern antebellum mansion than something belonging in West Virginia.

In its day, it must have been glorious, but that was decades ago. Now, what remained was being swallowed by kudzu, the leaves of which had already dropped in preparation for winter, leaving a dense, muddy exoskeleton ensnaring the mansion from ground to roof. It looked abandoned and left to rot.

"What's our cover story?" Wayne asked.

"I didn't think that far ahead," Carolina said. "I prefer to wing it."

He swallowed hard from behind her. "Just promise me you won't go and turn someone else's hands into hamburger."

"Wasn't planning on it," she said.

"Good. Cause I don't know if I'm comfortable with your style of winging it, and I thought I was the bad guy in this twosome."

She threw him her best attempt at a smile. "You're not a bad guy, Wayne."

"I feel like one."

Carolina didn't respond. She felt the same way.

CHAPTER FIFTY-SIX

Less than a minute after knocking, the front door swung inward, setting off a chime that echoed throughout the interior of the house. In the doorway stood a man who was eighty if he was a day. In the wide expanse of the doorway, he looked small and insignificant.

"May I help you?" he asked, his voice light and gentle.

He wore a shabby, moth-eaten pinstriped suit and had his white hair styled into a careful comb-over. A thin mustache, clipped razor-straight, set atop his upper lip. He adjusted his glasses to take a better look at the people on his doorstep.

Carolina grabbed onto Wayne's hand, leaning into him. "Yes, you certainly can. Thank you for coming to the door. We weren't even sure anyone lived here." She pointed to the road, which was out of sight behind them. "We were just driving along, minding our own business, when a deer jumped right out in front of us. I didn't have a chance." She pulled her hair back, revealing her wounds, then quickly covered them again hoping he wouldn't notice they were a day old.

"Oh, goodness. Are you all right?" the man asked, his eyes full of concern.

"I think so. Scrapes and scratches, but my car's out of commission. I tried to call a tow truck but didn't have any reception."

"Please," he said. "Come in." He stepped to the side, holding the door for them as they moved into a foyer, where the paint peeled from the walls, and the ceiling was dotted with rust-colored water stains.

Carolina tried not to be too obvious as she took in the poor condition of the house. "We appreciate this so much. If you wouldn't have answered, I don't know what we'd have done. We haven't passed a house in miles."

"No, you wouldn't have," he said. "This whole mountain is owned by the Weiss's. And thanks aren't necessary. Hospitality is the very least I can offer."

"You're a Godsend," Carolina said. "Mister..."

"O'Malley. But call me Lon. I'm the caretaker."

"You're a godsend, Lon."

Lon O'Malley flashed a tired smile revealing yellowed dentures. "Let me fetch you the telephone," he said, then hobbled away, using a silver cane to steady himself. He soon rounded the corner and was completely out of sight.

Carolina inhaled deeply through her nose. The air was thick and damp, leaving her lungs feeling oppressed. And the air reeked of rot. Of wood that had been wet for too long and never dried out. Of walls behind which black mold grew unchecked. But there was also a faunal aroma. Like she'd entered the carnivore section at the zoo.

When she turned to Wayne, she found him peeling a long strip of paint off the wall, then rolling it into a cylinder. He caught her staring. "Caretaker?" Wayne asked. "I'd say he's falling down on the job, wouldn't you?"

"This is it," Carolina whispered. "I can feel it. This is the place." She took another look around, another whiff, acclimating to the horrid aroma. "I'd bet my life on it."

Wayne threw down the tube of paint. "Let's hope it doesn't come to that."

CHAPTER FIFTY-SEVEN

Cyrus Mankey laid sprawled on his back atop the gigantic, mahogany table. His mouth hung agape, his eyes half-open and staring at the ceiling high above. Squadrons of flies swarmed around him, dive-bombing his face, crawling across his flesh. Laying eggs.

The lights were on now. No more candles. No more darkness. Not the physical kind, anyway. A genial, off-key humming filled the room. The singsong nature of the tune sounded like a lullaby.

Through the humming came a swish.

Swish.

Swish.

It was the hard, distinctive sound of a knife being sharpened.

A hand with four-inch-long fingernails, all thick and warped and the color of egg custard, reached across the table and took a fistful of Cyrus's hair, the slender fingers entwining themselves in his locks.

And then, that same hand pulled on the hair, and Cyrus's head left his body.

Der Todesbringer pulled the head in close, cradling it in his arms. His humming remained continuous as he pushed the dead man's eyelids closed. Then he set the severed head upright on a silver platter and gave it a long, loving caress.

The sprawling table was set as if in preparation for a lavish feast. Fine china, crystal glassware, genuine silver utensils. But it was all coated in a dense layer of dust, the accumulation of years of unuse.

But, today, the table wasn't for dining. It was for carving.

Der Todesbringer climbed onto the table, naked and moving on all fours, knees shattering plates, hands toppling glasses as he crawled over them. The destruction tore holes in his skin, but he never so much as flinched. Instead, he continued on until he was straddling Cyrus's corpse, which was also stripped bare.

He took hold of the freshly sharpened knife and carved a channel down the center of Cyrus's chest, one cut stretching from his neck to his crotch. Upon completion of the cut, the knife was set aside. Those long nails plucked up the dead man's skin, and his fingers wormed their way under the flesh. The hands pushed in further, deeper, separating the skin from the body, loosening it. Making it easier to remove.

Der Todesbringer was in up to his elbows when Lon O'Malley's voice entered the room.

"Sir, I regret being a bother, but it appears we have guests."

The humming stopped.

CHAPTER FIFTY-EIGHT

As Lon's footsteps and the hard clack, clack of his cane approached, Carolina and Wayne reverted to their appreciative and desperate faces. The elderly man handed over a cordless phone with a smile and nod.

"Here you go, Miss."

"You're a lifesaver," Carolina said as she took the phone and handed it to Wayne.

"Call AAA. My number is on this card," she said, pulling a card out of her pocket and pressing it into his free hand.

The card wasn't for AAA, though. It was Elven's business card, and it was the best she could do at the moment. Because, as reckless as she knew all of this was, the idea of backup, even if it was hours away, comforted her. If nothing else, they'd find her body before the maggots hatched.

Wayne glanced at the card and caught on immediately. He was a smart kid, just turned the wrong direction. Carolina was glad he'd come along, not only for the camaraderie but also because his presence allowed her next move.

She put her hand to her head, squeezing her eyes closed as her fingers explored her wounds. Then she looked at Lon.

"I feel like such a pain in the ass, but my head is splitting. Would you have any Advil? Or maybe Tylenol?"

Lon gave a curt nod. "Of course." He was halfway through turning when she spoke again.

"And some water to wash it down, please."

No response came. Just his retreat back into the bowels of the mansion. She was being a pain in the ass, and his mild annoyance was understandable, but she suspected there was more to it. And she needed to move fast.

As soon as Lon was out of sight, she spun toward Wayne. "If he gets back before me, tell him I felt nauseous and went looking for a bathroom."

"You shouldn't go alone," Wayne said. "That old dude, he just doesn't seem quite right; does he?"

He wasn't just smart; he had good instincts. Sometimes, that was even more important. "Hold tight and tell Elven you're calling for me. Tell him where we are and that I'm sure this is the killer's house."

"What's he going to do? Dupray's three hours away."

"Tell him to send in the state police. The fucking cavalry if he has to."

Wayne opened his mouth to protest further, but there was no time. She left him alone and turned down the hallway opposite the one that Lon O'Malley had just entered. Because, as much as she trusted her gut, she also needed evidence.

SHE STEPPED into a spacious billiards room, where the green felt had been savaged by mold. Her feet squished through damp carpet underfoot, the wetness seeping through her shoes. On the wall beyond the pool table, a row of paintings, each six feet tall, hung askew in ornate, gold frames.

They were family portraits, some appearing well over a hundred years old. All showing various versions of the Weiss's over the years. She went to the last in the line, the most recent. It showed two parents, the man in a suit, the woman in a gown, and a pale-skinned, fair-haired boy. All stood stiff as boards in front of this very house, although it was in far better condition in those days. She noticed a spot of color on the father's jacket and moved in for a better look.

There, just inches away from the nearly life-sized painting, she realized it was a family crest. And the design had a familiar shape. An oval with slashes through the top. The same mark she'd seen carved into the tree at the Devil's Teeth. The one Viola Shafer had said was the mark of the Todesbringer.

Carolina stared at the boy in the painting, convinced he was the man she'd been chasing. She tried to see something in his eyes, something foretelling the killer he would grow up to become. But it was only a painting.

"I'm close, motherfucker," she said.

She moved to the next room, the library, where books filled the walls from floor to ceiling. It even had a rolling ladder to make reaching the impossibly high-up books on the top shelves possible.

As she crept through the room, she dragged her fingers across the damp spines. Several had swollen and split in the humidity. A few shelves had rotted loose, spilling their contents onto the floor in random piles. She stepped past them, continuing to a grand oak writing desk.

The surface was littered with papers, most with Appalachian Mine Company logos. They were receipts, bills, and letters from business associates. Most were addressed to Mr. Weiss, but she saw a few slips with a name written in pristine penmanship on the signature line: Emil Weiss.

Was he her guy? Was he the Todesbringer? Her gut said he was.

As she sifted through the papers, she found a leather-bound notebook, its cover worn and smooth. Emil Weiss was imprinted on it.

When she cracked it open, she realized it was a journal, each page filled with the same perfect writing. But the words weren't perfect. They were nonsense. Gibberish. The ravings of a madman. Drawings like the devil-deer crest, along with other bizarre, occult symbols, were a common occurrence.

She kept flipping and came to a drawing of a prepubescent girl lying naked in the grass, while a hooded figure stood over her, holding a cleaver above its head. On the sidelines, other figures watched.

Maybe those watchers - men like Donnie Westfall - got their rocks off on the beating and the raping, but the man with the hood, the one who was clearly in charge, was an entirely different type of monster.

As she moved out of the room, she saw a quilted throw humped on the floor behind the desk. Its positioning made it look intentional, and the way it was strewn gave the impression there was something underneath.

She stepped toward it, taking quick glances at the doorway to ensure she was still alone, then grabbed one corner. It was cool and moist, the dampness making it weigh four times more than normal. She expected, was almost certain, she'd find a body under it. Maybe Cyrus. Maybe some new missing girl.

Instead, she found broken floorboards and a mound of raw earth. Worms undulated in the loose, stygian soil. Just like the worms the Rouschs found crawling in Cece Casto's mouth when her body was found.

Carolina pulled the pistol from behind her back, ensuring she would be ready for anything coming her way.

CHAPTER FIFTY-NINE

"Yeah, thanks," Wayne said into the phone. "As soon as possible, please."

Wayne clicked off the phone, hoping the man he'd just called would get there in time. Carolina had a lot of faith in the guy, but to Wayne, he was just a voice on the other end of the phone. A voice which sounded downright panicked upon learning where they were and what was happening.

All he could do was believe in Elven and Carolina. Believe they were somehow going to come out of this on top.

We will, he told himself. Because it was time for the good guys - or at least the non-evil guys - to win. After the nightmare fuel he'd seen in the photos, after seeing his sister naked and bleeding and terrified, he had to believe it, because anything less would mean the world was more fucked up than he had ever imagined. And a world where men who did those kinds of things to little girls could go unpunished wasn't possible.

Was it?

The picture. Damn, why'd he have to see that picture? For the rest of his life, it was how he would remember Sue Ellen. Every time he closed his eyes, he'd see her and remember the horror of her last hours. He'd thought not knowing was bad, but the reality was worse. So much worse.

Behind him, the floor creaked. He figured it was Lon, back with painkillers and water for Carolina, and prepared to answer the obvious question—where did she go?

To the bathroom, he reminded himself, trying to make the story sound real and convincing in his head. She got sick and went to the bathroom. Yeah, he could do this.

He spoke as he turned. "Hey, Carolina felt like she was gonna hurl and—"

But it wasn't Lon. And it wasn't Carolina.

Before him stood Der Todesbringer. The man was gigantic, his naked body thick with muscle. His flesh was so pale it was almost translucent. There wasn't a single hair on his body. There was only blood; his arms were covered with it.

Oh, shit—he got Carolina, Wayne thought, as the knife sunk deep into his belly.

The pain seared into him, and he opened his mouth to scream, but Der Todesbringer held a meaty hand over his mouth, muffling his cries.

"It's over now, little lamb," Wayne's killer whispered into his ear. "Your suffering is almost done."

Wayne could feel the man's hot breath against his skin. The spittle from his frothing lips splattering against his forehead. But none of it mattered because Wayne's existence was nothing but white-hot pain.

"My purpose is to set you free." The killer jerked the knife upward, the sharp metal slicing through Wayne's guts, all the way up until it clattered against his rib cage.

Then came a release. A feeling like a dam had burst, and freedom came with it.

Wayne looked down and saw his intestines spilling from the gaping hole in his abdomen. Saw them bombarding the floor in heavy, wet splatters that sent fecal matter misting out in hollow explosions. He saw organs for which he didn't know the names join the fray. And he saw blood. So much blood.

He died, still on his feet.

CHAPTER SIXTY

After twisting and turning through the labyrinth of rooms and hallways, Carolina came to two large double doors. She wondered how long she'd been gone. Surely, Lon had returned by now and it wasn't fair to leave Wayne alone with him, fumbling through an alibi.

But she needed more. The crest and the worms, were circumstantial evidence at best. The notebook was better, but still not proof. And she wasn't leaving this house without proof Emil Weiss was the man responsible for decades of death.

She pushed open the doors and found the horror that Der Todesbringer had left in his wake in the dining hall.

Headless skeletons were propped in chairs surrounding the table as if ready for Thanksgiving dinner. Leathery scraps of tissue still clung to some of the bones. Their heads sat on plates in front of them, as if they were the main course.

There were more than twenty in total, and although their height was hard to judge in a sitting position, she knew the score. These were the missing girls.

The fetid smell of death and rot hung heavy in the room, and

Carolina put her arm across her face to hold it at bay. She knew she needed to get out of there, return to Wayne, get out of this madhouse, and wait for backup. She'd found the killer's haven, his perverse collection. She didn't need to keep investigating, but she couldn't stop herself.

A silver-and-green bow hung loosely around the neck of one of the skeletons. It was the same bow Sue Ellen Tanner had been wearing in the junior cheer photo her father had shown both her and Cyrus when they interviewed him. I can't let Wayne see this, she thought.

Then her mind went to her other sidekick—to Cyrus. And she knew the decapitated torso on the table belonged to him, even though his head was nowhere to be found. Wide swaths of skin - the loose flesh which had shown he was wasting away - were gone, showing exposed ribs and muscle. His hands, at least, were unmarred, and she grabbed one of them, squeezing so hard he undoubtedly would have sworn at her if he'd been alive.

She knew this wasn't her fault, but she still blamed herself. Although Cyrus was the one who'd gotten her involved, she felt responsible for him. And she failed him. Inside, she'd known he was dead, but seeing him like this, butchered like a hunter's fresh kill...

"I'm so fucking sorry, Cyrus," she whispered. "But I promise, I'll make this fucker pay."

***

Carolina jogged through the mansion, trying to retrace her steps, but it was hopeless. She had taken too many turns, slipped down too many passages. She was lost in a maze where everything looked the same. Dilapidated, peeling, moldy, withering.

She picked up her pace, flying through the corridors, and finally saw a familiar hallway. The one which led down to the entrance. She slowed down, tried to get her breathing under control, pushed the pistol into her coat pocket but kept her finger on the trigger guard, one snap away from shooting, if it came to that.

As she neared the foyer, she'd almost convinced herself that somehow, by some miracle, this would be okay. That her ruse had worked and Lon O'Malley believed they were stranded motorists. That she and Wayne could slip out of the house, retreat to the road, and wait for the big dogs to come in and save the day. Because Carolina didn't need to be a hero. Someone else could play that role.

But when the foyer came into view, neither Wayne nor Lon were there. Instead, there was a pile of guts sprawled in a pool of blood. The flies had already found them, laying eggs that would be maggots within the day.

She was under no delusion that Wayne had somehow eviscerated Lon or Emil Weiss. He was dead. Another body on her conscience. And this one *was* her fault. She had dragged him into this and left him alone to get slaughtered.

Time doesn't suffer sissies, she thought. It was something her mother would say to her or Scarlet when something bad happened. Bea's way of telling them to buck the fuck up and not cry. Because crying was for the weak. Carolina bit her inner cheek hard enough to draw blood, but she didn't cry. She wasn't a sissy.

Instead, she drew her gun and followed a set of bloody, bare footprints trailing along the floor.

Her pace was slow, deliberate. The further into the house she went, the darker it grew, as every single window was covered with blankets, tarps, and bedsheets. There was no natural light in the house, only bare bulbs hanging from cords. The kind that screamed fire hazard and would send any building inspector running for his violation book. But no one like that had been within these walls in decades. This house was now an animal's den. The outside world was unwelcome.

She heard the faint, dull tapping of Lon's cane somewhere

ahead and moved even slower. Nobody was going to catch her off-guard now, even with the pills dulling her senses. The tapping became louder, two rooms away, and coming in her direction.

Carolina slid beside an antique grandfather clock in the hallway, waiting. And wondering what role Lon played in this. Was that even his name, or was he Emil Weiss? Maybe the boogeyman wore old suits and needed a cane to get around, that's why he had men like Donnie Westfall around, to do the heavy lifting.

She doubted it, though. No matter how hard she tried, she couldn't turn the diminutive, fragile-looking man who'd greeted them into her monster. Maybe an Igor, but not the monster.

Clack.

Clack.

Clack.

Closer. Maybe five yards away.

She pushed herself tighter into the wall, making herself as small as possible so she couldn't be seen from the other side of the clock.

Clack.

Clack.

She planned to jump him. To catch him off-guard and smash him in the face with the gun. Then get him on the ground, press the barrel against his forehead, and demand answers. To make him tell her who the Todesbringer was.

Clack.

She waited for the next clack of the cane against the floor, but before it happened, the grandfather clock next to her went off. The thunderous chimes rattled the floor and her brain.

This close, they were like canons going off next to her, and she instinctively tucked her head, closing her eyes, as if doing so could stop the assault. The timepiece was on its third strike when she opened her eyes, forcing herself to endure the audible onslaught, only to see Lon's cane jabbing at her.

The tip connected with her throat, a stabbing pain cut off her air and sent her into unstoppable coughing at the same time. The old man reared back, coming in for round two. His small face was twisted in rage, his perfect, prissy mustache an angry caterpillar on his lip.

She reacted just in time, bringing up her left arm and knocking the cane off-course. It buried itself in the plaster wall behind her, four inches deep.

Lon fell forward, tumbling into the clock, which was now up to its fifth chime. He struck the case with enough force it began to tip, rapidly picking up speed, then hitting the point of no return. It crashed into the floor, a chorus of clanging metal and breaking wood, but finally, thank God, the chiming had stopped.

Lon hit the floor at about the same time, a sharp cry bursting from his mouth as his knee bent at an obtuse angle. He moaned as his hands went to his injured joint.

Carolina stood over him, pistol in hand. She only wanted to ask one question, even if she already knew the answer. Because she'd looked at Lon's feet, and he wore plain black dress shoes.

"Are you Der Todesbringer?"

Lon threw his head from side to side. "No! I'm not him! I'm—"

She didn't need to hear anything else and put two bullets in his chest.

CHAPTER SIXTY-ONE

Carolina tracked the bloody footprints through the house, down another series of hallways leading to a bedroom. She paused outside the open doorway, steeling herself for whatever, whoever, might wait inside. Every breath she took hurt, thanks to Lon and his silver cane. She wheezed as she rubbed the point of impact on her neck, feeling a hot bruise which had already bloomed.

She did a slow five count in her head, raised the gun, then stepped into the room.

Her eyes flew across it, searching each corner and crevice. It was even darker than most of the house—no overhead light here. But no people either. She checked behind the door; it, too, was empty. The room was clear.

The walls and ceiling were covered with symbols and drawings, including more than a dozen varieties of the Todesbringer's mark. On the floor, in front of the bed, lay Wayne's body. He'd been placed on his back, arms folded in the typical pose of the dead. His sweet, innocent face looked at peace, and she supposed that should count for something, but it didn't.

The bed itself was a special kind of awful. Bloodstained ropes dangled from the bedposts. A bare mattress set atop box springs. No sheets, no blankets. Just a kaleidoscope of stains. Blood. Puke. Feces. Urine. It was a psychopath's abstract painting. Beside it, a pile of girls' clothing was heaped three feet high. Dresses, jeans, blouses, undergarments. It turned her stomach to see it, to know those clothes came from the girls who died in this room, on this bed.

On a nearby dresser were various weapons and tools. Machetes, saws, pliers, more knives than she could count. And beside the weapons sat a Polaroid camera, several boxes of film, and another stack of photos.

"Shit," Carolina muttered as she went to them. She already knew what she was going to see and didn't know how much more she could handle before the accumulated perversion drove her crazy, but she felt she owed it to the girls. That they deserved to be seen by someone other than their killers. After everything she had been through, the paths this case had dragged her down, she had to know everything, no matter how dark it became.

She stopped flipping through the photos when she saw a familiar face.

Cece Casto. The sweet, innocent girl whose death pulled her into this mess.

In the picture, she was nude and battered. Yellow and purple bruises marred her face, her abdomen. She was bleeding from the nose, mouth, and groin. Her legs were tied to the bedposts, as was one arm. The other was being stretched behind her, toward the fourth post. Carolina could see a man holding her arm, but his face wasn't in the picture, just half his body, the rest out of frame.

She flipped to the next photo. Cece was completely bound now. Her mouth was open in a silent scream. The same man was in the shot, but now, his back was to the camera.

It's you, she thought. Der Todesbringer. Let me see your face. The next photos showed Cece being tortured. Then a hand holding a cleaver over her neck.

Carolina wanted to quit. Wanted to stop seeing this. She had to look away, staring up at the ceiling, where cobwebs hung like nylon tulle. She had to brace herself before she could keep going on.

Behind her, beside the bed, the pile of clothing moved. Slowly, at first. A pair of shorts rolled off the pile, then a few shirts. Then the mass of fabric began to rise, growing in height, more clothes falling away like a mudslide.

She was ready. She could look again. And Carolina went to the next photograph.

The first thing she saw was Cece's lifeless face. Then she realized she was looking at her severed head. Fingers were in each side of her mouth, pulling her lips into an askew, abominable smile.

One more picture. This one was a wide shot. It showed Cece's body. The man sitting on the bed beside her. He held her head by her hair like it was some kind of trophy.

The man was Denton Mankey at seventeen years of age, pimply-faced and sporting the same aw-shucks grin he'd used to win her over in prison.

"You cocksucker," Carolina said, realizing he had been guilty the entire time. That Cyrus had been wholly wrong about his son. That she'd been wrong, too. Denton was as much a part of this as Donnie Westfall. As Lon O'Malley. As the Todesbringer.

She'd been played.

The mound of clothing was now six feet tall and still rising, clothes raining from the mountain being birthed from the bedroom floor. And when Carolina slammed the photos down on the bureau, she saw movement behind her via the filthy mirror.

She spun around, raising the gun, ready to shoot at whatever was becoming.

But Der Todesbringer was now free of his camouflage and, before she could pull the trigger, he blew a handful of white dust into her eyes.

"No little bird. You're not ready to see me yet," he whispered as she went blind.

She fired the gun, heard the bullet slam into the wall. She swiveled to the left, shot again. More exploding plaster. She knew this was a waste of ammunition, but she couldn't see anything but darkness and shapes, and for the first time in a very long while, she realized she wasn't ready to die.

She heard breathing to her left; so, she spun, fired, missed.

The presence of someone brushed past her.

Another shot. Another wasted bullet.

She forced herself to stop, to listen, to focus.

There was nothing but silence. She was alone.

Carolina blinked her eyes rapid-fire. They burned and watered - not tears, I'm no sissy, mother - and felt full of grit. She didn't dare rub them in case there was something dangerous, something that could scratch her lenses and put her permanently in the dark.

The waiting was horrid, but slowly, gradually, her vision came back. Everything was still a blur, like she'd put on a stranger's pair of glasses, but she could see enough to move. Using her free hand to help guide the way, she exited the room. And that's when she smelled the smoke. It was faint, but there.

She shuffled down the hall until she found a cramped water closet. There was no sink, just a toilet. But she had to make do with what was there, and Carolina splashed handfuls of the stagnant toilet water into her eyes. She held her breath to keep out the stench and kept her mouth pinched closed so none could find its way inside. She scooped over and over again until her vision cleared, then she was ready to finish this.

Carolina followed the smell of smoke. It led her to the dining room where, through the open doors, she saw the fire raging.

All the bodies. All the evidence. All disappearing.

If the entire house went up in flames, which she had no doubt would happen in short order, every bit of proof Emil Weiss was the Todesbringer, the killer, would be gone with it. And then he could vanish again, gone like the boogeyman when the lights are turned on.

That couldn't happen.

She was almost at the front entrance, certain he'd escaped into the daylight, when she heard footsteps above her.

He hadn't gone outside.

He was upstairs.

CHAPTER SIXTY-TWO

When Carolina reached the second floor, the first thing she saw was the ladder to the attic. It had been pulled down, twelve steps to the dark abyss above. And if she had any doubts the killer had gone there, his voice dispersed them.

"Up here, little bird." His whisper drifted down. "Fly, fly."

She sneered, knowing his sick voice was probably the last thing dozens of girls had heard before they died.

Climbing up there, into the pitch black, where he had high ground, where he would see her coming, was a probable death sentence. But what other options did she have? If she fled the house, she couldn't watch every exit. She would never know if he had escaped. And with the profusion of bodies inside this place, they would never determine with certainty whether a particular set of bones belonged to him.

Entering the attic might be suicide, but the girls deserved justice. They deserved finality. And there was only one way to ensure it.

She ascended the steps, keeping her head tucked, the pistol ready to fire. But she was aware only one bullet remained. Damn, why hadn't she brought a spare magazine? She knew why though. Because her head was fogged from the Oxy. This was her own fault.

At the third step from the top she was able to peek into the attic. She held her breath, half-expecting him to be there, to lash out with something long and sharp and lop her head off before she'd even have a chance to react.

But all she saw were boxes and dusty furniture. She climbed further, hitting the top step and then moving into the attic, keeping her head on a swivel all the while.

Where had he gone?

Her pounding pulse filled her ears, the acrid smoke her nostrils. The heat of the fire hadn't yet reached her, and she hoped it was a good sign. An omen she still had time before this entire deteriorating structure collapsed into itself in a fiery inferno.

A frenzy of motion exploded in her peripheral vision. Carolina whirled toward it, finger on the trigger just as—

Three crows flapped past her head. The wings of the third brushed against her cheeks as it passed by, cawing all the while until they escaped out the attic's lone and broken window.

An attempted murder, she thought, even managing a smirk. But before she could laugh at her own terrible joke, two oven-mitt-sized hands grabbed hold of her head from behind, wrenching her neck sideways. An electric shock burned through her shoulders, head, and neck, one all too reminiscent of being shot and the constant pain thereafter.

The hands spun her around, lifting her like she weighed nothing, and turned her face to face with the killer.

Carolina didn't waste time thinking. She shot, but in her haste, the bullet plunged into his abdomen. He flinched but didn't drop her. Instead, his hands squeezed harder, like vise grips around her skull. He lifted her off the floor, her feet kicking, trying to find hold but catching only air.

"Don't fight it, little bird. It's time to end your misery."

He was right. She felt it coming to an end, the life ebbing from her. He was either going to crush her skull, or her neck was going to snap. Either way, it was winding down.

For the first time, she could get a good look at him. He was no longer naked. Now, he wore a long, hooded robe made of flesh. Much of it was old and weathered, gone gray with time. But up top, the hood was comprised of Cyrus's skin. She could tell by his tattoos. The macabre bodysuit covered the killer's own pale, translucent skin. Everywhere except his face.

The veins under his flesh gave the only color. They looked like small highways on a road map, crisscrossing his cheeks. Even his irises were empty and achromatic. He had no stubble, no eyebrows, no eyelashes. It was like looking into the face of an alien.

But he wasn't an alien.

He was Der Todesbringer.

Even though Carolina had seen sights she could not have imagined in this house, she wasn't buying into the backwoods hoodoo bullshit of this legend. She didn't believe in magic. She didn't believe this monster before her had any special powers. She didn't believe in the boogeyman.

She used her remaining strength to wrap her legs around his waist. With the pressure off her neck, she could get a good breath; then, she dropped the gun and brought her hands to his face.

Before he could react, her thumbs went to his eyes, clawing and digging. Her right hit it dead-on. Bullseye. Her thumbnail pressed hard against his eyeball, then punctured it. She felt hot vitreous fluid shoot out in a quick burst.

And then she was loose and on the floor, crab-crawling backward. She only stopped when she collided with a box, tipping it, spilling the contents. Silverware tumbled to the attic floor, and she searched through it for a knife but only found spoons and forks.

Ahead, Der Todesbringer, Emil Weiss, covered his ruined eye with one hand, but he'd regrouped and was coming for her.

She grabbed a fistful of flatware and hurled it as the charging man, but it bounced off, useless. He was on top of her, had a meaty paw filled with her hair, and used it as a fulcrum as he flung her into the nearest wall. She hit hard, ribs breaking, her breath knocked out, making her see stars.

As she blinked to clear them, she saw his bare foot coming down, ready to crush her skull. She rolled to the side, and it just missed, sending up a cloud of dust, making her hack. It wasn't only the dust. Smoke flooded into the attic as the house beneath them burned. It was only a matter of time before the entire place was ablaze.

She fished around the floor, searching for something, anything she could use to defend herself. Then, among the forks and spoons, she found a meat tenderizer and took hold of it. She looked back to Weiss as his foot was coming down again, but she rolled out of the line of fire.

This time, when the foot hit the floor, she swung the mallet into his toes. There came a spray of blood, and his big toenail was sheared clean off as he howled and stumbled backward.

Carolina jumped to her feet, still holding the meat tenderizer, and this time, it was her that charged. She swung with everything she had in her, and the mallet smashed into his chin. Pieces of teeth flew from his gaping maw as he finally fell, his heavy body sprawling into the scattered utensils.

As he pushed himself to his knees, Carolina was running at him, ready to finish him off. To finish everything off. Because death was the only way this would ever end

She was almost on top of him, mallet at the ready, when she saw the steak knife in his hand. Her momentum, coupled with him lunging forward, made it impossible to avoid the collision, and he plunged the knife into her breastbone.

She dropped to her knees, hands clawing at her chest, desperate to pull the knife before it nicked her heart and she bled out, but she knew it was probably too late. That she'd used up all her luck. And that she didn't deserve all these second chances, anyway.

But there was no knife embedded in her chest. Her empty hands came away clean, no blood. She looked down and saw the bird medallion Hester the witch had put around her neck, a long gash now added to the crude design.

Then she looked to Weiss and saw the steak knife still in his hand, but the blade was bent at a near ninety-degree angle. They stared at each other for a moment in shared shock; then, he tossed the knife to the side, reached out with his arms. He couldn't speak through his shattered mouth and instead roared.

But he only looked pathetic. One eye. Broken jaw. Missing teeth. Smashed foot. Bleeding gut shot. The daylight seeping through the attic window behind him even managed to make his skin suit look less horrifying. In the light, it looked like cheap leather, rather than pieces of people.

"You don't scare me," Carolina said, then dove into him.

He fell backward, slamming into the window, shattering the remaining glass as he plunged through it. Carolina went with him, her upper body breaking the plane, and it was only a frantic, flailing grab, during which her hands caught the window frame, that kept her from plunging to the ground thirty feet below.

She pushed herself back into the smoke-filled attic, knowing she had to get out fast, but before she could, she had to take one last look down.

Carolina half-expected the ground below to be empty. That she'd realize she was wrong, and he was some supernatural force of evil had escaped death, yet again. But when she peered down at the ground, she found his body, twisted, bleeding and broken, on a concrete slab.

CHAPTER SIXTY-THREE

CAROLINA HEARD THE SIRENS APPROACHING IN THE DISTANCE, but they were faint, miles away. The cavalry was coming, but they wouldn't arrive in time. If she wanted to live, she had to save herself.

Her whole body was howling in pain as she descended the attic stairs, dropping into a space where dense, sable smoke dominated. She pressed a hand over her nose and mouth, trying to filter the air as she stumbled toward the staircase.

But when she made it there, she saw orange flames filling the ground floor, and the heat rising was so hot she felt like she might spontaneously combust. There was no going down those stairs, and she spun away from them, seeking another way out.

There probably was, but the house was a maze, and if she got lost in it again... well, then, her luck really would be spent. As the smoke billowed into the hallway, she plunged into a nearby bedroom, slamming the door closed to hold some of the fumes at bay.

In that room, like all the others, the windows were covered, this time, by a tattered bedsheet. She raced to it and ripped the sheet away, staring into the daylight, into her only hope. The drop to the ground below looked dangerously far, but she'd take a broken ankle, or even a cracked skull, over going down in this pyre.

Carolina grabbed the window frame and pushed. It didn't budge.

She tried again, grunting, giving it her all.

But the window gave nothing in return. The wood frame was swollen and locked in place.

She had to get out one way or another, though, and wrapped the sheet she'd just thrown aside around her arm. Turning her head to keep her face out of the line of fire, she closed her eyes and slammed her fist into the glass.

It disintegrated in a hailstorm of chunks and shards, one of which plunged into her bicep, skewering it like the world's biggest splinter. Carolina hadn't expected this to be easy, but it was getting a little ridiculous at this point.

She bit into the sheet and ripped with the other hand, tearing off a long strip she then fashioned into a tourniquet. Then, as she grabbed hold of the eight-inch long piece of glass, ready to yank it free, she had an epiphany. Her hand dug through her pocket, coming up with the baggie of pills. She chucked two into her mouth and chewed them because, at this point, why not?

After she swallowed down the bitter paste of pills and saliva, she returned her attention to the foreign body in her arm, grabbing hold, gritting her teeth. Then, she pulled.

It came free easier and less painfully than she'd expected, but some of it, hell, most of it, was probably the Oxy. Tossing it aside, she turned back to the window, kicking out random pieces lingering in the frame. Once they were gone, she looked down.

I can do this, she thought. Easy peasy.

She didn't believe her own lies this time but went ahead with the plan anyway. She climbed out the window, holding onto the frame, then let her feet drop from under her.

Her poor, injured body bounced off the wall, but she kept her grip tight. She was only 5'4", but she'd drop a few less feet by lowering herself as far as her arms would stretch. Once she was maxed out, she let go.

Tuck and roll, she thought on the way down. Tuck and r—

Then she was landing, rolling. She forgot the tuck part. But it was okay because she was on the ground, and although she felt like she'd just emerged from the business end of a meat grinder, that didn't matter.

She looked up at the sky, still alive. And grateful.

Then her heavy eyelids couldn't stay open any longer.

CHAPTER SIXTY-FOUR

A LANKY, BALDING PARAMEDIC WITH A WOOLY MUSTACHE shined his penlight into Carolina's eye, forcing her to flinch; her head rolled to the side. That meant yet another new flash of pain.

"Asshole," she said.

"I should have warned you about her," Elven said. He was standing beside the ambulance, while she sat in the rear of it. A second paramedic was busy tending to her surface wounds.

"You may be concussed," Baldy said.

Carolina tried to shrug her shoulders, which brought about an avalanche of agony.

"I'd say a ride to the hospital's due," Paramedic Number Two, a middle-aged woman with carrot-orange hair and a plain, doughy face added. "This stab wound on your arm might require surgery, and I'd bet a month's salary you've got at least a few cracked ribs to go along with your concussion."

"So, in other words, I'm fine?" Carolina asked.

"Only if you have a very low definition for fine," the woman, who seemed to be the leader in the duo said.

"But I'll live."

"You're not bleeding out, if that's what you mean."

"Good enough for me."

Carolina looked to Elven, whose attention drifted between her and the fire engines, shooting gushing arcs of water on the blazing remains of the Weiss mansion. They were just putting in time, though. It was a lost cause.

But no real loss, Carolina thought.

"Are you declining medical treatment against my advice?" the female paramedic asked. "It's your right to do so, but I need to hear you say the words. Liability, you know."

Carolina nodded. "I am declining medical treatment against your advice."

"All righty, then." She added the last strip of tape to the bandage on Carolina's arm, then yanked the bloody latex gloves off her hands. "You're one tough bitch, but let me get you something for the pain."

"I'd hold off on those," Elven said.

The paramedic checked him out, eyes drifting to his badge. "Whatever you say, boss."

Carolina climbed down from the back of the ambulance, and Elven was at her side immediately, arm around her waist to make the transition easier. As soon as she was on the ground, he wrapped his jacket around her shoulders. She wasn't cold, but she appreciated the thought.

They drifted away from the crowd, both staring at the inferno on the hill.

"I'm real glad you're okay," Elven said, not looking at her.

"Me, too."

He reached over, taking her hand and giving it a gentle squeeze, then didn't let go. She turned to him and met his eyes.

"No, I really mean it," Elven said.

She smiled. "I'm not gonna lie. There were moments when I had my doubts."

"You did it, though. I thought you were half-crazy, the way you carried on about it. The boogeyman, The big conspiracy. Crooked cops. How they were all connected. But you were right."

"Half-right," she said. "I still can't believe I fell for Denton's line of shit."

"It was for the best you did."

"How so?" she asked.

"If you hadn't, none of this would have come out. Emil Weiss would still be out there, killing, and doing God knows what, with impunity."

Carolina glanced toward the road, where a group of young girls walked their bikes. They gawked at the scene, trying to steal a good look at the chaos. Seeing them ruined the decent mood she'd been in. Because they reminded her of Cece Casto, Sue Ellen Tanner, and all the others.

She kept watching them as she spoke to Elven. "Two men grabbed me that night at the boardinghouse. One of them was Donnie Westfall. I still don't know who the second was."

"You have any guesses?" Elven asked.

"I still don't trust Bando. Maybe him."

"I'm not saying to trust the man," Elven said. "But I'd say it's safe to cross him off your list."

The remark shocked her. Did he know something, or was he covering for a fellow sheriff? If the latter, she'd be disappointed in him.

"Why?" she asked.

"Because he's the one who pulled you away from that hellfire," Elven said, tipping his jaw toward the mansion. "If he wanted you dead, all he'd have needed to do was leave you there. I'm sure the heat and smoke would have taken you out."

"Bando saved me?" she asked, even though he'd just said that.

"He did."

"I figured it was one of the firemen."

Her eyes scanned the crowd and she found Reed Bando standing in a throng of other middle-aged men, conversing. He must have sensed her watching him, swiveled his head, and their eyes met.

Bando gave her a brief, professional nod, one Carolina returned. Somehow, despite their differences, they understood each other.

Beside her, Elven motioned to an oversized bodybag that looked ready to burst. Weiss, Der Todesbringer, was sealed inside. "It was probably the big brute who grabbed you."

She shook her head. "No, the other guy who took me was normal-sized. Not XXL like Weiss."

Elven stood in silence. It was obvious he didn't have any answers for her. And she wouldn't be getting them from anyone else, either.

Her focus drifted back to the girls, who gossiped like hens. One of them, a pretty thing with blond hair that hung halfway down her back, clad in thrift-store specials, realized Carolina was staring at them.

The girl dropped out of the conversation with her friends, raised a hand, gave a sweet and innocent smile, and wagged her fingers at Carolina. Carolina waved back but couldn't work up a smile in return.

"I may have killed the man," Carolina said. "But I didn't kill the boogeyman."

She looked to the body bag, then to the burning house. "You can't kill evil. Not in a place like this."

EPILOGUE

CAROLINA SLEPT IN THE BACK OF ELVEN'S WRANGLER, oblivious to the potholes and rough road. She'd earned a good nap. But it was cut short.

Elven shook her gently. "Carolina?" he asked in a loud voice, in case the little push wasn't enough to wake her.

Her eyelids fluttered. She was reluctant to return to the real world so soon. "What?

"Your phone's been ringing nonstop for the better part of an hour. Thought you might could check it. Just in case."

She'd gone so long without a working cell that she'd almost forgotten she had one. When she pulled it from the pocket of her jeans, it was still ringing. The caller ID said Bea, and below it were fourteen missed calls. All from her mother.

Carolina sighed.

"What is it?" Elven asked.

"My mother."

She saw him grin via his reflection in the rearview mirror. "Aw," he said. "She probably wants to know you're all right."

Carolina rolled her eyes as she sat upright, the movement

bringing misery along with it. "She probably wants to make sure I didn't crash the Volkswagen."

"Either way, answer the poor woman before she has a coronary."

"Why do you hate me?" Carolina asked him as she swiped the phone.

"Yeah," she said, her voice hoarse from sleep and smoke.

"Carolina?" Bea asked.

"Yeah," she repeated. "It's my phone. Who else would answer it?"

"My God, Carolina," Bea said; then, her voice broke off.

There was a noise in the background, one so foreign it took her a long moment to decipher. Her mother was crying. But that was impossible—Bea Boothe didn't cry.

Carolina pressed the phone tighter against her ear, then plugged her other ear canal with her index finger. Elven kept shooting her glances and mouthed, *What's wrong?* Carolina ignored him.

"Mom? Are you there? What's going on?"

"It's your sister."

Half-sister, Carolina thought but didn't say because this didn't seem like the right time for snark. "Scarlet? What happened?"

"She isn't answering my calls. Something's happened to her."

———

Want to read what comes next? Check out "Her Deadly Double Life" which is available now.

FROM THE AUTHORS

Thank you for reading book 2 in Carolina's adventures! We hope you enjoyed it. Carolina is a wonderfully fun character to write and we have so many stories planned. Hopefully you decide to stick along and see if she can get her life back on track! You can order book 3 now.

Her Deadly Double Life

As authors without million dollar ad budgets or huge publishing houses at our backs, reviews are very important to both the success of the book and our careers so, if you enjoyed the book, please consider a quick jaunt to Amazon or Goodreads to share your thoughts.

Again please accept our most sincere thanks & happy reading!

-Tony

-Drew

Join Drew's mailing list - http://drewstricklandbooks.com/readers-list

Join Tony's mailing list - http://tonyurbanauthor.com/signup

MORE FROM TONY & DREW

Made in the USA
Coppell, TX
08 July 2024

34410086R00169